CIT SURV THE ..ED BOOK

MINISTRY
OF
SURVIVORS

RICHARD DENHAM
MARYANNE COLEMAN
M. J. TROW
KYT WRIGHT
JULIA COWAN
FAYE IRWIN
JUSTIN ALCALA
BETHAN WHITE
SAMANTHA EVERGREEN
TALIESIN TROW

Paperback ISBN 978-1-913762-82-7

A catalogue record for this book is available from the British Library.

Cover art by Andy Johnson.

Illustrations by M. J. Trow.

EST. 2019

BLKDOG

www.blkdogpublishing.com

Other titles in the *Citizen Survivor* series

Citizen Survivor's Handbook

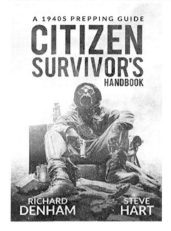

Citizen Survivor Tales

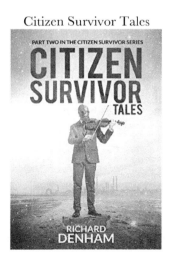

'Those who cannot remember the past are condemned to repeat it.'

- George Santayana
The Life of Reasons: The Phases of Human Progress

WOT?
NO SURVIVORS?

FACTIONS

Arbitrators: Courts, run by anonymous members of the community, charged with keeping the peace and settling local issues and disputes. Despised by many for their secrecy and esoteric jargon.

Blue Lampers: A broad term for individuals and groups opposed to local constabularies, arbitrators and politicians, often anarchic and violent in nature.

The British Union of Survivors: An outlawed fringe political paramilitary group, purged by Parliament as terrorists and extremists.

The Church of the Remnant: An ultra-orthodox religious group which has split from the Church of England and live in enigmatic seclusion. Distrusted by others.

Ferals: Gangs of wandering children that exist throughout Britain.

Free Corps: British citizens who have volunteered for military service on behalf of the government.

Home Guard/Dad's Army: Soldiers charged with policing their jurisdiction, keeping the peace and eliminating local terrorist/resistance elements.

John Bull Co-operative Society/The Co-op: A loose network of organisations and individuals believed to be involved in criminality and the black market.

The Ministry [of Survivors]: A shadowy governmental department, unknown to the public, whose purpose is not clear.

Reivers: Criminal gangs and racketeers that operate in remote and lawless areas of Great Britain.

The Roundheads: One of the prominent resistance movements, despised by many for their violence and for viewing everyone not with them as being the enemy.

XXII Committee: The chief authority of Great Britain, a committee of twenty-two men who oversee the king and Parliament.

FOREWORD

BY RICHARD DENHAM

'There are a terrible lot of lies going around the world,
and the worst of it is half of them are true.'

- Winston Churchill

I've always found the most chilling stories to be those
that are *almost* believable. Think of Franz Kafka's
work, Joseph Conrad's *The Heart of Darkness*, Samuel
Beckett's *Waiting for Godot* and even *The Prisoner* and *The
Twilight Zone* television series. Although far fetched, what
made these stories so unsettling is the fact that the
characters could never be trusted to act in the way you
hoped or assumed they would. These people could never be
taken on their word, their behaviour couldn't be predicted
and for me, this is much more terrifying than any amount
of over-the-top gore and lazy jump scares found in today's
horror movies.

The Second World War is *the* hotbed for alternative and
speculative fiction, the likes of which the world has never
seen before. No period of human history has fascinated
writers and readers quite so much. And the most tantalizing
question is, 'What if the Nazis had won the war?' Famous

examples include Robert Harris' 1992 novel *Fatherland* and the 1964 movie *It Happened Here* and *Swastika Night* by Katherine Burdekin, under the pseudonym of Murray Constantine (writing as a female was considered unwise and this title was, oddly, actually written *before* the war and published in 1937).

This obsession continues to the modern day, with popular retellings such as the televised series *Man In The High Castle*, originally a 1962 novel by science fiction writer Philip K. Dick, and the BBC series *SS GB*, originally published in 1978 by Len Deighton.

There are so many hypothetical questions that intrigue us; what if Germany continued its relationship with China and did not ally with Japan; what if Japan attacked the Soviet Union instead of the US; what if Finland fell to the Soviet Union and the Molotov-Ribbentrop Pact was fulfilled; what if Spain or Turkey joined the Axis; what if Roosevelt did not stand or win a third term as US President; what if the US entered the war before Operation Barbarossa had begun - the list goes on and on. I've always found these stories fascinating, but they are all a bird's eye view, an overarching political and military view on events – I wanted to zoom in and know what it would be like for ordinary people simply trying to live their day to day lives.

So what can we use as a source? The occupation of France can only give us a rough comparison but the accounts of survivors of this, from all sides, are fascinating. The first eight months of World War Two were odd in the west, even being referred to as the Phoney War by the Allies and Sitzkrieg by the Germans. The French tentatively moved into Saarland in September 1939, before withdrawing the following month to their starting lines.

Hitler launched his invasion of France on 10 May 1940, interestingly the same day that Winston Churchill took the reins in Britain. Churchill had opposed Nazi Germany from the beginning; was Hitler hoping for a more accommodating politician and a last attempt at reconciliation with the British before burning his bridges and going all in or was this purely coincidence?

The attack on France shocked the world; the devastating Blitzkrieg of the Wehrmacht caught the French and British by the backfoot. The British forces fled back across the English Channel to avoid capture in the famous Dunkirk evacuation while the French surrendered on 25 June. It was a dark miracle, Hitler, the insignificant but brave corporal from the First World War had achieved in just forty-six days what the Kaiser couldn't achieve in over four years. Not to mention sweeping up Poland, Denmark, Norway, Belgium, the Netherlands and Luxembourg too. The messiah of the Reich was validated and France, the long-term enemy of Germany, was defeated.

It is important not to downplay the fall of France. France was stunned, it had huge armies still in the field and many couldn't comprehend why their government surrendered so easily. Britain had lost its only ally and its foothold in Europe; it could not hope to make a significant impact in Europe until D-Day four years later. The Soviet Union was also bewildered, they had secretly allied with Nazi Germany in the Molotov-Ribbentrop Pact, quietly carving up Eastern Europe between them. Stalin's motives are still debated, many claiming that he hoped that Hitler would be entangled in a western war for years while he built up his strength. If this was his hope, he would be sorely disappointed, and Hitler's eye would turn to the east the following year, launching the largest and bloodiest assault in history, Operation Barbarossa.

Historians still debate Hitler's motives. It seems madness to us now that he didn't finish off Britain before moving East. Plans to invade Britain, Operation Sea Lion, were discussed but it's debated how serious this was. Hitler's advisors didn't believe it could work, the power of the Royal Navy and the Royal Air Force was still a force to be reckoned with, and, even if it was possible to cross the English Channel in a sort of reverse D-Day, could the Axis have reasonably placated the British?

It seems that invading Britain was never high on Hitler's agenda. Hitler believed the British were fellow Aryans, and he longed for an alliance with them, against what he perceived to be the enemies of the Aryan people, the subhuman Bolsheviks of the Soviet Union and the decadent and effeminate liberal France. Hitler discusses in depth his hopes to join forces with Britain in his largely forgotten book, *Zweites Buch* (literally 'Second Book'). He fantasies of Germany ruling Europe and Britain ruling overseas, he even planned to offer Wehrmacht soldiers to police the Empire and thought one day the British and Germans would attack the United States of America together! The 1936 Anglo-German Naval Agreement encouraged Hitler for his long hoped for alliance, but he misread the British motives and no alliance was to come. The British were clear they would not tolerate any huge power shift on the continent. Ultimately, we can conclude that for Hitler, delusional as his reasons were, his heart was never in occupying Britain, and with the fall of France he thought it was only a matter of time before the British listened to his 'appeal to reason' and saw sense, coming to some sort of conditional peace with the Reich. Many history books don't like the fact that Hitler offered peace to the British, it doesn't fit in with the warmongering narrative (world domination is far fetched too, he'd probably have been content reaching the Ural Mountains, the unofficial edge of Europe). For more on this, read up on the bizarre and enigmatic one-man-flight of Rudolf Hess, second-in-command of Nazi Germany to Scotland in 1940. A free-hand in the east against the barbaric Red Army of the Soviet Union seemed a fair trade to him for the British to have a free-hand with their Empire, which had not quite begun to ebb. Interestingly, it was the British fighting Hitler that meant they were too weak to keep their Empire together and nation after nation, peacefully in the main, declared independence.

So, if we assume Hitler could not, or would not, defeat the British by force, it would have to be some sort of deal. The Italians had offered to mediate between Britain and Germany in peace talks, and it could be said that it was only Churchill's pride and stubbornness that stopped these talks dead. Britain was close, very close, to peace talks and, arguably, why not? The evils of Hitler's regime were unknown and the Holocaust wouldn't begin in earnest for another two years. Britain had very little benefit, if any, from fighting Hitler, apart from pride and maintaining the balance of power and we mustn't forget the Great War, the link of which is so easily dismissed by historians. It was only twenty-one years since the horrors of the Great War had ended, the most insane, needless and bloodiest of conflicts that had already shattered Europe that generation. Those men who argued for or against war again knew they would be sending their sons into the same madness they had survived.

In other words, Britain only loses/leaves the war through diplomacy and politics, it has to be Britain's choice. If the British did throw in the towel, what sort of government would we have had? How would they justify this to 'Joe Public', the ordinary man on the street? What terms and conditions would Hitler's Reich have demanded to allow Britain to run itself? This brings us to the world of the Citizen Survivors.

The stories within never happened of course, but with a liberal splash of artistic licence and imagination it is just about feasible that the stories or similar things *could* have happened.

Did the Church of the Remnant exist? No, but many Christians were pushed to the absolute limits of their faith such as Maximillian Kolbe and Bernard Lichtenburg. Did the British defend Brighton Beach against a seaborne invasion? No, but the plans, as part of Hitler's Operation Sea Lion were seriously considered and the accounts of Wehrmacht defenders at Normandy during the D-Day Landings (a sort of reverse Dunkirk) are just as terrifying. Did the British arrest and imprison a woman for being a witch? Actually, surprisingly yes, her name was Helen Duncan, and there were countless baffling ways a person could end up in prison or a concentration camp for reasons completely out of their control. What links the Citizen

Survivors is that every story has some real world comparison, even if this is obscured by layers of fiction.

In our world, reading survivors of the Second World War's accounts, what is most uncomfortable for me is how people really did behave in a way the writer didn't expect; they really did live through a nightmare. Neighbours whispering to authorities, brainwashed children reporting their family to their teachers, conscripts thrust into the most hellish battlefields imaginable, refugees returning to their homes after the war to find it being lived in by disinterested strangers, people having their worlds turned upside down with really no way to escape. We learn that experience and reality are subjective. Ten people can view the same event in ten different ways and be adamant that their truth is *the* truth. We often have to remind ourselves that this all happened, just about, in living memory.

If you have read *Citizen Survivor Tales* prior to picking up this book, you may notice that the interviews from that title often disagree with, or openly contradict, the accounts in this book, this is deliberate. Those of us with an interest in history will know there is always a huge gulf between a person's versions of events and what actually happened – the old cliché, 'history is written by the victor' very much rings true. Are the interviews in *Citizen Survivor Tales* reliable? Did *The Southern Herald* even interview these people or did the journalists fill in the gaps themselves, and why were these particular individuals of interest to them. In other words, what was the motive of the staff at *The Southern Herald*?

Why did the Ministry of Survivors produce and publish their cryptic survival guide, *The Citizen Survivor's Handbook*? Who was the intended audience? We know that in our timeline secret books were produced. *The Countryman's Diary 1939* by Highworth's Fertilisers, for example, was actually a clandestine manual for resistance fighters on how to use explosives!

What links the Citizen Survivors is that their knowledge of what is happening outside their own worlds is limited, they simply don't understand how the war is progressing or what is happening outside of Britain, and as is human nature, they will fill in the gaps themselves. This is not as far-fetched as it appears. For example, during the real world evacuation of Dunkirk, there are harrowing eyewitness accounts of stragglers arriving at the beach to see tens of thousands of soldiers desperately waiting to get home; to them it seemed like their world was ending or the war was well and truly lost – or perhaps they were regrouping for a last ditch counter attack? And, again, the (highly censored) news of this wouldn't reach Joe Public for weeks after, if at all.

We will always have the benefit of hindsight with history and have the luxury of seeing things at a strategic level, but this is not what contemporaries found. Their only access to the bigger picture was the highly censored newspapers, radio or the dubious word of their superiors.

I hope you enjoy these stories and the world of the Citizen Survivors. Not quite true, not quite a lie; not quite a comedy and not quite a nightmare. You may finish this book more confused than when you started, is it a horror anthology, an attempt at black humour or something else entirely? That's what history is, and like history, you can interpret this book however you like. We are as in the dark as the characters in this book!

It is my hope that this title may inspire you to read more on the real world, and take comfort that *this* book, by a hair's breadth, is and will always be fiction.

However we interpret our version of reality, we owe a debt to those who experienced the real nightmare and to never forget them.

My great appreciation and respect go to all the talented authors who have contributed to bringing this title and the world of the Citizen Survivors to life: Maryanne Coleman; M. J. Trow; Kyt Wright; Julia Cowan; Faye Irwin; Justin Alcala; Bethan White; Samantha Evergreen and Taliesin Trow.

Various Authors

THE INMATE

BY MARYANNE COLEMAN

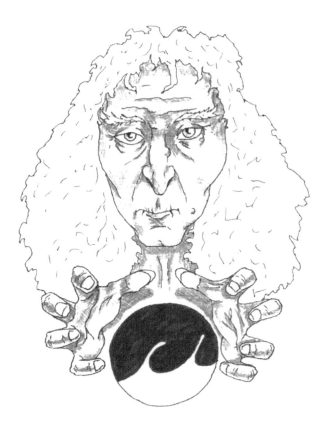

Various Authors

THE INMATE

The woman sat hunched over the remains of a fire, smoky now and filling the space with an evil smell compounded of wet wood smouldering, ox bones burning and an indefinable stench of age and … could it be? … evil. The man sitting opposite her was all but indistinguishable as a human, wrapped in furs and old scraps of loosely woven wool, anything to keep the cold out, to repel the damp. He peered as best he could through the smoke, his eyes stinging and his throat already raw, to see what she was doing, to hear what she was muttering.

She had a skin in front of her, flayed and cured so long ago it was no longer possible to see what animal it had once clothed. In it, a selection of bones, thrush bones as light as feathers, which, as they rubbed together, gave off a hint of long-sung song. Knuckle bones from sheep clunked together and brought a smell of damp fleece, a sound of dull teeth grinding hard, salt-laden grass. She stirred and listened, stirred and listened and then suddenly threw them in the air, making the man on the other side of the fire flinch back.

She caught them expertly on the skin and looked at them through eyes seemingly impervious to the smoke.

'I see men,' she said, in an unexpectedly young voice, making the man look again, past the layers of grime.

He was amazed to find she was little more than a child. 'Men with helmets on their heads, sandals on their feet. An eagle. I ...' she cocked her head, like a bird listening to a worm. 'I can't understand ...' she listened a moment more, then nodded, half to herself. 'Yes, I have it now. They are soldiers. They don't want to leave their home. It's warm there and here they are cold. The sea is rough and they are sick. They don't want to come.'

The fur-clad heap opposite clambered to his feet. 'But they *are* coming, then? That boat load on the beach are not the only ones?'

She threw the bones up in the air, higher than before, and caught some as they fell. She held out her fist over the fire and dropped the bones into the sullen flame. They flared up and, just for an instant, the man saw what she saw, ships by the dozen, tearing up the beach and grounding in the shingle. They moved in silence, like water breaching a riverbank, sliding inexorably over the land. The man gasped and immediately clapped a hand to his mouth. He was the leader here – he must show no weakness.

'Where is that ... where is that happening?' he whispered. 'We must call our people together, withstand these men.'

'It hasn't happened ... yet,' she said. 'There are still things that must happen first.'

'What things?' The man sat down again, leaning forward, eager to learn.

'A leader must rise, here, on our soil. He must be brave, clever, bold and resolute.'

The man across the fire tried to look like all of that, and more.

'He must gather his men and women – don't dismiss the power of a woman fighting for her children – and meet this force head on. He must wait until the tide is coming in, carrying the boats with it. They must hide in the dunes and strike at just the right moment.'

She looked up at him, brushing her hair from her eyes. The man across the fire drew in his breath. Gods in heaven, she was beautiful! Her eyes were as clear as water and her skin was like milk. Why she hid herself in this frowsty hut, he would never understand. When he had repelled these hordes, when he had become leader of his people, why then ... then he would make her his queen.

'You are above yourself,' she said and the air between them froze. 'I am no one's queen but my own. Think not about what you will do with me when this is over, but what you will do to raise your people, to keep your country safe. The future depends on you, and you alone. Don't forget, a powerful man will by the very nature of things have powerful enemies.' She threw the bones in the air again and caught just one and handed it to him. 'Keep this bone in your bosom at all times and it will keep you safe. Don't forget, at all times.' She lowered her head and she was a crone in the smoke again.

The man in the furs scrambled to his feet again and stood, irresolute. It was clear she had said her piece and he ducked to leave the room, pushing aside the skins which were her only door. Outside, in the frosty air, the magic of the fireside seemed less strong. What would his kinsmen say when he told them what he had seen? He laughed quietly to himself. They would call him a fool and that would simply be the politest thing. It didn't do to let men know you had listened to a woman, even the crone in the smoke who everyone knew was mad. He looked down at his right hand, still clenched in a fist. He opened it and saw a bone, white in the clear starlit night. It was ... he turned it this way and that. He was a hunter, he knew what animals looked like when they had met their end and had gone through the pot, but this was a mystery. Deer? Goat? He smiled. If he didn't know better, it looked like nothing so much as a finger from his own hand. He laughed as he turned to make his way through the woods, back to his village, tossing the bone in the air as he went.

It twirled high, almost sparkling as the frosty light touched it in its path. As it hit the ground, there was a soft groan and a thud, with the imperceptible sound of a man's life blood gushing from his throat.

He hadn't even seen the knife.

Inside the hut, the woman sighed and shook her head. It was all one to her whether she shared her land with the oaf she had just warned or the men from across the sea, but she did wish that they would listen to her, sometimes.

* * *

The woman sat in the sparse, stone-built room, her hands spread on the table on either side of a dish full of black water. Her hair was intricately knotted at the nape of her neck and her gown was modest, high-necked and of a simple weave and cut. Her face was unremarkable, not plain, not beautiful, but the man opposite her found much to see in the placid immobility of her mouth. Her eyes were downcast, but slewed slowly from side to side as she read the smooth surface of the water.

Her visitor held himself well; his clothes were immaculate, and his beard and hair had been trimmed by someone else, that much was clear. No one with a knife and a polished metal mirror was ever going to manage that kind of precision – this man had servants, to tend him and his body, to feed him and his household, to make sure that his life went along the lines he wished it to go. But still, he was concerned, that much was clear. His foot tapped relentlessly on the flagstone floor and his nails were bitten to the quick.

He was not a patient man; anyone who knew him would say that, even his friends. But he had been told, by the men who had sent him to this woman in her little stone cell out in the woods, that he must wait, quietly, while she did what she must do. He was like a coiled spring, waiting, waiting …

The woman lifted her eyes and he was immediately caught in their beam. They were almost colourless, like water, with wide pupils and black lashes, sweeping up now and framing her eyes, making them like windows into her soul, if he had had the skill to see. 'What are you here to ask?' she said. It was the first time she had spoken since he had arrived and her voice had a husky quality that made him think of warmed sheets, of soft candlelight and unspoken promises.

'I need to know ... my colleagues in the Witan need to know, whether the rumours we have heard are true? That men from the North are coming, as they came long ago, to steal our lands, to steal everything we own. To make themselves our rulers?'

She pulled a face. 'Men from the North are *always* coming,' she pointed out. 'Don't you want to find out anything new?'

'This is new, though,' he said. 'We have heard ... stories. That the men from the North will come and invade from the sea. That our lands in the South are not safe. We ... we wondered if you knew about it.'

She shrugged. 'I know everything, of course. That is why you're here, I suppose.'

He remembered that he had been told to be humble. 'Of course, of course you know everything,' he said and let his voice die away.

'Let me look,' she said. 'I have a sister in the North. Perhaps she will help me. But first ... I don't want to bring money into it, I really don't. But ... well, I must live ...'

The man looked askance. No one had mentioned money. It was true that his shoes were of the softest pigskin money could buy. His cloak had been brought overland and by sea from the best weavers in Normandy. His gown had just the right amount of silk from the lands of the Far East woven into it to make it as soft as a kiss and as hardwearing as he needed it to be. But he didn't get these things by throwing money away on one who could only be described as a common cunning woman. What did she need money for? She had no *things*. She had no need for anything that money could buy. He hedged.

'I don't travel with money,' he said. 'The roads are so wild and ... with no disrespect ... the path to your ...' he wanted to say 'hovel' but stopped himself just in time, 'home is wilder than most. I have an idea. Why don't you tell me what I want to know, and I will send a boy with the money, as soon as I get home.?'

She looked at him, dubiously. He was so washed, so scrubbed, so outwardly clean; it was a shame it hid a heart as black as a raven's wing. She fixed him with her stare for a moment, and then smiled. 'Of course, my lord. That would be quite acceptable. As soon as you get home, mind … as I said, I must live.'

'Of course.' He could hardly hide his smile. 'Now, tell me what you see?' He craned over, trying to see the pictures in the water, but could see nothing. Afterwards, he would realise how odd that was; he could see *nothing*. Not even a reflection of the ceiling, of the cunning woman's face. Just … nothing.

She dropped her extraordinary eyes again and the man found he could breathe more easily. He stared out of the window, which framed a view of a clear blue sky. Far above, a hawk fluttered, stationary on an updraft. Suddenly, it dropped like a stone and his heart with it as the woman spoke. Afterwards, he could never see a hawk plummet without almost collapsing with the horror of what came later.

'I see men, charging up a beach,' she said. 'They have iron on their heads, their shoulders are cloaked with fur. They carry axes as tall as a man. They have their children with them, wild as feral dogs, women too, who look ready to kill. With them is a man who leads; they look to him as their king. I …' she put her forefingers to her temples and pressed hard. 'I … his thoughts are not warlike, he would rather rule with intelligence than force. But he knows that force will come first. He doesn't care how many heads his men break, if those heads will bow to him one day. He will make his court at … Wintan-ceastre …' She looked up. 'Do you know it?'

'I know of it,' he said, grimly. It was almost in his demesne; he wanted no foreign king there.

'You have it in your power to prevent this man,' she said. 'All you need to do is to gather your forces and billet them along the coast. Look for bays, inlets, look for an island off into the sea. Guard them well and no harm will come.'

The man slapped the table and the black water swayed in the bowl. Afterwards, he wondered why he hadn't noticed that it hadn't slopped over the side; that was surely something that was odd. But he was in such a hurry to go and tell the fyrd how they must prepare that he noticed nothing. 'I must away,' he said. 'I must tell ...'

'Of course you must,' she said, leaning back and fixing him with her strange eyes. 'You won't forget my money, though, will you?'

'No, no,' he flapped a hand at her as he ran out to his waiting horse. 'No, no ... as soon as I get home. I promise.'

She sat at her table, her eyes focussing on nothing. The raven which her visitor hadn't even noticed sitting up in the rafters swept out after him and she rode with him, using his eyes. She saw, from above, the man leap from his horse and race through his courtyard, calling men to him and shouting excitedly. She saw them ride their horses to all points of the compass, lathering them to reach far places in times almost unbelievably short. But she didn't see him go near his coffers. She didn't see him send a boy. She unhitched her eyes from her raven's and leaned over the mirror water.

'Sister,' she hissed. 'Sister, are you there?'

A face swam up to the surface and hovered there. A face like hers, but with an etch of the frozen North about it. 'Here, sister.'

'Have you had a visitor, a king perhaps, asking about my land?'

'Just this morning.' The mouth moved but the sound arrived deep in the woman's head, not through the air. You couldn't be too careful.

'What did you tell him?'

'He has gone home to fetch money.' The lips laughed silently. 'Funny how they always come with purses empty.'

'If he comes back,' the woman said, holding out a hand to the raven, which flew like night in through the open door and smoothing its glossy head, 'if he comes back and brings you money, tell him to attack in the North, along the river they cannot bridge. They don't expect him there; I think my land could do with one more honest man.'

* * *

The woman sat on a settle, pulled up into the inglenook in the kitchen. She had sat there every day for as long as anyone could remember and yet no one knew her name. She was there, or so it was said, to turn the spit so the meat roasted evenly and indeed, the meat in that great house was said to be as moist and well-roasted as any in the kingdom. And yet, no one could be found who had ever seen her put so much as a hand to the handle. It was best not to stare, though – you could lose an eye that way. The cook and all the minions below him had stopped seeing her – like anything or anyone who was in the same place night and day, she had become, to all intents and purposes, invisible.

Sometimes, a woman of the household would come into the kitchen and walk up to the woman and whisper in her ear. Sometimes, the woman would follow her, walking through the scurrying scullions as if they weren't there. Sometimes, she stayed in her seat. Today, she followed, cutting a path through the sweaty humanity like a hot knife through new butter.

She followed the woman up a winding stair until they were in the sunlit chamber that ran all along one side of the house, grabbing every ray of sunshine that came its way. The summer had not been kind so far this year, with storms and portents which unnerved the gullible but ruined everyone's crops, whatever they believed in.

The man sat by the fire at one end of the long room and lounged there as the women approached him. When they were within earshot, he spoke. 'Thank you, Dorcas,' he said to the serving woman. 'You can return to your mistress now. And ...' he clicked his fingers and the woman turned to him, with a bobbed curtsey. 'Tell your mistress I shall want her in my bed tonight. Oh, and Dorcas.' Again, there was a bob. 'I want you there this afternoon. As soon as I have finished here.' The bob this time was accompanied by downcast eyes and the woman from the inglenook felt the revulsion sweep from the serving girl like gall.

The man lounging among the cushions gestured with his head for the woman to sit. A hard chair had been placed at a respectful distance, with a low table in front of it. Someone in the house knew what was needed, though this lord had never lowered himself so far as to consult the woman before. That was for women and lovesick boys. But this was serious – otherwise she would never have got this close. He had heard ... things ... and had no wish to tempt fate. As far as he was concerned, simply having the woman in the room was reward enough, though he did have a small silver coin in his purse, should push eventually come to shove.

She took her seat and waited, her hands folded politely in her lap, her eyes downcast. He looked at her; he had heard of the old hag by the kitchen fire, but this was no hag but a woman just approaching her prime. Not much meat on her, but he didn't much mind what shape his bedfellows were, or even if they were that willing. He stored her in his mind, to come back to later, when he had time. She felt the thought and shuddered inwardly, casting a casual spell as she did so. If Dorcas did visit his bed that afternoon, she had made sure it would be to little avail.

He was finding this woman oddly difficult to talk to. He tried several times to address her in his usual hectoring tone, but for some reason, the words wouldn't leave his tongue. Eventually, he gasped out, 'I would ask your advice, madam, if I may?' He was aghast to hear the words but didn't seem to have much control over them.

'So I gathered,' she said, polite enough, though the words seemed to have a touch of ice in them. 'About what?'

There was really only one matter on everyone's minds right now – the war with Spain – but she didn't believe in letting anyone down easily, if she could help it.

'We hear that Philip has an Armada, all built and

ready and gathering in the sea-roads, waiting to pounce.'

She nodded. She had definitely heard that, and much more besides which she would, for now, keep to herself.

'Our Admirals are, of course, the best in the world.'

Again, a nod.

'As are our ships.'

'Indeed.'

'Our sailors are second to none.'

'Agreed.'

'And our guns, of course, could outgun any other navy on any ocean.'

'All of this, sir, is as it should be. So ... I wonder ... why am I here? Surely, you don't intend to speak to all your servants, separately, to tell them how wonderful our navy is.'

He sat up, his brows bristling with anger. The starched ruff around his neck suddenly seemed to be three sizes too small. 'Insolent! Insolent hussy!' Spittle flew from his lips. 'How dare you speak to me like that?'

She got up, her hands still demurely folded in front of her. 'You are upset, sir,' she said. 'Shall I fetch someone? Your wife? Dorcas?'

'No, no.' He fell back on his cushions. 'No. But you should not try me, woman. This is a testing time for all of us with ships at sea. Or in port. I have heard ... and I mentioned it to some men too important to name in front of the likes of you ... I heard that ... well, I heard you can control the weather.'

She sat down and looked at him, a half-smile on her face. 'Really, sir,' she said. 'You shouldn't say such things. You'll get me burned.'

He looked at her through narrowed eyes. That was certainly true. Something to hang on to for later, perhaps.

'And you, of course, for harbouring a witch under your roof all these years. Letting her physick your household. Make sure your little by-blows don't cause trouble. Making sure your neighbours' fields and flocks don't outshine yours.'

He sprang up again. 'I never asked ...' He saw her eyes for the first time. Pale as water, fringed with lashes black as sin.

She smiled again, that smile with no humour in it. 'But who knows that?' she said. 'By the time I have finished telling the judge and jury that you beat me until I did it, well, who would they believe?'

'You have no marks of beating,' he said. 'They'll not believe you!'

She pulled up a sleeve and held out her arm, with the tender underside uppermost. As he watched, stripes and wheals began appear on the milk-white skin. She looked up at him, her mouth insolent now.

He slumped back on his cushions. 'I see,' he muttered. 'I see.'

She leaned forward, pulling down her sleeve. 'I merely mean, sir, that you shouldn't *say* it. I don't say it isn't possible. But when you say 'control' the weather, it is a skill which isn't as precise as we should like. I can ... influence ... the weather. But if Philip of Spain has ... someone like me, then the outcome isn't certain.'

The man on the cushions relaxed again. 'Philip!' His voice was full of scorn. 'He wouldn't have a ... have someone like you. The man is a rabid Catholic and wouldn't be seen dead with ... that person. So, you'll be working free and clear, I am almost certain.'

'What is it you want?' she asked and sat looking helpful, back straight, face alert. With the sun on her hair and her attentive posture, she was certainly a fine figure of a woman. He waited for his usual stirrings in his codpiece but there was nothing – but, these were serious times. Sometimes even a man's manhood had to take second place to affairs of state. Even so, he glanced down with a worried look and missed the smile on her face, this time with enough humour for them both.

'We ... that is to say, the navy, would like the weather to be ... well, shall we say in our favour. Winds and so on. To drive the Spaniard back and scatter his fleet. We don't mind where it ends up, as long as it isn't in a concerted attack up the Channel.'

'Hmm ... well, that shouldn't be too difficult. I would need some peace and quiet.'

He gestured to the room where they sat. 'You have it.'

'I shall need a pot of fresh water. Also, a pot of urine fresh from a virgin – I would imagine that around here, that might take some time, so ask for that first, if I were you. I shall need some rosemary, rue, feverfew and ... let me see,' she put her forefinger to her lip and looked heavenwards. 'Oh, yes, a wafer from the communion plate and ... she leaned forward and suddenly he felt a pain in his chin, 'a hair from the chin of an honest man.'

He looked furtive. 'You *are* an honest man, are you not?' she said. 'True to your wife. Fair in your dealings?' She looked at him intently, waiting for his reply.

'Oh, oh, yes. As true as true.'

She smiled and his bowels turned to water. 'That's all right, then. If I could suggest you start the search for the virgin's water first, then the rest of the things. I'll just put my feet up here and rest. This won't be easy, you know.'

He jumped up and made for the door. As he looked behind him, he saw to his horror that she was laid out among the cushions of his chair, her noisome boots kicked off and her feet on the arm. He shuddered and made a mental note to have the cushions burned and replaced. No – make that the entire chair.

She was still asleep when he got back with her ingredients carried by a servant scurrying along behind him. The virgin water was still warm. She sat back in her hard chair and assembled everything on the table. When the servant had left, she began her work, pulling the leaves from the herbs and weighing them in her left hand, sprinkling the spring water and the hairs from an honest man's chin into the pot of virgin water. She took the man's hand and, without speaking, indicated that he should extend his middle two fingers. She used them to stir the pot, round and round and round until a little whirlpool was created. She glanced up covertly and was delighted to see his look of horror so she stirred for a little longer.

'Oh! I almost forgot. Do you have a silver coin? Quick, now!' She let go of his hand and watched with delight as he tried to open his purse without using the two wet fingers. 'Drop it in and keep stirring,' she commanded. 'I must now recite the incantation!'

He stirred, but without enthusiasm, so she held his hand and pushed it further into the virgin's water, now merely tepid.

'Gadewch i'r dydd fod yn iawn a llongau Sbaen yn fuddugol.'

'What was that you said?'

'I can't tell you, sir. Or the weather gods from olden times won't listen to me.'

'What language was that?'

'The language of the Druids, sir. Now, *stir*!'

'My hand is tired.'

'Do you want Philip to prosper?'

'No. No.' He stirred as he had never stirred before.

After another ten minutes, in which she muttered to herself, twining her fingers together and rocking in her seat, she held up her hand.

'Enough!'

He stopped stirring so suddenly, the mixture slopped from the bowl all down his breeches. He swore under his breath and leapt back.

'Well, sir,' she said, her eyes sparkling. 'I think that was a job well done. It was the hair from the chin of an honest man which clinched it, I can't help thinking.'

And she made for the door, trying desperately not to look round; she knew she would laugh if she did. She trotted down the stairs, too pleased with her afternoon's work to worry whether anyone would notice she wasn't a little old lady. In the hallway leading to the kitchens, she met the steward of the house, who was surprised to see her out of her chimney corner.

'Good afternoon,' she said, pleasantly.

He nodded and held open the door. Like most below stairs, he was wary.

'Oh, by the way,' she said, as she passed through, 'do you speak Spanish?'

'Ummm …' That was an odd question. 'No. Why?'

'Hmmm. Pity.' And she went on her way, humming.

* * *

The woman sat in an ante-room of the Admiralty, a cold, bleak place for anyone to sit in, but someone of her stature, she felt, deserved more. Ever since the flunkey had appeared at the door of her lodgings that morning, she had been treated with considerably less than respect, and she was beginning to get a little testy. Already, the plant standing on a plinth in the corner, always looking peaky, had died and a canary which had been singing happily in a cage in the window had fallen silent and was hunched on its perch, looking very seedy. She pulled her tattered lace tippet around her shoulders and tweaked her grubby fingerless gloves further up her bony wrists. Her hair was coming loose again and she tucked it, rather randomly, under her bonnet. This had better be important; she had been about to set off for a weekend of fortune-telling in Berkshire; very profitable, Berkshire, in her experience.

The door opened finally and a lad entered. He was in full Naval fig and looked a bit like a child who had been let loose in the dressing up box. Although all his clothes fitted him, he nevertheless had the look of someone who had bought them to grow into.

He bowed and she looked for irony but no, he seemed like a nice enough lad.

'Good morning,' he said, politely.

'Afternoon,' she snapped. 'It was morning when I got here. It's afternoon now.'

'My word!' He looked distraught. He had gone to an extremely good school and believed that punctuality was the politeness of princes, though not many of the princes currently enjoying that position. 'Did no one bring you tea? Biscuits? A light lunch?'

'No.' Her mouth shut like a trap but she was

immediately sorry. He did seem such a nice, polite boy. Just the kind of boy she would have loved to have had, had she ever been so blessed. 'But I'm not hungry,' she said, in a more pleasant tone. 'Just a little disgruntled and also somewhat confused. I wonder if you have me mixed up with someone else.'

'I'm not sure,' the lad said. 'I was asked to fetch you and unless you have moved into your lodgings in the last six hours, I am quite sure I have the right person. What I am not sure of is how you can help us.'

'Well, if you don't know,' she said, 'why not go and fetch me someone who does?'

'I have a letter for you,' he said, fishing it out of his inner pocket. It was quite small, folded over and over on itself and sealed with an extravagant amount of sealing wax.

She looked at it, checking the name on the front. She hadn't used that name precisely for a good long while, but it would do. She sniffed it. It smelled of bay rum, always a sign of class. And the wax was hard and brittle, denoting that the man who wrote it wasn't skulking in a room upstairs. She started to break the seal.

'Oh, no, no …' the boy backed away. 'I was told not to be in the room when you opened it.'

'My goodness.' She smiled at him. 'It's not a bomb, is it?'

'If it is,' he said, 'then someone has invented something rather special. No, apparently, the contents of the letter are rather … inflammatory.'

They both smiled at the potential play on words.

'All right, then,' she said, pausing with her thumb behind the seal. 'Off you go. Where will you be, if I want you?'

He pointed. 'Just through there.'

'Wonderful. I'll let you know.' When he was safely gone, she pulled the wax free, unfolded the letter and read it, muttering to herself. 'Madam,' the letter said, 'I do not know if you remember me, but we met some years ago at a review of the fleet in Portsmouth. I was the naval captain with, you were kind enough to say ...' her mutter dropped lower; she didn't want even her own ears to hear his description, let alone any the walls might have and she hoped there were no eyes to see her blushes. He was quite accurate, though, even after all this time. 'I am now on the staff at Plymouth and am concerned at the way this war is going. My superiors are, to a man, idiots. They don't take that little Corsican half seriously enough, in my opinion and what they need is a damned good scare. Jevons got into hot water lately, by saying that he thought the French would come, though not by sea. I think the mad old bugger was trying to be a bit clever, because, after all, what other way is there? But the admirals and such took such umbrage I thought they would tear him limb from limb. So, my dear, and in fond hopes that our weekend together might dispose you to think well of me, I would be so grateful if you could work your wiles in some way, so as to give these petty little men a scare. Yours, fondly ...' and his signature was a squiggle.

She sighed and folded the letter into her bodice. He was asking something very serious and he couldn't see it. It wasn't simply a matter of giving them a scare. She could do that if they were all in the same room. She could easily raise a spirit to give them the willies – she did that every day of the week in parlours and great houses across the land. But ... this was bigger. Possibly *much* bigger. And in her long life, she had had enough of invasions. Great swathes of men, rampaging across the country. Raping. Pillaging. It was easy to have enough of that, that was for certain. Having to learn a new language every couple of centuries or so – though it was intriguing how quickly the native tongue reasserted itself. But it had been a while. She sat back in her chair, relaxed and let herself drift away.

In a drawing room, not very far away as a crow flew, a small but brilliant emperor suddenly felt sleepy. He sent away his advisors, who had been wearing him out anyway, with yelling, screaming, pointing, shoving and pushing, all trying to convince him that their idea was the best. He was tired not just physically, but mentally; he had had steam ships, he had had rafts, he had had balloons, all pushed in front of him as drawings, designs and models – in one rather unusual case made of straws by a more than usually disgruntled English prisoner. But for now, all he wanted to do was sleep. And, as he was the emperor, sleep was what he got.

It was an unusual dream he dreamed. A rather unkempt woman of indeterminate age appeared in front of him and seemed to shake him awake. She picked up a raft and with a ribbon unravelled from her cap, she attached a balloon to it. In his sleep, the emperor smiled. That was *it*! Now, all he needed to do was to remember the dream when he awoke, and it should be job done.

* * *

The woman sat in an austere room in the Office of Works. She was wearing a cotton dress under a hand-knitted cardigan. The bodice and skirt had once been from two garments. Times were hard and she tried not to think of appearances, but really – it was too demeaning. But in the heat of a Spitfire Summer, her more formal clothes were too hot and she wanted to look cool and collected. In front of her sat a testy-looking gent in a crisp uniform. His chest seemed to almost bristle with medals and although she knew quite a lot of military chaps – quite a few had come her way over the years – she didn't recognize all of them and wondered whether this upright field marshal might be a little bit original when it came to the absolute truth.

'Not really comfortable with this,' he barked, his grey moustache blowing in the angry breath. 'One of Mister Ravenley's lot I've heard. But you come highly recommended.'

'I'm sure I do.'

The door opened slowly and another man entered, dressed casually in a creased shirt and trousers gone baggy and shiny at the seat from too much sitting at a desk. His hair was ruffled as if he had run his hands through it once too often. He smiled and slipped into a chair placed crosswise at the end of the desk, a middle-man in every way.

'Thank you for coming,' he said, just a little too late. 'You do indeed come highly recommended. We believe you can help us prevent this invasion which is threatened.'

The woman shrugged. 'Time does what time does,' she said. 'No one can change it.'

The man with the ruffled hair looked dubious and cocked his head at her, questioning. The military gent harrumphed and his moustache blew out again.

'Ruddy nonsense,' he barked. 'Waste of my time and yours. Should be had up for vagrancy, whatever law we could find to suit.'

The man in the shirt held out his hand but it was too late. The woman looked across the desk in silence. The ancient Tarot pack, slick with use, whispered in her hands as she shuffled, shuffled and shuffled again. Finally, she was ready and held out the pack to her military opponent.

'Take a card,' she said. 'Any card.'

THE REVEREND

BY M. J. TROW

THE REVEREND

Spring is everyone's favourite time of the year, isn't it? Waking to the sound of birdsong, going to sleep with the blush of sunset still in the sky? Since that 'spring forward, fall back' nonsense was abolished, there are not even those few disordered weeks when you don't know whether it's breakfast or dinner. No, definitely, Spring is the best time of year. People used to like Spring because of Easter, too. Chocolate, mostly, that was what the draw was. Chocolate eggs, rabbits, chicks – just chocolate, in any shape or form. Then, of course, came rationing and so that went by the wayside and then ... well, somehow Easter never really came back.

The Reverend Alexander Green, BD Oxon., rector of an idyllic little village loved the Spring. He missed the old days, though, the church packed to the gunwales with people he wouldn't see again until midnight mass on Christmas Eve; the hats – as a single gentleman, he never really worked out the hat thing; the flowers, massed in the windows, on the altar and at each pew end. The catch in the throat when singing the Easter hymns. He loved it all – from the moment it kicked off on Shrove Tuesday until Ascension Day, he felt his faith restored enough to take him through the rest of the year. But Spring was always a joy, Easter or no Easter. And this year, he feared, would be a no

Easter year.

Until rationing hit, the village had had cake sales, beetle drives and every conceivable form of fund raiser to make enough money to buy the sheaves of flowers for Easter Sunday. Because, no matter how mild the season, there were not enough acres of garden in the village to provide the thousands of blossoms which the Young Mothers, Women's Institute, Townswomen's Guild, Flower Association and all the rest demanded. Then, the cake sales had gone by the wayside, killed off by lack of sugar, fat, eggs and all the rest that made cakes taste like ... well, cakes. Then the beetle drives had gone, killed by the blackout. These were followed by the demise of the various associations – the Church of the Remnant, though denying it, had siphoned off almost all the women and now his once-packed village hall meetings had dwindled down to just him and the cat, in his kitchen.

It's hard to enthuse about flowers for the church when the only person even remotely interested – and the Reverend Green suspected, as the cat was cleaning her bum quite carefully, that this was not the case – is the cat herself. He could remember the days when they had to leave the doors open so that people who couldn't squeeze in could take part from the churchyard. He could remember the days when the church was thrown open on the afternoon of Holy Saturday and stayed that way for the next week. Sitting there alone at his kitchen table, the Reverend Green sighed.

'More tea, Vicar?' He put on a funny voice, as the cat had yet to speak.

'I don't mind if I do, Eglentyne,' he said – he was something of a Chaucer fan. 'Shall I do the honours?'

'Please,' said the cat's voice. 'As you know, it's tricky without opposable thumbs.'

The Reverend Green bent down and smoothed the cat's sleek head. 'Do you know,' he said, in his normal voice, 'if anyone had stopped me when I was an undergraduate swinging down the High without a care in the world, if anyone had stopped me and told me that before I was as old as any of the dons who taught me that I would be putting on funny voices to talk to a cat, I would have thrown myself in the Isis and no messing.'

Eglentyne looked up at him, affronted. Who was this cat of whom he spoke? She couldn't see a cat in the room, just two pals having a chat. She pressed her head up into his hand and purred. Sometimes, she could honestly believe he understood every word she said.

'You're a good girl,' he said. 'My best friend, in fact.'

Eglentyne purred and licked his thumb, with a tongue like a file. He wasn't a bad old chap, one thing taken with another.

He turned away and put the kettle on, making sure, when he filled the kettle, that some water splashed on his thumb. He wouldn't hurt Eglentyne's feelings by washing, but she had, after all, just been licking out her bum. There were limits, even when a person lived alone.

'Biscuit?' he asked himself in the cat's voice.

'Oh, no, really. I couldn't take your ration,' he said.

'Nonsense,' he replied. 'Treat yourself.'

'Oh, all right then. You've twisted my arm.'

He took down a metal tin from the shelf, one of the few things he had to remind himself of his mother. It was an old Britannia metal thing, hand hammered by the look of it, and although not handsome, it had a nice tight fitting lid so his meagre store of biscuits lasted as long as he needed them to without going stale. He prised the lid off and peered inside. One Garibaldi with ... he blew on it ... only one real dead fly. And a Marie. Not exactly a walk on the culinary wild side. He pretended to think things over and then chose the Marie. Boring, but then he at least knew he had the Garibaldi to look forward to.

The kettle came to the boil and the whistle reached a mad crescendo, almost out of the range of human ears. Eglentyne shook her head and, jumping down from her chair, made a bolt for the door, standing open to the mild Spring day.

The Reverend Green sighed and measured out his tea, almost leaf by precious leaf. Things were getting hard to find, not just luxuries now but the basics of life. Never much of a cook, now that his housekeeper had left, he was reduced mainly to things on toast. Except that, without her baking skills, that very quickly had become things, without the toast. And then, thing. He smiled wryly as he thought that he was probably the only person he knew who could make a tin of sardines last a week. He looked down ruefully at what had once been his paunch and was now simply the fabric of his cassock, gathered in by a broad leather belt. He was a shadow of his former self, in more ways than one.

He poured the hot water on his tea leaves and stirred them in ruminative mood. His mother and father had always disagreed about making tea. *She* always rushed to the kettle while it was still bubbling and poured it, still singing and spitting little spots of super-heated water, onto the leaves, having warmed the pot first, of course. *He* always let it rest a while – one whistled verse of *Tiger Rag* – and only then added it to the leaves. To be honest, he had never been able to taste the difference but nowadays, when he was alone so much, it was good to be reminded of them every time he made a cup of tea. Good people, both, in their way, and he was glad they hadn't lived to see this. Before so much as a buzz bomb had sung through the skies of Hampshire, they had been long dead and gone.

He lifted the lid of the pot and peered in. The few leaves looked quite lonely, swirling around in the pale liquid, but they were doing their job and as soon as they were brewed, he could have a drink. His housekeeper, before she had disappeared, had used a lot of leaves per pot, but had then dried them on the windowsill to use again. And again. And again. The trouble with that, as he pointed out to her, often while spitting one out, was that it was a slight gamble vis a vis how many flies got in the mix. Garibaldis, in fact, had nothing on her ninth incarnation tea.

He solemnly put the Marie biscuit on a plate and set it on the table. He got one of his grandmother's Sevres cups and saucers out of the dresser cupboard and put it alongside. There was a milk jug and sugar bowl to match, but it scarcely seemed worthwhile. He allowed himself one sugar cube once a week and today was not the day. Sometimes, one of the smallholders at the edge of the village would leave him some milk at the door, or a few eggs. But mostly, as today, tea was just tea. Or faintly brown water. It was a matter of perspective.

He carried the teapot over to the table and placed it on a crocheted doily, one of the many things his housekeeper had left behind when she went. He didn't really see the point, but she had always been very strict about such things and, well, at his age, he was finding that old habits died hard.

He gave the pot a final swirl and tutted to himself. He got up and went into the sitting room and got the silver tea strainer from the shelf. He had once had many nice things, most of them gone now, some sold to provide necessities and some, he was sure, stolen during his meetings. He sighed as he gave the strainer a light buff with a corner of his cassock. It was true that indeed, you never truly knew anyone, when the chips were down.

There was nothing else for it, he couldn't put it off any longer. He had to pour the tea. He did it slowly, watching the leaves all join together into a thin, brown mat in the strainer. He paused and checked. Actually, not at all bad. It looked quite like tea. Not gnats' piss, as his father used to sometimes call it. Not the old builders' tea which sometimes needed a spade to get moving; the days of builders' tea were long gone, along with most builders. If people's houses started to get a bit wobbly these days, they just moved the furniture to hold the walls up, hide the damp, whatever the problem might be. But – he tapped the strainer against the cup and replaced it in its holder – as tea went, this was all right. Okay, as the soldiers used to say, before they went away.

He looked into the cup. The surface of the liquid was still moving, almost oily in its enclosed circle. Blue lights shot off the surface and reflected its own version of the ceiling. Now it was ready, it didn't look that appetising, but it was a drink and that was important. He remembered a nice VAD he had met – how long ago, was it? – and she had told him that keeping hydrated was a very key thing when it came to health. She had told him a lot else, as well, in the sweaty dark, and he didn't remember it all. But sometimes, in the long nights, when he remembered her, he had to get up and splash himself with cold water. That kind of thoughts never helped anyone, in his experience.

He took a sip. Not at all bad. If you took a sniff before the sip, the smell could take you right back, to the meetings with all the associations, with cakes on the table and the boom of the echo in the church hall ringing with the talking and the tapping of the gavel on the wood. Here, in his silent kitchen, it wasn't quite the same, but he brought the meeting to order, nonetheless.

He proffered the plate around, with its single biscuit. Everyone declined it and so he took it, with polite demurs. To dunk, or not to dunk. That was the question. Was it the milk in the tea that made the biscuit taste better, or was it the biscuit that made the tea taste better? He wasn't sure, but decided against anyway. It was always so shame-making when a biscuit fell in half and had to be scooped out with a spoon.

Spoon! He knew he had forgotten something and went back into the sitting room to get one. Might as well have one of the nice ones, an apostle spoon from his grandmother's set. He had always hated going to grandma's house. Having to be quiet on a Sunday and not speak unless spoken to. Which, in practice, was never. She had had seven indoor staff, she always told him, before the war. She would always sigh at that point and look at his father with a frown. All her sons, she would say, had died in the war. 'Not me, mother!' his father would say, with mock brightness. And she would sigh again and look away. There was a story there, he knew, but now anyone who knew it was dead. Now. What had he come into the room for? Oh, yes. A spoon. He chose St Matthew, for no other reason than that he was the only one who mentioned the Three Kings, his all-time favourite part of the Christmas story. He polished him as he went back to the kitchen. Don't start thinking about Christmas yet, he told himself, let's get Easter over with first.

He stirred his tea automatically. Did tea need stirring when there was no milk and no sugar? He fished out an errant tea leaf, a piece of dust, really, which had escaped the strainer. He tapped the spoon on the table. 'Will the meeting come to order?'

Pairs of invisible eyes turned to him, pairs of invisible lips stopped talking and they all waited.

'As always at this time of the year,' he announced, 'we meet together to discuss the Easter flowers. The ladies of the flower rota ...' He smiled round the table and invisible heads bobbed back, '... know more than I about what is needed, so I will let them take the floor.'

He took another sip of tea and tried to focus on their faces. Sometimes, he could recognise them, sometimes they seemed to merge, to become those faces he had seen above those dun-coloured clothes, working in the fields, worshipping with the remnant. He put the cup down but had to search for the saucer with trembling fingers. Something was definitely not right. For some reason, the women crowded around his kitchen table just wouldn't keep still, he couldn't concentrate on any one face.

He pushed his cup away and leaned back, closing his eyes. From previous experience, they would argue themselves to a standstill and everything would be done exactly as it had been the year before and the year before that. They didn't need him ...

To his surprise, he found himself no longer in his kitchen, but sitting in a meadow. He knew the one, it was just outside the village and was where they used to hold the church fetes, in happier days. The sun was shining, but there was a freshness in the air which told him it was still Spring. So that was all right then; he hadn't missed Easter. The stalls were going up around him, women were happily chattering and calling to each other, passing the ends of bunting to their men, teetering on ladders up in the trees. The bunting was a bit bright for his taste. Red, white and blue, all very patriotic, but he liked a nice yellow and green theme for Easter, very … eggy. But he didn't say anything; he left all that kind of thing to the women. They did all that kind of thing. It was warm in the sun and he closed his eyes. They would be glad that he wasn't poking his nose in; there had been problems about that, in previous years. It was good just to rest in the sun, letting it warm his bones. He didn't know why he felt so cold. It was unseasonably warm for April, after all.

He opened his eyes as a loud noise split the sky. Not one but dozens of aircraft were going overhead, making a noise fit to wake the dead. The women putting up the stalls looked up, shielding their eyes from the glare of the sun and some of them were crying. The men up in the trees seemed to have gone; the Reverend Green looked about him, wondering what could have happened to them. They usually could manage a few hours off work to help out for the fete, but … a faint memory stirred. Was their disappearance anything to do with the planes, perhaps? But no – these were just men from the village; what would they know about planes?

The bunting was starting to look a bit tatty. The red, white and blue had faded and some triangles were interspersed with bits of floral fabric, clearly cut from a dress which had long outlived its usefulness. When a dress had been a blouse then a waistcoat, there was nowhere for it to go but into the duster box or for bunting. Without the men, they were having trouble attaching it at the ends. He started to struggle to his feet (somehow, his cassock had become entangled and it wasn't easy) but his housekeeper, seeing him trying to rise, scurried over with a cup of tea and a slice of rather flat-looking cake.

'Don't worry, Reverend,' she said. 'We're managing. Just you rest here in the sun.'

He tried to explain about the cassock around his legs, but somehow it wasn't that important. He didn't tell her that the cake was certainly not one of her best. He settled back again and watched the women work. They always made the fête a success. They didn't need him at all. He just said thank you. He didn't ask where all the men had gone or why the planes had been going over. As long as the fête was a success, that was all he cared. The Easter flowers wouldn't buy themselves.

He woke to a chill in the air. The weather seemed to have changed and the sky was very overcast. Nonetheless, the village women were manfully erecting the stalls and at a quick glance, they all seemed to be the same as ever. No cake stall, perhaps – and that was a shame, it was the biggest earner, regularly, every year – and the second-hand clothes looked fourth or fifth hand now, but the white elephant was there and so was the book stall. The Reverend Green looked around and noticed that his housekeeper seemed to be elsewhere. Without her beady eye on him, he could get up and wander around. As long as he didn't change anything or get in the way, surely, that would be all right.

He wandered over to the bookstall. There were fewer books than usual, but he knew in these difficult times, not so many were being printed, so that might explain it. He had a small but rather special collection of religious books back at the rectory and many, if not most, had been found on stalls just such as these. He ran his finger along the spines. There were books on wildlife, gardening, sewing, carpentry. There were books on how to bring up children – it had never struck him before that it was necessary to have some kind of manual – and how to groom your dog. There were a few on history, but he noticed that it was very ancient history; Romans, Greeks, Phoenicians. He looked closer. Some of the books looked to be in bad shape and he tutted; just because this was a village fête, there was no excuse for bad merchandise. He pulled one out at random. A once-lovely copy of Browning's poems. Sometimes a little too saccharine, but the man could get to the heart of the matter sometimes. *My Last Duchess*, for example – they had discussed that for weeks, back in the sunny days at Oxford, floating down the river, young men with their lives ahead of them.

The book flopped open, lifelessly. There was the engraved bookplate, from one of the big houses in the village, now commandeered by some secret government office. And then … nothing. Not even the Pied Piper had been able to use his charms to escape the censor's knife. He looked around. Who was in charge of the stall? Who was responsible for this desecration? He picked up other books and flung them down one by one. All, all had been cut about and spoiled. Just a few had the odd page left. How to turn the heel of a sock. How to prune apple trees. How to plane a plank. How to chastise a child. Apart from that, nothing. He felt sick with rage and held on to the edge of the table.

Kind but firm hands were leading him back to his deck chair on the edge of the meadow. Someone pressed a cup of tea into his hands. He looked around wildly and, as he began to get calmer, noticed, fluttering against the darkling sky, bunting, made of dun coloured fabric, almost too coarse and stiff to flutter in even the stiffest breeze.

He woke on the edge of the meadow. Except that, for some strange reason, it was no longer a meadow. It had been ploughed in uncertain rows by untrained hands. Women and small children, all dressed alike, were walking slowly down the rows. They all carried a basket with seedlings laid in rows and they were planting them regularly in the turned soil. Watching them was quite hypnotic. Step, step, step, bend, plant. Step, step, step, bend, plant. He found himself reciting the creed, in time to their work, but it made a nonsense of the words and after a while, he had to stop. 'I believe in God – the Father Almighty, Creator of heav – en and earth, and in – Jesus Christ, His on …' Splitting the word 'only' to match their rhythm was just too much; he would finish it later, when his head could be more silent.

He started watching the workers carefully. There were faces which he thought he knew, but the life and spark which had made them who they were seemed to have gone. Perhaps it was simply the repetitive task which had done this to them; it didn't seem any time at all since the children had been lining up at the fete to see who was the prettiest baby, who had the knobbliest knees.

One thing, though – there were now at least a few men about. In some cases, though not many, they worked with the women and children, wearing the same brown clothes and wearing the same rather inconvenient hats, which often fell off and landed in the dirt. When this happened, a red-cloaked man with one eye covered, would swoop down the line and drag the wrongdoer upright, berating them with much pointing upwards and gesticulating. The Reverend Green was reminded of his priest at Sunday School when you couldn't remember your catechism, but even he had love behind his ready tongue and readier cane. This seemed a loveless thing indeed.

Behind the sowers, the leeks – if such they were – heeled over limply, as if they had given up too. Again, he thought of scripture. 'A sower went forth to sow and some seed fell on stony ground.' The seeds which Matthew said was devoured by the birds of the air were the plants trampled by the men in red who didn't care where their sandaled feet fell when going to chastise the workers for a dropped hat. Forgetting the scriptures for a moment, the Reverend Green was reminded of a saying of his grandmother's. Throwing the baby out with the bathwater.

He looked down at his lap. He seemed to have a very small bath in his hand – no, it was a cup of tea. Looking back at the workers, they were now being visited by a very bent old woman, ladling out drinks into their cupped hands. He looked closer. Could that be his housekeeper, back again after all this time?

A tear gathered in the corner of his eye. He dashed it away with the back of his hand, and sipped his tea. A nice cup of tea. That always made him feel better …

'So.' The policeman was curt and the sobbing woman was finding it hard to concentrate. What she needed was some sympathy, not this.

'So, this here is the Reverend … what, did you say?

Purple? Blue? Sounds a bit unlikely to me.'

She blew her nose. 'Green. The Reverend Alexander Green. He is rector of this parish.'

The policeman looked around him, at the sparse kitchen, the empty cupboards, the empty cup, cold teapot, the single biscuit on the plate in the middle of the table. It didn't look like the rectories he remembered from his choirboy days.

'Are you sure?'

'Of course I'm sure!' The woman was not so much upset now as annoyed. 'I was his housekeeper for more years than I can count.'

The policeman jumped on what he thought was the salient word. '*Was*. Why was you his housekeeper?' That didn't sound right, but it wasn't his habit to correct himself; it was demeaning.

The woman was confused. 'Well … I suppose I needed a job and he needed a housekeeper.' She wasn't sure why that wasn't clear to the man.

'No, I mean, why are you no longer his housekeeper?'

'Oh, I see. Well,' she held out the brown skirt, pointed to the hat under her arm, 'I joined the Church of the Remnant and … well, it didn't seem right. I couldn't live here anymore anyway – as you know, we sleep in dormitories in the Remnant – so I just … well, I left him.'

'Did he mind when you gave in your resignation?'

She looked shamefaced. 'Well, I didn't, as such,' she said, muttering now as if a low voice would hide the low act. 'I just … went.'

The man looked at the peaceful face of what remained of the Reverend Alexander Green, BD, Oxon. 'Wasn't that a bit … thoughtless? Old chap like this?'

The housekeeper looked at the man's face too. 'To tell the truth, I never thought he was that old. A bit set in his ways but … now I come to look, he does look old, doesn't he? Not *lined*, you know. Just … weary.'

'Death does that,' the policeman said, snapping his notebook shut. 'Irons out the lines. Have you never heard people say they have never seen their deceased loved ones look so well as when they're laid out for the coffin?'

The housekeeper wasn't sure she had, but was prepared to concede this could be so.

'Did he have any family?' the policeman asked.

'Not as far as I know,' the woman said. 'A few cards at Christmas, but I don't remember him celebrating his birthday. You do that, don't you, when you've got family?'

'Hmm. Well, it looks like it will be a government job then, burying him.' He flicked out a pad of forms and wrote for a moment, muttering as he filled in the bits he already knew. 'Name ...hmmm. Age ... unknown. Address ... hmmm.' He looked at the woman. 'Any religious beliefs, do you know?'

Her eyes widened. 'He's the *vicar*!' she said.

'Doesn't necessarily apply,' the policeman said, on his high horse. 'But let's assume 'yes'.' He made a tick with a flourish, checked down the rest of the form and signed it with a terse initial. 'Right, that's that.' He tore the triplicate form off the pad. 'Right, that's one for him,' he slapped one on the Reverend Green's bald head, where it stuck automatically with a built in glue strip. 'One for me.' He folded it and slipped it into his pocket. 'And one for the office. They'll send a van shortly.'

The woman stifled a sob.

'You all right?' It was automatic, no more.

'I ... I should have visited him more. I should have kept an eye on him. I ... to find him like this. It's just terrible.'

'Don't blame yourself, Missus,' the man said. 'Can't be everywhere, can we? 'Specially now. These days, know what I mean. Still, it's nice you brought him flowers.' He gestured to the daffodils, massed in vases all around the room, their honey scent overlaying the stale air. 'Bit over the top, perhaps, but nice.'

The woman looked at him, eyes wide. 'Flowers?' she said. 'I didn't bring him flowers.'

THE POLICEMAN

BY KYT WRIGHT

Various Authors

THE POLICEMAN

Old Bill Dixon arrived home in the early hours to sit heavily in his chair and stare blankly into the dying embers of the fire, feeling detached from reality, as if underwater.

'Is that you, Bill?' called his wife Maureen coming down the stairs in her fleecy dressing gown.

'Who did you think it was you daft bat, the milkman?' he asked, trying to pretend everything was normal, *how can I be making jokes, must be shock?*

'No, I always leave a bottle outside with a note in it so he knows it's safe to come up,' she responded and they both laughed. Mo, as she was known, was slightly younger than him but they had been happily married for over thirty years. 'Want a cuppa tea?'

'No thanks, me duck, I'll just sit quietly awhile if it's all the same to you.' *They're bastards, the whole lot of 'em!*

'Well, I'm having one now I'm up,' she glanced at his ashen face and dishevelled uniform. 'Are you alright? You don't look well.'

'Yes, Mo, 'ad a bad night, don't wanna talk about it. Be fine after a bit of kip,' replied Bill, *he'd had a bad night right enough, no doubt of that!*

* * *

It had started last week when Dixon set off on the night beat with PC Richard Thomas, a young lad exempt from conscription because of his position in the police. Old Bill, being considered a safe pair of hands, had been given charge of the new recruit.

'I'm thinking about joining up, Bill,' he announced as they strolled the bomb-damaged streets in the vicinity of what remained of the cathedral.

'What? Don't tell me, Gloria's mates 'ave bin on at 'er again, haven't they?'

Young Richard was smitten with a girl called Gloria, she didn't mind that he hadn't served in the army but her gaggle of friends kept on ribbing her about walking out with a *conchy* or Conscientious Objector, which of course he was not.

He pulled a face. 'I dunno, Bill, perhaps I should, you know, King and Country an' all that?'

'Don't be a fool, lad, you're serving the nation as much here as in some far corner of the Empire. Coppers risk their bloody lives every time they step out during the blackout, there's many of us been stuck with a blade or bricked over the head, to say nowt of Jerry dropping bombs on everybody!'

'I know Bill but …' he started.

'No, no, don't make no excuses. Does your girl want you to leave her all alone and bugger off to war?' interjected the older constable.

'She says not but …'

'If she says not then her mates can go and be damned!' he interrupted again.

Before his companion could answer they heard a muffled scream, Dixon motioned to him to be quiet and they headed in the direction from whence it came, as unobtrusively as possible in regulation boots. A further noise from a bombed-out building told of something going on within but as they entered, Bill trod on some fallen plaster that had once been part of the ceiling and it broke with a loud crunch. There came an exclamation from the next room, followed by further muffled cries so both policemen dashed in to shine their torches on a woman, clothes in disarray, cowering in the corner.

Dixon took stock of the situation immediately. 'Where is he, me duck?' The woman pointed to the broken window as a clatter was heard in the backyard. 'Dick, get after him, I'll catch up!' then he turned to see the woman dashing from the room. 'Don't worry love, we'll sort the bastard out when we get him and I'll make bloody sure he can't do it again!' he yelled after her as she fled. Dixon wasn't surprised at this, even though they'd virtually caught him in the act he'd doubtlessly get away with it. Some poor girl had come to the station the other month saying she'd been raped and because she'd no proof the damned Sergeant had her arrested for wasting police time.

'It might not be the same bastard as done it that time but he was going to get his balls crushed when I catch him up!' thought Dixon setting off in pursuit.

He had nearly caught up when the thick clouds broke, briefly allowing the moon to illuminate his colleague clambering over the rubble-strewn landscape while the culprit could be seen entering a derelict house. Then there was a bright flash and the building collapsed taking half the terrace down with it, *bloody hell, there must have been an unexploded bomb in there!*

The old policeman carefully made his way through the pall of smoke to see PC Thomas standing dazed, a thin trickle of blood marking a red streak down his dust-covered face. 'Are you alright Dick?'

'Yes, Bill, but that chap?'

'Didn't stand a chance, brown bread without a doubt, never thought I'd say this but Jerry's just done us a favour.'

'Eh?' said Thomas, looking askance.

'Well, I was gonna give him a right good kicking, especially in his meat and two veg but this saves any paperwork, all nice and tidy and the bastard's never gonna do it again neither!'

'What about the woman?' asked the younger man, incredulous at his colleague's sangfroid.

'Done a runner and I don't blame the poor lass one bit, she wouldn't get no bloody justice would she?' replied Bill.

PC Thomas nodded in understanding.

'Well, best go and check this fella's really dead I suppose?' suggested Bill and they began making their way towards where the house had once stood.

'Ugh, is that a bit of him?' asked Dick, they were picking their way carefully up the pile of rubble that had once been someone's home and a red fleshy scrap had been picked out in the light of the younger policeman's torch.

'Yep, don't ask me what though?' Bill shone his torch in his companion's face to see the shocked expression and grabbed his shoulder firmly. 'Come on, lad, shape up; if you're serious about joining the army you'll be seeing much worse than that.'

They crested the mound to see the house had collapsed into what had been the cellar but it was so dark that their torchlight could not penetrate to the bottom.

'Bloody hell, Bill, that must have been a big 'un!' remarked Thomas.

'You're not wrong there, son, wonder how long it's been there? We ought to try and find the bugger's ID card but it's too bloody dark tonight, I'll pop back and have a look tomorrow before I start me shift.'

As they made to leave, a slithering noise came from the darkness and they shone their lights down, once again to no effect. 'Anyone down there?' called Dixon.

There was no answer so they started to walk away. 'It's just stuff sliding down the hole.' the younger policeman said nervously.

'Yes!' agreed the other, nodding.

Then there was a guttural growl that chilled the very marrow of their bones.

PC Thomas froze. 'What was that?'

'A stray dog probably' replied Bill, nerves on edge. He had an uncomfortable feeling that hidden eyes were watching them.

'I'd swear it came from that hole.'

'Just an echo, come on let's be on our way, shall we? We'll tell Sergeant Mardy-arse about the bomb but we won't bother about the other thing; justice has been served in my eyes and I doubt we'll see that poor woman again.'

'But that growl?'

'Could be anything, do you want to check it out in the dark?' asked Dixon.

'Er, no,' responded Thomas.

'Right then, I'll pop over tomorrow like I said and have a look.'

The pair duly reported the explosion and the dour sergeant, whose name was really Mardment, wrote it all down saying he would phone the UXB squad when he had a chance.

* * *

Bill got up late the next morning and read the paper while listening to the radio; none of it made much sense to Bill. There'd been no news of what was happening in Europe, there was vague talk of countries he was sure he had never heard of before. In fact, Bill couldn't remember the last time he had heard any real news of how the war was actually going. *Official secrets eh?*

After he'd fed the chickens in the backyard, Bill tended his tiny plot, *dig for victory they said, they won't win much with my garden!* Then he sat down to dinner and Mo had done them proud, they each had a small lamb chop with their potatoes and cabbage, a nice change from Lord Woolton pie. But potatoes, always potatoes. If Bill never saw those stupid cartoon characters Potato Pete and Doctor Carrot again, he could die a happy man. Part of the perks of the job was turning a blind eye in exchange for the odd favour and today's meat had been paid for with petrol coupons he'd *acquired* a few nights before.

He put on his smart blue uniform, admired the shine on the toecaps of his boots and after picking up his gasmask gave Mo an affectionate peck on the cheek before setting off.

Bill walked along the same street as the previous night, noticing the spire of the cathedral rising proudly over the houses. It was one of the few parts of the building intact and stood as if to affirm the enduring power of the almighty. Although Dixon had been confirmed as a boy, he didn't hold much faith in religion but nevertheless the sight of the edifice gave him some comfort. They would doubtless rebuild the city after the war and Bill hoped it would try to recreate what had gone before and not just be a horrendous nightmare cooked up by some bloody modern architect.

After continuing past the house where the cries had been heard Dixon rounded the corner to arrive at the row of empty terraces, which now had a large bite out of it, to see workmen erecting barricades and danger signs across the street.

'Howdo Bill?' said the man in charge and Dixon recognised him as Marty Bickley, Air Raid Warden and garage mechanic.

'Afternoon Marty, I saw this bugger go off last night so I thought I'd have a look in the daylight.'

'We've not had a raid for nearly a year so that thing must've have been sitting there all that time, amazing innit?' He looked furtively over his shoulder as if relating a great secret. 'We're supposed to be cordoning it off until the Army get here but since you're a copper it won't hurt.' He surveyed the damaged street. 'It must have been a blockbuster to do that much damage! Ere, I bet you didn't know this row was built over an old tunnel system?'

'What, you mean like sewers?' asked the policeman.

'Nah, definitely not sewers, there's a bloody big arched tunnel smack under the cellar!' replied the ARP. 'Tell yer what, we've got a ladder down there, I'll take you meself.'

Dixon accompanied the ARP man and scrambled up the rubble to see clearly that the hole went well below the level of the cellar and, despite being partially filled in, a tall stone arch was visible with a gap where the fallen masonry did not quite reach. 'See, mediaeval, I reckon,' said Bickley with assumed confidence.

'Have you taken a look through?' asked the policeman.

'I did shine a torch in, lotta rubble the other side but the darkness seems to swallow the light up very quickly so I couldn't see much else. Tell you what tho', it must lead somewhere 'cos there's a hell of a cold draught comes out,' answered Bickley.

'Yes, goes right to Yarmouth!' Bill chuckled. 'I reckon a person could squeeze through that gap, have you thought about going in and having a look around?'

The ARP man gave him a look. 'Are you kidding, Bill? I wouldn't go in there for all the tea in China, old Jonesy up there reckons he heard summat moving in all that dark,' he waved at the worried-looking figure stood at the top of the ladder.' And there's summat else, can't you feel it?'

Now that it had been mentioned Dixon could feel a chill in his bones just like the night before and again there was that feeling of being watched.

'You're right, it is a bit cold down here and you said he heard a noise?'

'Like wheezy breathing, he said, reckoned it made him feel funny' replied the ARP man. 'It was probably just the wind though?'

'Yes, I'll bet it was,' Dixon shuddered. 'Let's go up, this place is giving me the willies.'

Once at the top the policeman realised no mention had been of any human remains so asked. 'You haven't found a body or any bits of one in the rubble?'

'Nah, were we supposed to, oh no don't tell me we've got to dig through this lot?'

'Noo, noo,' he answered reassuringly. 'I just wondered if some old dosser might 'a set it off or something.

'Nuffin,' Bickley shrugged and shook his head. Dixon pondered on this, he'd spotted a few other gory remnants after PC Thomas' grim discovery but now they were all gone. *It'll have been that stray dog ...*

* * *

Dixon and Thomas were walking the beat next evening and putting the world to rights, Dick mentioned that Gloria had told him how much she admired a man in uniform but when he reminded her that he wore one she had fluttered her long eyelashes to say. 'No, I meant a proper one, like a sailor's or the RAF, they look so smart in their uniforms.' She had raised her eyebrows at this and smiled but when he had shown his dismay, Gloria had insisted he would look just as good in a soldier's uniform.

'I would give 'er the elbow if I were you, son,' said Dixon sagely.

'I like her, Bill, and she likes me too.'

'I'm not having a pop, Dick. It's just that you're reading too much into this thing with Gloria.'

The younger man harrumphed and the pair continued in silence after that. They were checking shop doors, making sure they were locked up tight, when the sound of breaking glass drew their attention. The policemen proceeded briskly towards the sound and sure enough, upon their approach, a figure darted from a chemist's shop doorway.

'Oy, police stop where you are!' yelled Dixon, the shadowy figure did not stop but instead ran as fast as possible in the other direction.

They gave chase, with Thomas easily gaining on the man and pulling down him. 'Got ya!' he cried.

Dixon caught up and as they dragged the weaselly man to his feet, bottles of pills fell from his pocket. ''Ello Johnny, up to your old tricks, are yer?'

The man muttered inaudibly before being swiftly frogmarched to the station where after a quick booking and an even quicker cuppa, Dixon and Thomas set off once more into the night. They had just returned to the very same street when a police whistle could be heard and following the sound they discovered PC Wyatt kneeling by a prone figure on the ground and attempting to staunch a bleeding wound on the man's neck with his handkerchief.

'Bloody hell, Tony, what happened?' asked Dixon.

'Some bastard stabbed this poor sod in the throat and did a runner! Jock's gone after him, the bastard's headed towards the cathedral.'

'How long ago?' asked Dixon.

'Couple a minutes at most, we almost bleeding fell over them, went that way!'

The older policeman looked in the direction Wyatt was pointing. 'Right, Dick, go find a telephone. I'm going after Jock, let's see if we can't bag another piece of scum tonight!' *it was a long shot, but …*

A few minutes later Dixon saw something lying on the pavement in the moonlight; it was a wallet that must have belonged to the victim, empty of course but at least he was going the right way.

'Did he stab that bloke just for his wallet?' asked PC Andrews, emerging from the shell of someone's shattered home.

'Who knows, Jock?' replied Old Bill. 'Could be some kind of grudge or maybe he hadn't paid his dues, the robbery might be a cover-up job.'

There was a sound of slipping masonry from a nearby bombsite followed by a cry of alarm.

'Do you think that's him?'

'Might be, hopefully, he's fell and broke his neck or something,' replied Dixon.

'Bill, ain't you got any charity in you?'

'Been at this game too long mate and think of the paperwork it'll save.' He grinned mirthlessly at this. 'Keep your wits about yer and remember this sod's handy with a blade.'

They split up and cautiously climbed the precarious pile while trying to make as little noise as possible but of the knife-man, there was no sign.

'I can't see anyone, Bill,' called Andrews some distance to his right.

'Me neither,' he responded. 'Well, better press on just in case!' and with that Dixon started down the other side of the debris but his foot slipped on something and he slid awkwardly downslope on his backside.

'You alright, Bill?' asked the policeman, who had seen his ungainly descent.

'Yes, I might need a rubber ring for a while,' he stood stiffly, half smiling.

'What's that on your trousers?' Andrews, shining his light, could see something smeared on the seat of his pants and his left boot was covered in it too.

'Dunno, I stood on something up there and lost my footing, felt like a sack of something soft. Bloody hell, it don't half whiff!' he had squatted to examine the toe of his boot by the light of his torch and it was no longer shiny but covered in a putrid-smelling ooze.

'I'll go and have a look,' announced the other constable.

Careful, it's a bit precarious, like,' called Dixon after him.

He watched PC Andrews' torchlight as the policeman stepped nimbly up. *Oh to be ten years younger*, he thought before hearing his colleague cry in horror. It was followed by the unmistakable sound of vomiting.

* * *

Even the usually unflappable Sergeant Mardment looked askance at the officers when they made their report. Finally believing what had been said, he called in forensics who examined everywhere as best they could in the dark; when dawn came they were able to take photographs of the full horror exposed by the rising sun.

Dixon had quite literally put his foot in what was left of Stanley 'Knife' Phipps, according to the ID found close to his remains. He had a reputation of being a hard man who would see to anyone for a price. The unfortunate hoodlum had been reduced to a meaty skeleton, its internal organs bizarrely intact and the pathologist asserted that it had been in one piece until the policeman had put his size ten boot in it to slip on a mix of viscera and bodily fluids.

Inspector Tennyson ordered them all to his office and Dixon, wearing a pair of new trousers, his boots cleaned but not shiny, decided it was time for the truth. He related the incidents of the rapist and the bomb and when he had finished, the Inspector stared at the officer with a tic in his left eye. 'So, apart from not reporting a crime and the death of a member of the public, is there anything else you haven't told me?' He was incandescent with rage but holding it in remarkably well.

'Sir, I don't think that body could have belonged to Phipps.'

'And why not, Dixon?' asked Tennyson curiously.

'Well, he didn't have that much of a head start on us and it would take a while to do that much damage to a soul. It was like someone had carved the best cuts off him?'

'Well thank you for that, Constable, I must have missed you getting that degree in pathology,' remarked the Inspector sarcastically.

'But, sir?' continued Bill.

'Police Constable Dixon, the pathologist is still examining the body and will give his verdict in good time! Is there anything else any of you might have overlooked?'

'Well, there was that growling noise,' chipped in PC Thomas before Dixon could speak.

'Growling noise?' snarled Tennyson and Bill reluctantly told of the strange sound heard after the first death.

The inspector ordered Andrews and Wyatt out of his office then took a deep breath and said, as calmly as he could. 'By rights, I should put you two on report but since we are very short-staffed no further action will be taken, for now!' he then took a deep breath before announcing. 'But, since this terrible situation may be attributable to that bomb-hole in some strange way, the boundary fence will be guarded at all times and guess what? You lucky pair have the night watch. Good day constables and consider yourself lucky there's a war on!'

'Thank you, sir,' croaked Dixon, horrified at the thought of spending his shift there.

Thomas seemed quite exuberant as they left the station. 'If we were to catch this killer, we'd be in the papers!'

'Look, Dick, this is bloody serious and I don't mind admitting it, I'm worried.'

'Why?'

'You didn't see the body, it couldn't 'ave been Stanley Knife; it'd have taken a long time to do that to him.'

'But you found his ID card?'

'I found *an* ID card. What if someone had just dropped the body there and that cry me and Jock heard was Phipps being collared by whoever did it, what if the ID had just fallen out his pocket?'

'Who in the name of God would do that?'

'Someone evil!' answered Dixon.

'Oh don't be such an old woman!'

'What!'

'We'll look out for each other Bill, it'll be fine.'

'Hmmph!' growled Dixon walking sharply away.

* * *

Bill Dixon had been a copper since he was Dick's age and was now past retirement; if not for the shortage of recruits he would have been pensioned off years ago. The fact was, he had been seriously considering jacking it in for some time *but the country needed him*, he would tell himself trying to justify staying on but the truth was he was scared to leave, scared at how corrupt the force had become since the war started and how much further it might sink when all the old-timers left.

One bad apple can spoil the barrel so they say? Bill wondered how many there were in the Warwickshire and Coventry Constabulary.

He slept fitfully that morning and on getting up sat at the table staring at his unappetising breakfast, reconstituted powdered egg sitting on a slice of toast made with the barely palatable National Loaf.

'Bill, love, eat your breakfast before it goes cold,' said Mo, concerned at his strange mood.

'Sorry duck, I'm not hungry at the moment, a cup of

tea will do just fine,' and his wife cleared it away, tutting at the waste of good food. He sat disconsolately, listening to the light programme, the thin newspaper unread on his lap. Later in the afternoon, he gave his surprised wife a long hug saying quietly, 'I love you, Mo,' before setting off, determined to do his duty no matter what might happen.

Having checked in at the station early it was still quite light when he arrived at the barricade. Thomas was nowhere in sight, but an elderly man was there, leaning on a walking stick while peering at the mound of rubble.

'Evening,' said Dixon in greeting; the man reminded him of someone.

'Good evening, constable,' replied the man in a refined voice.

'I'm sorry, sir, but you really can't be here.'

'Oh, that's all right, officer, I just saw the barrier and thought I'd have a nosey.'

'Well, I don't want to insist ...' said Dixon, trying not to insist. The man smiled and nodded in understanding then walked off at quite a lively pace using his walking stick, pausing only to say good evening to Thomas who was walking towards them.

'Who was he?' asked the younger policeman.

'No idea but he seemed rather interested in that bomb hole.'

'Looked a bit like that politician bloke, Darnley?' Thomas mused.

'Too old,' grunted Dixon in reply. Darkness had begun to fall and they huddled around the night watchman's brazier someone had left for them. *Probably Marty*, thought Bill.

They had hardly spoken a word since starting their duty so Thomas decided to break the ice. 'Bill, sorry I was being a bit hot-headed this morning.'

'S'alright, Dick, I am getting old and I think it's high time I packed it in.'

'Go on, you're the lynchpin of the station. How would we cope without you?' retorted Thomas jokingly.

'Tell that to old Mardy-arse and bloody inspector

Tennis-court!'

'Woo, watch your language,' laughed Dick. 'In all the time I've worked with you I've never heard you effing anything before?'

'I'm in a mood, son, Tennyson's going to hang us out to dry.'

'You reckon?'

'I reckon.'

The policemen stood stoically at their station until the early hours when Dixon heard heavy breathing close by.

'Bill, did you hear that?' whispered his colleague anxiously.

'Yes, it came from behind that wall' replied Dixon in hushed tones.

'We ought to look, oughtn't we?'

'Bugger that!' The older policeman's heart was in his mouth.

'Bill we're coppers, I'm going to look,' and with that, Thomas set off across the rubble. Dixon watched him for a second then followed cursing under his breath.

They rounded the broken wall shining their torches to see ... nothing.

'Nothing here, Dick let's go back,' suggested Dixon.

'It could've come from down there?' Thomas shone his beam into the inky blackness of the cellar.

'I hope you're not thinking what I think you're thinking,' Bill said, but before the young policeman could answer the sound of police whistles echoed in the distance. 'We should see what the trouble is!'

'But the inspector said we were to stand guard here?'

'We have done, all bleeding night, and our shift changes in an hour, come on let's see what all the fuss is about!' asserted Bill, *anything to get away from this creepy place.*

A few streets away, a cluster of Bobbies marked where the incident had happened; a couple of them looked horrified while another leaned with one hand against the wall, his supper on the pavement by his feet.

'Now then, what's all this, then?' asked Bill.

'We've found another bleeding body!' replied PC

Andrews shakily.

'Christ! Let's take a look,' Dixon made his way into a dark jitty and shone his torch on yet another vision from hell. The greater part of the skin had been removed along with most of the muscle tissue leaving something that resembled an anatomical model. The skull had been split by something like, at Dixon's best guess, an axe or a butcher's cleaver. Disturbingly, some of the remaining flesh had what looked like teeth marks in it.

'It's a bloody mess and no mistake' stated Andrews, who had steeled himself to follow.

PC Thomas had decided not to look at the body.

Dixon noticed a tattoo on the left forearm where the skin remained. It was a dagger with a rose briar growing around it. 'That's quite distinctive, might be able to identify the poor bugger from it?'

'Don't need to, it's Stanley Knife,' replied Jock, a little queasily.

'Don't tell that to Tennyson, he tore me off a strip for suggesting the first one wasn't him.'

'Well, I've felt his collar often enough and that's his tattoo, very pleased with it he was.'

The Inspector turned up at the scene to see for himself and listened grimly while Jock related his observation. 'You're mistaken Andrews. Has it not crossed your *or* Dixon's mind that anyone could have a similar tattoo?' and he glared at Bill before walking off angrily. The older policeman noticed Tennyson stop at a large black car to briefly converse with the stern driver before it disappeared into the early morning gloom.

* * *

Bill shuffled lazily into the sitting room, rubbing his eyes after another awful night's sleep. He opened the curtains and pulled back the net curtain over his window. Ruins, grey, cold, heartless ruins. Coventry had taken a beating, all right. It was said his town even gave birth to a new word for a city devastated by the bombs, 'Coventrate'. Bill tutted; his city was coventrated enough alright. Among the ruins though there was a bizarre beauty, Rosebay Willowherb, 'fireweed', flourished, its beautiful magenta flowers thriving among the ash of former fires. Like the poppy fields that covered the senseless slaughter of the Great War, nature didn't take long at all to conceal the worst of humanity.

Bill snapped out of his daydream and sat down in his favourite chair before the fire to read last night's *Coventry Telegraph* after breakfast. It didn't take long for him to swear aloud, something he rarely did at home.

'Bill, there's no need for that!' scolded Mo from the kitchen.

'Sorry, Luv, some stupid bugger's written in the paper that there's a monster roaming the streets, tearing people up and half eating them!' He shook his head in disbelief. *And this morning's killing hasn't made the news yet!*

'Mrs Whelan reckons the Luftwaffe secretly parachuted a wild gorilla in at night like a sort of secret weapon,' stated Mo assuredly.

'It's not very secret if she knows about it,' grumbled Bill.

'It's not true is it?' asked his wife.

'Don't be daft, Jerry's got better things to drop on us than that, it's just some nutter. We'll catch him soon enough!'

'Bill, you will take care when you're walking the beat, won't you?' Mo was concerned.

'I always do, Luv,' he assured her.

'I just worry, especially now.'

Tennyson had relented on making the two policemen stand guard on what was, as he said 'a bloody hole in the ground!' so Bill walked the beat with Dick Thomas, as usual that night but, while the pair were picking their way along Pepper Lane, they spotted a man leave the Golden Cross to scurry towards the cathedral ruins. Bill gave his colleague a look and they hurried after the figure to see him glance furtively about before making to cross the wooden barrier.

'Oy, what's your game?' shouted Bill. The man froze, then relaxed on recognising the policeman.

'Oh, it's you, Constable Dixon, nice evening, ain't it?'

'Don't give me that, you bleeder! Dick, meet Tommy, better known as Dodgy, Smith, king of spivs, if you want it he can get it. So, what're you about?'

Dodgy nodded to PC Thomas then addressing Bill said. 'Just trying to do a bit of honest business, PC Dixon' replied the man. He was wearing a long khaki trench-coat with his hat pulled low; if it was supposed to make him inconspicuous it wasn't working.

'You wouldn't know honest if it smacked you in the face, which could happen if you're not too careful!' retorted Dixon. 'What's fallen off the back off a lorry today then?'

'Funny you should ask, officer, ciggies, tinned peaches, nylons, chocolate?'

'Are they dented, then?' asked Thomas.

'Eh?' both Dixon and Smith looked at him in askance.

'If they've fallen off a lorry?' suggested the younger constable in an attempt to explain.

Dodgy laughed wheezily at this and Bill continued. 'And how much would you be robbing the poor old general public for if they wanted to buy any of your ill-gotten goods?'

'Since it's you, I can do one of each for fifteen bob the lot,' announced the spiv, producing a small case from behind a large slab of stone.

'Naff off, Dodgy, that's far too much. I think I might run you down the station and you can have a nice sleep in one of our cells!' stated Dixon.

'Bloody hell!' cried PC Thomas, who had opened the case on the slab to reveal a veritable cornucopia of illicit treasure, including the tinned fruit and chocolate of which he had spoken.

'Ay up, take care, that's me livelihood you've got there!'

'You know, if you were put in a cell overnight there's no telling what might 'appen to that case?' suggested Bill.

'Ten bob!' said the spiv in panic.

'Seven and six,' responded Dixon reaching for his handcuffs.

'Alright but you're ruining my profit.' Dodgy knew when he was beaten.

The policeman handed over his money and helped himself to two tins and a bar of chocolate; all had the arrow of the War Department printed on their labels. 'And I believe you mentioned nylons?'

The spiv reached into his voluminous coat to produce a packet then handed it over, saying. 'You owe me for this.'

'Don't worry, I'll look the other way, for now,' replied Dixon, then, 'Watch out for yourself, Dodgy, it's not safe out after dark at the moment.'

'It's not been safe anywhere since they started dropping bleeding bombs on us!' he replied.

'You know what I mean, you bugger,' said Dixon.

'Yes, the bleeding monster. Don't worry I'm all tooled up.' Dodgy had a Colt 45 automatic in his pocket.

'I hope you ain't carrying,' Dixon said and the spiv shook his head and the policeman looked at him disbelievingly. 'I'll give you the benefit of the doubt this time, take bloody care anyway.'

PC Thomas watched the wide-boy slink into the shadows in incredulity. 'I can't believe you've just done that?'

Bill laughed. 'Mo likes a bit of chocolate and the peaches'll go nice with a bit of evap.' There was a tin of it in the Dixon's pantry, courtesy of a previous deal with Smith.

'But it's the Black Market, it's not legal!' stuttered Thomas.

'Of course it's bloody illegal!' retorted Dixon. 'People miss their luxuries, coppers included and it's nothing as bad as what some turn a blind one to. You really are wet behind the ears, me lad.'

'But …' started Thomas.

'Dick, these are for your Gloria' Dixon handed him the nylons. 'She's got nice pins and they deserve something better than gravy browning and pencil.'

'Well, it's only a little indiscretion I suppose?' *she did have nice legs.*

'Good lad, with any luck she'll be so pleased you might get a leg over,' he grinned.

Thomas felt grateful for the blackout as his face flushed and they continued on their beat. The shift was remarkably uneventful following that but when they returned to the station in the early hours it was a hive of activity.

'What's going on, Ted?' asked Bill.

PC Joiner, on desk duty, replied. 'Guess what, another bloody corpse and this time it was found right near that MP, what's his name er, Darnley's house. Anyway, word got around and the bleeding newspapers have turned up, one's even come from London on the milk train and Sergeant Mardy-arse is trying to deal with them until Tennyson gets here,' the policeman's face split in a wide grin. 'I'll bet he's right pissed off at having to get up at the sort of time us poor plods do.'

'Serve the bastard right,' laughed Dixon before it occurred to him that Darnley's creepy old pile wasn't on his beat but it was on the other side of the cathedral. 'Who's the poor victim this time?' *not Dodgy surely?*

'Another crook, Ron Smedley, in between jail sentences,' answered Joiner.

'Bloody hell, this bugger's doing our job for us!' exclaimed Bill.

Tennyson arrived with a face like thunder to be followed shortly by a policeman with a lot of silver braid on his shoulders and another smartly dressed individual with a very familiar face. 'Bugger me!' muttered Jock Andrews, who had just come in off shift. 'It's the Chief Constable with our local bloody MP.'

'What's he want here?' asked PC Thomas.

'I dare say we'll find out soon enough' expounded Old Bill.

They did. Tennyson gathered everyone present in the canteen where the Chief Constable addressed them to explain that forensic evidence suggested the killings were likely due to an escaped wild animal, such as a lion or a tiger and in response to this, police in the city centre were to patrol in pairs and would carry a firearm between them.

The police station had been issued with a small stock of rifles at the start of the war, ostensibly to fight off the enemy should they decide to invade; they were old Canadian issue dating back to the Great War but quite accurate and were kept well maintained. Thus it was that each two-man patrol was issued with one rifle and twenty rounds of ammunition, along with the dire warning to use it if only necessary.

* * *

The following night another 'half-eaten' body was found, this time a respectable shopkeeper who had been 'stocktaking'; to Dixon this meant doing a bit of Black Market trading and there were mutterings of the Chief Constable asking Dad's Army for help.

By now the newspapers were in full swing and reporters from Fleet Street were arriving in droves to report on what was being called 'The Monster of St Michaels', although only one body had been found in the vicinity of the ruined cathedral and one esteemed publication surpassed itself to ask. 'Is a Nazi Ape-man stalking the streets of Coventry?'

'It's no bloody ape done this!' raged Dixon while he walked the beat with Thomas the next evening.

'But that's what they're all saying, even Frobisher the pathologist?' remarked the younger policeman.

'Come on, he's following the official line. What animal skins its prey and carves prime cuts off it? Gorillas don't eat meat as far as I remember reading and lions and tigers tear animals apart and they eat their innards as well,' stated Dixon. 'Anyway if it is a wild beast, where's it come from? There's no circus or zoo round here.'

'I'll shoot the bugger, whatever it is,' declared Thomas excitedly; it was his turn with the rifle. All duty constables had been given a quick refresher on the firing range used by the local Home Guard, five rounds each.

'Be careful with that bloody thing!' snapped Dixon,

the younger man was swinging it round to aim at various imaginary beasts.

'Sorry, Bill' replied Thomas, putting the strap over his shoulder. 'Gloria is dead excited about me going out tooled up as they say at the flicks.

'You both need to grow up,' said Dixon shaking his head. Mo had been worried at the prospect of him going out with a wild beast prowling the city centre, even though he assured her it was just a load of rubbish put out by the newspapers.

'She liked the nylons, by the way,' said the younger PC.

'Yeah?' asked Dixon, raising his eyebrows.

'Yeah!' replied Thomas, Dixon thought he saw him grinning in the dim light but didn't want to push it.

They were walking past the end of the terrace where the bomb had gone off when a noise attracted their attention, the sound of a yell suddenly cut short.

'You hear that?' asked Thomas slipping the rifle off his shoulder.

'Yes, I don't suppose we can ignore it?' suggested Dixon before spotting movement near the bomb-crater, a misshapen figure was hurriedly climbing over the wooden barrier in the dim light. It could have been someone carrying a large load on its back, perhaps? *And it was definitely not an ape-man, no way!* he told himself.

'Come on, Bill, let's get 'em' cried the younger policeman, setting off towards the bomb hole.

'Take it easy, lad!' Bill blew his whistle to summon help then set off in an attempt to keep up with Thomas, who was sprinting ahead.

He caught up as the younger man crested the rubble surrounding the hole and they looked down into the inky blackness, the waning moon was still casting its pale light but it was of no use down there. There was a scraping, sliding sound and Dixon knew something was going through the gap below the archway and possibly dragging something with it!

'Come on, Bill, it's got to be this so-called monster!'

and with that Thomas half scrambled, half slid down the slope holding his lamp next to the rifle.

'Wait a minute, Dick, I've got older legs than you and besides, you can't aim a bloody gun with one hand.'

Dixon followed PC Thomas down in much the same fashion but on reaching the rubble-strewn bottom discovered there was no-one there.

'Dick?' called Bill nervously, there came no reply so he reluctantly climbed to the gap under the archway to shine his torch through and saw stone piled on the other side in much the same manner, *getting out will be easy anyway!* 'Dick, are you there?' he asked in more hushed tones. Receiving no answer, Bill pushed his way through onto a floor of slippery slabs in a dark, stone-lined tunnel which stretched into the distance, a musty smell hung in the air mingled with something else, the sickly sweet odour of decaying flesh.

A single echoing shot grabbed Bill's attention and he fancied he saw a brief glow in the darkness beyond the torch's beam. Every instinct told him to go back but he couldn't, it was his duty as a policeman to investigate and besides, Dick might be in trouble! Summoning up his courage, he moved cautiously along the tunnel, torch in his outstretched left hand, truncheon at the ready in the right and after what seemed an interminably long five minutes his foot kicked something lying on the floor; it was a police helmet.

Bill played the torch around and shuddered, spotting something at the utmost range of the beam. Moving closer he felt himself go weak at the knees as the light illuminated the shape on the floor. 'No, please, God, no!' It was Dick Thomas, head split open, a look of horror upon his dead face. 'Oh, you stupid bleeding sod, why didn't you wait for me?' whispered Dixon, then seeing the rifle glinting in the light he snatched it up to walk resolutely into the blackness, torch clasped tightly along the barrel and revenge in his heart.

Noticing dark doorways here and there along the tunnel, he nervously checked a couple to find they were empty cell-like chambers, *for long-dead monks?* Spying a distant glow, he walked forwards and it grew in brightness as he approached, Bill could now see it was coming from one of the cells, *whatever it is can't see in the bleeding dark!*

Bill peered cautiously around the chamber's entrance to see a figure wielding a butcher's cleaver bent over a tall bench and busily working on something; on closer inspection the *something* turned out to be a man with a face he knew well. Even in the dim flickering light of the Tilley lamp that was the chamber's only illumination, Dixon recognised it as a very deceased Dodgy Smith!

He watched in horror as the figure hewed away a piece of the ex-spiv and chewed at it then noticing strips of rotting flesh hanging on hooks on the wall, Dixon realised this was the creature's butchery and larder.

Bill summoned up his courage to step into the light raising the rifle as he did so. 'You're dead, you bastard!' he yelled and as the figure turned he pulled the trigger.

There was a click but nothing happened and Dixon barely managed to get the rifle up in time to block the cleaver as it swung down at him. The blade stuck in the stock and the policeman, taking his chance, pushed the figure backwards as hard as he could before stumbling into the hellish room himself to land on the floor with the assailant in front of him.

The rifle had landed out of reach and the man, who had a familiar cast to his face in the dim light, was slowly getting to his feet, growling gutturally. Bill's hand touched something cold and metallic, it was Dodgy's automatic fallen from a pocket in his voluminous trench-coat. The spiv had not had time to draw it when attacked. Dixon wasted no time in grabbing the weapon, and pushing up the safety catch fired several times. He was shocked to see the face of the MP Darnley in the bright muzzle flashes before the man sagged to the floor, where he lay with his breath making a strange sucking noise until life finally left him.

Bill didn't know how long he had been sat there, with no noise but the hiss of the Tilley for company, when two stern-faced men armed with revolvers and brandishing powerful flashlights appeared. One appraised the bodies while the other helped the old policeman firmly but politely to his feet before walking him quickly along the tunnel for a distance, to finally enter a large cellar through a rough hole in its wall. Dixon was then escorted upstairs to be left alone in a luxuriously appointed room, not one of them had spoken on the way here but he knew the type, tough men, ex-services and probably now working for the Government. The lock clicked and Bill realised he was now their prisoner; he'd killed a Member of Parliament and no matter what the bastard had done, he'd take the rap and most likely swing for it!

The door opened and the old man from the other day walked in leaning on his stick, he nodded sadly to Dixon then poured two glasses from a large crystal decanter before handing one to him. 'Brandy, it's good for shock.' He motioned to a chair. 'Please sit.'

Bill did as asked then scrutinised the elderly gentleman. His resemblance to Darnley was so unmistakable that the man could only be his father.

He sat silently and the man, seeing Bill was not willing to speak, continued. 'I knew this was going to happen one day and when he broke through the cellar wall into the old tunnels. We let him be, where could he go? Then that damned bomb opened a way out and well, you know the rest. Officer, whatever follows from this awful night I do not hold you responsible for his death, he is at rest now and people will be safer for it.'

Bill found his voice. 'Why didn't you block the sodding tunnel up?'

'There are so many bomb-sites for him to hide in, the detectives tried to find him to no avail so we left the way open so we could capture him upon his return but tonight was the first time he did so,' replied the man wearily.

There was a knock at the door and one of the detectives looked in to beckon Dixon silently, the elder Darnley nodded again and the policeman followed the heavy into the hallway where he was astonished to see the

MP, alive and well.

He was unable to meet the policeman's eyes. 'Constable Dixon, please understand my brother was a very sick man.'

Bill did not dignify him with a response and once on the street, he immediately recognised the front of Darnley's tall house before being bundled into the back seat of a very familiar black car where he found a stony faced Tennyson waiting for him. Bill was then dropped off outside his house with the stern warning that he was to speak to no-one and report straight to his office at the start of shift in the afternoon.

* * *

After Mo had made his tea she left him alone to his thoughts and he found tears running down his cheeks. He could not but help think of PC Thomas, a young man with his life cut so tragically short, *poor old Dick, what a terrible way to go!*

The day dragged until finally it was time and he walked slowly to the station where, on his arrival, most of his colleagues seemed reluctant to acknowledge him.

Jock came forward and clapped him on the shoulder. 'Sorry to hear what happened to young Dick, we'll miss him,' he said aloud before continuing in a quieter voice. 'Bill, we're on your side you know, me, Ted and Tony,' he assured him then walked with him to the door of the Inspector's office.

Once inside, Dixon stood before Tennyson's desk but the inspector was sat to one side as the Chief Constable had taken it over with another man sitting opposite, the stranger was smartly dressed but certainly cut from the same cloth as the pair from the Darnley house.

'Dixon,' started the Chief. 'While your actions last night put the end to a rather difficult problem, killing a member of the public should not go unpunished. Darnley's father, however, has insisted on leniency so, Constable Dixon, you are to be discharged from the force immediately on the grounds of corruption and consorting with the Black Market. You will be allowed to receive your pension and you should consider yourself lucky that is as far as it goes. Furthermore, you must never speak of what happened again as it would not be good for the country if it was known a member of the government had a twin brother who was, shall we say, unwell?'

'Bastards!' the numbness had finally left him. 'That bugger was chopping people up and eating bits of 'em and you're telling me to keep quiet about it, what about poor old Dick Thomas, all his life ahead of him and that loony ends it just like that! He had a girl who he doted on, what about her and what about his mam and dad?'

'Dixon, it is a great pity that that young man lost his life carrying out his duty but people are dying all the time; there is a war on you know?' retorted the Chief Constable. 'He will, of course, receive a posthumous commendation.'

'How dare you sit there and spout that bollocks?' Bill was boiling with rage. 'No-one deserves to die like those people did and no-one is above the law in my eyes, not even the likes of the bloody Darnleys!'

'Steady on, man!' started Tennyson.

'Constable Dixon!' the well-dressed man spoke for the first time. 'Is your wife Maureen in good health?' he asked in an oily voice.

'What?'

'And your daughter, Sharon, currently in Grimsby, I believe?'

Bill had a cold feeling in the pit of his stomach. 'Are you threatening my family?'

'Constable Dixon, this is Britain, not Peking, but I was thinking how terrible it would be should anything happen to them,' continued the man.

'So, I have no choice but to keep quiet, that's what you're saying?'

The man produced a sheet of paper with *Official Secrets Act* written on the header. 'I think if you were to sign this it would solve a lot of problems.'

Bill read through it quickly then reluctantly signed at

the bottom. 'There you are, you bastard, I hope you're bleeding satisfied.'

Tennyson looked at the ministry goon with ill-concealed disdain while the Chief Constable stared fixedly at the floor but the man just smiled mirthlessly. He folded the paper then put it into his attaché case saying, 'Thank you, constable, or should I say, Mr, Dixon.'

'Thank you, Dixon, you may go' the Chief dismissed him.

When Tennyson had led him into the corridor he turned to Bill 'Look, Dixon, I didn't want this to happen.'

'Bugger off!' Dixon snarled, dashing his helmet to the floor. As he checked in his warrant card, handcuffs and truncheon at the desk the majority of his fellow officers turned away as if to disassociate themselves from this corrupt policeman leaving only Andrews, Joiner and Wyatt to shake his hand. Noticing the Chief Constable exiting Tennyson's office Bill stopped at the main door and shouted. 'A barrel of rotten apples the lot of yer, rotten from the bloody top down!'

THE AGENT

BY MARYANNE COLEMAN

THE AGENT

Mrs Williams was often described as 'comfortable' and she wouldn't argue with that. She was comfortably off, even in these uncertain times. Mr Williams – God rest his soul – had prepared for his own death almost from the moment he was born. He was careful, frugal, if you were a friend. A mean bastard if you were not. But now he was gone, with all his cheeseparing ways, Mrs Williams looked back with gratitude on his habits, because, she was very comfortable indeed.

She was also very comfortable to look at. She wasn't fat – no one would call her fat – but she was certainly carrying a few extra pounds. But, she would say, smiling smugly, they were all in the right place. Men liked something to grab hold of, she would simper, though when a man last grabbed anything belonging to Mrs Williams was becoming a bit of a distant memory. But she knew that, when Mr Right came along, she would have all the equipment, in all the right places, to be grabbed as the occasion demanded.

And it wasn't just her figure that was comfortable. There was something very comfy about her face as well. Her eyes were just the right shade of blue to be likeable, not bright and hard as she remembered that awful man in the newspapers were. Her cheeks were pleasantly plump, with perhaps just the merest hint of peach fuzz now she had passed through the ch-nge of l-fe, as she always said it, her voice dropping away so that only those in the know would understand. Her friends would chime in quickly with the observation that it must have been a very early one, possibly preternaturally early, poor dear. And she would lift her teacup to her comfortably smiling mouth and nod ruefully. She and Mr Williams had not been blessed with children – the mean old bugger had been too tight to part with the you-know-what, the wags at the pub always said – but that didn't mean she didn't lead a full and satisfying life, change or no.

She always said she was glad that Mr Williams had passed away before All This Nonsense had begun. Mr Williams didn't like it when the world didn't wag the way he wanted it and it was fair enough to say that, these days, the world didn't so much wag as run around randomly, with no particular plan in mind. She had stopped going to church when that nice Reverend Green had passed on. This Remnant rubbish didn't appeal to her at all. She liked her services from the old prayer book she remembered from when she was a girl. She and Mr Williams – however unadvisedly – had promised to love, honour and obey and she didn't approve of the way things were done these days, a quick signature in a book and two people would be together until they fancied it otherwise. Where was the commitment in that? Mr Williams had promised to worship her with his body, and though that had been infrequent and not as much fun as it sounded, it had at least had the ring of seriousness about it. Turning up at some town hall in a borrowed hat and signing on the dotted line just wasn't the same. Although, to judge by the shape of some of the brides, quite a lot of worshipping had been going on prior. Mrs Williams tended to sniff her disapproval when she saw That Kind of Thing being flaunted about. Once, it had ended with her hat being knocked into a puddle, but principles were principles and Mrs Williams didn't intend to change now.

Mrs Williams didn't have that many friends, if she were to be honest. Acquaintances, yes, by the bucket load.

But only two real friends. One was Mrs Arbuthnot from over the road, a widow like herself, but not as comfortable, either in looks or circumstances. Mrs Arbuthnot had, to quote one of her sons-in-law, the one who was working at the Ministry of Supply, a face like a smacked arse and it had to be said that, civil servant or no civil servant, the man had got it right on the money. Mr Arbuthnot had not been careful, like Mr Williams. He had been profligate with both his money and his you-know-what so Mrs Arbuthnot hadn't got two ha'pennies to rub together and eight children, all now happily grown up and off her hands. Mrs Arbuthnot liked visiting Mrs Williams, to sit on furniture without more darns than fabric and to eat cake made with cake ingredients rather than potato. Mrs Williams liked Mrs Arbuthnot visiting – it gave her a warm glow to give her the cast-offs from her burgeoning wardrobe and see Mrs Arbuthnot's gratitude. For both women, it was a win-win situation.

Mrs Arbuthnot, for reasons which escaped her friend, genuinely mourned Mr Arbuthnot, who had been an early casualty of what Mrs Williams called Events. One evening, he had set off for the pub as usual and had said the wrong thing to the wrong person and – pouf! Just like that, no more Mr Arbuthnot and a stiff note to Mrs Arbuthnot that he was no more. She tried to manage, she really did, she once whimpered on Mrs Williams' ample bosom, but it was the companionship she missed. She had had a glass of sherry or would not have spoken so frankly, but Mr Arbuthnot, despite looking somewhat like a weasel, had been Very Active and had, apparently, been Hung Like a Mule. Mrs Williams had kept a bit of a distance for a while – she disliked all Smut.

Her other friend was unlikely to vouchsafe such bedroom secrets. She was Miss Miller and she ran what had once been the Post Office but since all mail had been taken over by central powers, was now just the corner store. Her stock had diminished but her gentility was undimmed. She was a mouselike little person, with hair scraped back in a way reminiscent of Olive Oyl in the pre-war cartoons and large, flat feet that she encased in sensible shoes. She didn't often visit Mrs Williams if Mrs Arbuthnot was there. After the Mule remark, whispered verbatim by Mrs Williams, she was afraid she might be put in a position where she would have to Say Something. She and Mrs Williams thought in capital letters a lot and despite their physical differences, they were sisters under the skin.

Nevertheless, Mrs Williams, in spite of her committees, good works, gardening and baking, seemed to have more and more time on her hands. She did her own housework these days, domestic staff being broadly speaking frowned upon, but she had the house all shipshape and so often, by mid-afternoon, she was at a loose end. She hated to admit it to herself and certainly wouldn't have admitted it to either of her friends, but Mrs Williams was lonely. She missed even the frigid presence of Mr Williams and she had begun to hanker for those rare occasions when Mr Williams would do his bit of worshipping – usually birthdays and, on one very memorable occasion, Shrove Tuesday. She saw women around town, with soldiers or other men in dubious uniforms on their arms and she wondered how one went about meeting people. People other than Mrs Arbuthnot or Miss Miller, that was. But as soon as the thought crossed her mind, she dismissed it. It really wasn't seemly, and she would be doing no such thing. Even so … and with a sigh, Mrs Williams would pour herself another glass of British Sherry, having forgotten by now that there was ever any other kind.

Mrs Williams was out in her front garden one late afternoon, weeding her pansies – she had given over the whole of her back garden to improving vegetables, but she refused to give up her little bit of colour, as she told everyone. She was bending over so didn't notice Mrs Arbuthnot at first, until alerted by a 'coo-ee' from across the road. Looking up, she saw her friend latching her front gate and, even as the woman crossed the road, darting out through the traffic in a most uninhibited way, she could tell there was something different about her. The arse was no longer smacked – indeed, it was positively glowing. An old discarded hat of Mrs Williams' from some seasons ago had been tarted up with ribbon and a bunch of fabric violets and the coat was ... surely not; was the coat *new*?

Mrs Williams carefully peeled off her gardening gloves – one might have to do one's own work, but there was no need for standards to slip – and went to the gate. Her friend was almost prancing on the spot with ill-suppressed excitement.

'My goodness me, dear,' Mrs Williams admonished. 'Do keep still. It's as though you have St Vitus' Dance or something.'

Mrs Arbuthnot laughed out loud, not because what Mrs Williams had said was particularly funny but simply for the joy of it. 'Not St Vitus Dance, dear,' she said. 'It's ...' and she clapped a workworn hand to her mouth.

'It's what, dear?' Mrs Williams was beginning to feel a little testy, though she scarcely knew why. 'Is it that new nerve tonic? Because if so, you've taken a tad too much, I would say.'

Mrs Arbuthnot had not forgotten what had happened over the Mule incident. She hadn't been invited to tea for almost a month. But, she reasoned, she wouldn't have so much time for tea with Mrs Williams from hereon in. She took her hand away from her mouth. It was now or never. It was a brave new world and she was one of the brave new people in it. 'It's not the nerve tonic,' she said in a rush. 'It's ... I've got a man! I've *had* a man!' Her eyes sparkled and her mouth was in a smile so wide it threatened to split her face in two.

Mrs Williams flared her nostrils and took a step back. Mrs Arbuthnot was briefly reminded of a startled horse she had seen once in the park. She almost heard the whinny and the huff of hot breath. 'Mrs Arbuthnot!' Mrs Williams and Mrs Arbuthnot, though friends, had never been on first name terms. 'I am *appalled*. You are a *widow*. A respectable *widow*!'

Mrs Arbuthnot grinned. 'That's true,' she said. 'I *am* a widow, but I am now a widow getting a good seeing to nightly from her new lodger.' She looked what she knew was her ex-friend up and down. 'And to be honest, you look as if you could do with the same.' With a positive skip in her step, she turned to walk down the road. 'Shall I see if he's got a mate?' And, still chortling, she walked away.

Mrs Williams looked down at her pansies and she could hardly see for tears. She had gone, in a heartbeat, from a woman with two friends to a woman with one. She knew she could never have tea with Mrs Arbuthnot again, could never again condescend to her over her featherlight scones made with real flour and butter. Her first thought was to get into the house, then she thought she must see Miss Miller. She would understand, as perhaps no one else would.

Her friend was behind the counter as she always was, a bright smile on her small, pasty face. There were, as usual, no customers in her shop, which was over-priced and under-stocked. But still she waited, day after day (except Wednesday afternoons) for the profligate and desperate housewife to come in to buy an emergency can of snoek, out of date by some years but still, as she always assured her customers, as good as new. She could immediately see that Mrs Williams was in sore need of tea and sympathy, so pulled down the blind, flipped the 'closed' sign over and ushered her through to what everyone called 'the back'. It was a cheerless little room at the best of times, but with a smoky fire on the verge of going out and its relentless smell of stale digestive biscuits, it wasn't ideal for a place to unburden a soul. Mrs Williams was reminded in a rush as to why they always met at her house. But this was no time to be picky.

'Oh, Miss Miller,' she sobbed, sitting down on a rickety chair and rummaging for a handkerchief up her sleeve. 'I've had such a shock!'

'I can see you have, dear.' Miss Miller filled her ancient kettle at the sink in the corner and put it on the gas, hang the expense. The fire wouldn't boil it if they waited until doomsday. 'What's happened?'

Now she was asked, Mrs Williams had a bit of a quandary to resolve. She needed to tell someone about Mrs

Arbuthnot's defection to the other side, as she saw it. But she also realised suddenly that Miss Miller was not the ideal person in whom to confide. What words could she use, to this respectable spinster lady? It would take some careful language and so she began, tentatively.

'I … I've just seen Mrs Arbuthnot,' she began.

'Oooh,' Miss Miller squeaked. 'It's all over town! She's got a lodger and apparently, he's very handsome.' She dropped her voice. 'They say …'

Mrs Williams stood up, affronted. That Miss Miller should be sharing such gossip with all and sundry was a severe shock, to say the least.

'Oh, don't go, Mrs Williams,' Miss Miller pleaded. 'I'm sorry. I don't know what came over me. It's appalling, it really is. And her a respectable widow.'

Slightly mollified, Mrs Williams resumed her seat and sniffed. She might yet get what she wanted from this encounter, which was sympathy and perhaps a decent cup of tea. A biscuit wouldn't come amiss either and if there wasn't one in a shop, where was there one, she would like to know. In a low voice, she started to tell the suitably embroidered story of Mrs Arbuthnot and how she had been brought lower than low.

Miss Miller tinkered with the tea and the only-just out of date plum cake she had fetched from the shop. She listened patiently but could tell, as Mrs Williams could not, that most of her problem was not outrage but plain jealousy. She believed she had an answer to the problem, but she had to let Mrs Williams think of it for herself – years of friendship with the woman had taught her it was the only way forward. Eventually, the hissed detail trickled to a stop and Mrs Williams took a restorative swig of tea and a big bite of cake.

While the woman's jaws were still stuck together, Miss Miller took her chance to speak and, as she had had a while to work out what to say, it all came out without pause, which was not her usual style. 'Mrs Williams,' she said, 'I have an idea. Why don't *you* put a card in my window, like Mrs Arbuthnot did, and get yourself a lodger.'

Mrs Williams held up a finger, but was still struggling with cake.

'No, let me finish. Of course, you don't have to go as far as Mrs Arbuthnot, but you can show her that anything she can do, you can do better. Let's see ...' she rummaged in a drawer, 'here's her card. What did she put? Hmmm, oh, yes, very basic. Just says there is a room to let, home cooking ...' The two women looked at each other and raised an eyebrow. That was a matter of opinion, that was for sure. 'Hmmm ... nothing about what kind of person she is after.' More raised eyebrows. 'Well, I think you can do better than that.'

Miss Miller took the discreet stub of pencil she kept secreted in her bodice and wrote, busily. After a while, she passed the card over to Mrs Williams, who read it aloud, having managed to subdue the cake.

'VACANCY.' Miss Miller's capitals were firm and black. 'Room in very respectable home. Professional gentleman preferred. References required. Apply within.' Mrs Williams looked at Miss Miller, a question on her lips. 'Apply within?'

'Well, dear, you don't want to go putting your address in my window, surely?' Miss Miller smiled. She didn't add that this way, she would know who had answered the advertisement.

'You're *so* thoughtful, Miss Miller,' Mrs Williams murmured. 'But ... do people *answer* this kind of thing? Do people *want* rooms in respectable homes?'

'Any number,' Miss Miller said, comfortingly. 'As I let you out, I'll pop it on the board and you'll have an answer as quick as a wink, I promise.'

Mrs Williams felt very much happier on her way home, but also very apprehensive. She set about cleaning the front bedroom as it had never been cleaned before, from the picture rail to the skirting boards. She emptied the wardrobe and the drawers of the bedside table, she relined the drawers of the chest under the window. She looked long and hard at the curtains but decided they would do – a good shake and they would last for years yet. Finally, she was happy with the result and closed the door on the room and went downstairs to wait for results.

Some days went by and Mrs Williams was on the verge of deciding to take the card down from Miss Miller's board, on the grounds that it was all too humiliating, when there was a strong, manly knock at the door. She leapt to her feet and rushed to answer it, pausing only to pat her hair into place in the hallway mirror and make sure she had no lipstick on her teeth. All was well, and she flung open the front door.

Standing on the step was possibly the blandest man she had ever seen. He was wearing a bowler hat which, despite its narrow brim, still managed to shade most of his face. Although the day was dry, he was wearing a mackintosh done up tightly with a belt and carried a furled umbrella. His trousers, peeping discreetly from below the hem of his coat, were pin-striped and his shoes were polished to a high glaze.

'Good afternoon,' he said and his voice was as colourless as his appearance. 'I have been sent by Miss Miller at the shop, who thought there might be a room vacant at this address.' He lifted his bowler, just a threat. 'She gave me this note for you.' He handed it over and stood, perfectly still, on the step while she read it.

'Mrs Williams,' the note said, and she could almost hear Miss Miller's breathless delivery, 'I *do* believe that this gentleman might be just what you need. He is *very* respectable – I have taken the liberty of looking into his references – and will be no trouble, I am sure. Yours, M. Miller.' Mrs Williams realised she had no idea what her friend's Christian name was. Surely, the M didn't stand for 'Miss'. She looked up. The man was standing there, quite still, as if stuffed. She looked closer. He wasn't very interesting, but he wasn't ugly, at least. And this was just a start. If things didn't work out … well, there were plenty more fish in the sea.

'This all seems to be in order,' she said. 'Let me show you the room.'

'I'm sure it is perfect,' the man said, in his colourless voice. 'If it is acceptable to you, I will fetch my luggage and return this evening. A meal, I understand, is included within the tariff.'

'Um … yes.' Mrs Williams hadn't remembered agreeing to that, but it was probably normal. 'It may be a bit scratch tonight, with it being so sudden …'

'I am sure it will be delightful,' the man said. 'I will return at six, if that is agreeable.'

'Er … yes, perfectly agreeable,' she heard herself saying. 'May I ask, what is your name, please?'

He doffed his bowler again, just ever so slightly. 'Smith,' he said. Then added, not really to her surprise, 'John Smith.' And he turned and went down the path, opening the gate and carefully closing it behind him, with just the slightest of bends. Without another word or gesture, he walked away and was hidden by the hedge.

Mrs Williams was at once in a twitter and disappointed. Mr Smith was not quite what she had hoped for, if she was to make Mrs Arbuthnot green with jealousy. On the other hand, he was clearly a professional gentleman – although Miss Miller had not specified what profession, exactly, nor who his referees were – and didn't look as if he would be any trouble. So, as a start, she could have done far worse. She went into the kitchen and checked the cupboards. She had the makings of a nice spam pie and a milk pudding to follow. She rubbed her hands together and assembled her ingredients. It was good to be cooking for more than one again.

John Smith ate like he did everything else. He held his knife like a pen, to her distress, but he was deft with his cutlery, didn't clash them together and didn't drag the fork across the best china. Everything was cut into equal sized pieces and was conveyed to his mouth with mathematical precision. At the end of each course, he had said, 'That was very pleasant, thank you,' and had placidly waited while she removed the plate and brought the next item for his attention. She had tried to make small talk, but it had been like wading through treacle. He worked in an office in what he called Town, which she assumed to be London, probably the City, which was a little confusing. His hours were 'to suit' but usually ten to five, so he would require his breakfast at seven and his evening repast – she hadn't heard it called that since her grandmother had died – also at seven would be ideal. He gave a small snicker at that and she realised he had made what passed for a joke. She watched him covertly now as he sipped his coffee – black, no sugar – and decided actually he was quite handsome, if a little difficult to pin down. His eyes were ... colour, certainly. His hair ... well, the same. But she could not have described him had her life depended upon it.

When he had finished his coffee, she asked him if he would like to join her in the sitting room, to read the evening paper, perhaps. To her surprise, he accepted and they sat on opposite sides of the fireplace like an old married couple, he deep in the paper, she picking at her embroidery. She smiled to herself. Even without the extras provided by Mrs Arbuthnot's lodger, this was actually rather nice. John Smith exuded a manly smell of pipe tobacco and bay rum on his slicked hair and when he asked if he might smoke his pipe, she agreed gladly. It was good to have a man about the place.

Morning after morning, John Smith ate his boiled egg and precisely two rounds of toast soldiers at exactly seven. At exactly seven in the evening, he ate in his usual pernickety way his two course repast and, whatever it was, from ham salad to roast dinner, he said the same thing – 'That was very pleasant, thank you.' Mrs Williams called him Mr Smith. He called her Mrs Williams. She stopped thinking of Mrs Arbuthnot and hadn't spoken to Miss Miller in weeks when she asked him, suddenly, one evening, 'Mr Smith, do excuse me, but what *do* you do for a living?'

He looked over his paper and blew out a stream of smoke from the corner of his mouth. 'It's a bit hush hush, Mrs Williams,' he said with what she had come to recognise as a smile. 'If I told you, I would have to kill you.' And with that, he retired behind his paper and soon began on the crossword, his sign that there would be no more talking.

Mrs Williams couldn't concentrate on her embroidery that evening. She felt that somehow, a line had been crossed and she wasn't sure whether it would end well. At bedtime, she got up as usual and went up the stairs first, tacitly giving Mr Smith and his manly habits last go in the bathroom. She was almost asleep when she heard the landing floorboards creaking and she turned over, suddenly alert. Her bedroom door opened slowly and not very far but when it closed again, she knew that Mr Smith was in the room with her. She held her breath.

Slowly, so slowly she was beginning to think she had imagined it, he lifted the bedclothes and slid in beside her. He was wearing nothing at all and she gasped in shock. With no preamble or so much as a word, Mr Smith proceeded to worship her with his body and she realised that, even on Shrove Tuesday, Mr Williams had not really come up to the mark, not even slightly.

When Mr Smith had gone, she lay there, a trembling heap. His words had not surprised her – 'that was very pleasant, thank you' – but that he had visited her by night at all had rocked her to her core. She wasn't sure how to proceed from here, though. Did they carry on as normal? Would he ever do this again? If he didn't, she thought she might go mad. But, the worm in her brain kept asking, what on earth did he do for a living?

The days that followed answered many of her questions. They went on as before, with the breakfast and the evening repast coming along exactly twelve hours apart and they were always very pleasant, as was the third course, in the dark of her room, on alternate nights of the week, regular as the clock. But she couldn't work out what it was he did for a living. Not anything manual, obviously – his hands were too soft and smooth for that. And she had a feeling it wasn't anything in the financial sector – the rent she charged was high and he never quibbled, as she knew Mr Williams would have done, optional extras notwithstanding.

One afternoon, her curiosity got the better of her and she let herself into his room with the spare key. She was somewhat disappointed that he still locked it, given their intimacy and the fact that he occasionally stayed to sleep the night away beside her. But lock it he did and it was his prerogative, of course.

Once inside the room, she stood for a moment, looking to see if anything obvious was in view which would give her an immediate clue and would mean that she didn't have to search, which somehow seemed so underhand. The room was, if anything, tidier than when John Smith had moved in. The surfaces were still clear of dust, the silver-backed brushes and comb on the dressing table were still aligned exactly in the centre, as she had left them. She eased open the wardrobe doors and there, hanging neatly in line, were six identical suits with dark jackets and striped trousers, with six matched snow white shirts, each with a dark tie around the hook of the hanger. Underneath them were six pairs of highly polished shoes, each with a pair of black socks rolled inside.

The drawer beneath held four pairs of pyjamas – she looked at them, puzzled, then realised; on every other night, he wore nothing but a light sheen of sweat and a memory of her perfume. She closed the drawer and the wardrobe door and turned round, looking a level beneath the obvious. She felt along the bed, pushing down the springs of the mattress until she reached a place where it didn't give to pressure. Reaching beneath, she found a folder, with coded words on the front. With trembling fingers, she opened it, to find a picture of Mr Williams, but not wearing his usual finicky expression. This man looked out from the picture challengingly, daring you to ask him anything. Beneath the picture were the words – Missing; find at all costs.

Mrs Williams stood there, the folder in her hands, lost in a world she could not have imagined just moments before. So intent was she that she didn't hear the familiar creak of the landing floorboards, the hush of the opening door on the carpet.

'Oh, dear,' said Mr Smith's voice from behind the muzzle of the gun that was the first thing she saw as she turned. 'Mrs Williams, I am truly sorry.' And to be fair to the man, he did sound it. 'But I did warn you.'

And before she could answer, he put a bullet, neatly, precisely, as he did everything, right between her eyes.

Miss Miller looked up as the bell above her shop door jangled and jumped. A customer, just as she was about to close; how trying.

'Miss Miller,' said the bland man in the bowler hat, 'I wonder if I could trouble you. I'm looking for another place to stay.'

Her hand reached out for the card – such a nice gentleman. Always so polite …

THE WIDOW

BY JULIA COWAN

THE WIDOW

The clock chimed the hour gently from the mantlepiece above the crackling fire. The bright yellow flames curled around the logs in the hearth. Catherine wiped her hands on the apron before reaching for the poker to stir the flames. The embers sizzled like fireflies as they chased each other up the chimney.

She turned to see the figure stood at the window, his hand pulling back the curtain. He had maintained this pose at regular intervals for the last few days, an almost constant watch at the window which led out directly onto their street.

'What is it Reg?' she quizzed, more out of curiosity than annoyance at his persistent stoic position.

'Hmmm …' he mused before letting the curtain drop and turned to face her. 'The Sealeys I think … looks as if they are the ones who are clearing out …'

'Lots of fuss about nothing if you ask me,' Catherine tutted in disapproval. 'All these neighbours taking off. Goodness knows what will happen to their houses whilst they are gone! What kind of a state will their homes be in when they get back? It will take more than a few bombs to shift us, eh, Reg?'

He smiled at her and nodded. 'We've been through worse in our forty years here, that's for sure.' Reg shuffled over to their wireless, which sat on the old dresser, facing the fireplace. He adjusted a few knobs until low, crackling tones could be heard.

'The news,' he called to his wife, who had retreated back to the kitchen, busily preparing their evening meal. After a few minutes, she emerged holding two plates and placed them on their dining table. Catherine watched as Reg remained bent over the wireless, one hand on top of it and a deep frown etched on his face.

'Anything new?' she enquired. However, before he had time to answer, she added, 'turn it over, we don't need to hear any of that ...'

Eventually, he smiled back to her and nodded. By the time he had sat opposite her, the dulcet tones of Vera Lynn soothed them. Catherine found herself humming along.

'Lots of news from Whitehall,' Reg was poised holding his cutlery. 'They say people are panicking, lots away from London, heading to the country ... Maybe that's why the Sealeys are leaving ...'

'As if they'll be any safer there,' Catherine tutted again. 'If we just sit tight ... everything will blow over soon enough. Just like we did with the last war ...'

He nodded in agreement. 'Reckon we're best to stay put for the time being. We've everything we need here anyway.' He used his fork to sift through the vegetables on his plate. 'There's no grocery shops to buy such good produce, that's for sure. Our little allotment out back has done us well this year.'

Catherine took a moment to study the man sat opposite her. They had married young and his working years outside had given him a permanent rugged, weathered face. Reg had served in the Great War, eventually being discharged with an injury that had left him with a limp. He had spent the time up until his recent retirement working in the local cotton factory whilst she had raised their children and kept the household in order. She breathed a sigh of relief that they had each other and their love was as strong as when they had first met, many decades ago. Gossiping with her neighbours had told her that other husbands couldn't hold a candle to Reg, his often-spontaneous bursts of impulsiveness still took her by surprise. Why, just recently during the Blitz, he had come up with the crazy idea for them to dance around the living room wearing their gas masks as the sky had glowed orange outside.

The thought still made her smile, this was the solid, dependable man she had married and they would see out their days together, in their own home and no invasions from overseas would drive them out anytime soon. Sadly, Britain was still at war, but it was important to stay grounded, pull up your sleeves and survive like they always had.

'Have you had enough dear?' she moved to clear his plate.

He nodded. 'Lovely, thank you,' his voice was muffled as he dabbed the corners of his mouth with his napkin. She moved around him skilfully, tidying up their dishes and cleaning as she went.

'Leave your shirt out for me to mend,' she reminded him. 'I'll start it straight after ...'

They were disturbed by a commotion from outside, the sound of breaking glass and raised voices dampened their spirits. Reg jumped up the best he could and resumed his place at the window.

'Kids ...' he called to his wife, 'I think ...'

He was surprised to find Catherine at his side. 'It's from next to the Sealeys' house, can you see?' she asked him. Sure enough, they could see several figures running away from the house, the front door left open as they fled. Neither of them spoke until the street was quiet again.

'Just kids,' she repeated. Silently, Reg walked over to their front door and moved the bolts in quick succession.

'Just in case,' he murmured. He shook his head, 'can't remember the last time we had to lock this thing so well ...'

Catherine nodded. He was of course referring to their street and neighbourhood in fact, where it was considered so safe that residents hadn't needed to lock their doors until now. She had noticed on her last walk that people had been quick to lock windows now and padlock their doors. There was a lot of curtain twitching, almost as though people didn't trust each other anymore. She remembered how it used to be in years gone by. She and Reg had been used to neighbours coming in during the day, just a quick knock to announce their arrival, followed by a gossip over a nicely brewed cup of tea.

Catherine and Reg were no fools. These gangs of hopeless children had already been labelled 'ferals' by the radio and the papers. A disgusting term, as if the children chose to be in that desperate state, as if they had somehow reverted back to some primal place that was always within them. The couple didn't doubt that many of the horror stories were true, but a starving person, even a child, would resort to any measures to get food in their belly, and it was easy for the two of them to judge as they discussed over dinner with a roof over their head. The street wardens, home guard and the police would round up the ferals when they could, sending them off to God knows where, but it was only the weak, starving and desperate of them that would let themselves be captured. You wouldn't know you'd have been the victim of a good feral until daylight the next day.

She forced a smile – a good cup of tea would be just fine before bedtime.

* * *

Catherine slept fitfully that night. There seemed to be constant noise from outside. Just as things started to quieten down, another lot started. Shouting, crying, screaming, each noise had blurred into the next in the end. Eventually the sun shone onto their net curtain. She rubbed her eyes as Reg moved around their bedroom.

'You're going fishing?' This was more of a statement than a question. She was used to Reg spending the day at the riverbank and more often than not, he would return with their dinner in tow.

'Yes,' he confirmed. 'Might have a look round the streets, awful lot of noise around last night …'

'I'll make you a packed lunch ...' she rose from the bed and searched under the bed for her slippers.

'No bother, love,' he stated.

'It will take me a few minutes, it's no fuss.'

He had a head start on her going down the stairs and she found him at the wireless again. Catherine shook her head and headed into the kitchen. She was able to see out into their garden from the kitchen window. All seemed quiet in comparison to the night before. Reg made his way downstairs fully ready for his day. She watched from the front door as Reg left for the riverbank and spotted Mr Sealey hurriedly pulling suitcases out of his door. They seemed heavy by the way he moved.

'You're off, then?' she called out, her tone light.

He appeared to freeze and turned to face her. Without warning, he marched over to her and in no time at all, was at her side.

'It's not safe ...' his eyes were wild, panicked. 'You and Reg, you can't stay here. I ... we can't leave you here, Mrs Lowe ...'

'It's Cath ...'

He shook his head, ignoring her correction. He held her arm with one hand, his grip urgent and almost painful. 'I can't leave you here,' he stated again, in hushed tones. 'They are watching, everyone is ...'

'Please,' she gestured to his grip. 'I ... we, myself and my husband are fine.' She stood tall, now having managed to release his vice-like hold on her. She smoothed down her house apron.

'Mr Sealey, I'd like to remind you that Reg and I have lived on this street for forty years. We are not leaving, now or ever for that fact,' she replied haughtily.

'Look around you!' he gestured up and down their street. The rows of terraced houses sat with a single road running down the middle. People took pride in their homes here. Catherine looked up and down the street to humour him though. She noted that some of the houses were boarded up, several had paint thrown on the outside. Her immediate neighbours, who she had often envied for their potted plants on their doorsteps ... she frowned as the pots lay smashed in the road, their wilted flowers strewn on the pavement. For a moment, she wondered whether her neighbours had contacted the police about the damage. *Maybe there is a delay,* she thought. *Too busy with troubles the war is causing ...*

'It's not safe,' Mr Sealey seemed calmer now. He used his hands to smooth down his hair, a once respected member of their community seemed somewhat unhinged, on edge.

'Reg has gone fishing. He'll be out for the day. We'll discuss this when he returns later.' Her tone was clipped now as she brushed him off.

He shook his head. 'Keep your door locked,' he nodded to her open front door. 'And your wits about you,' he muttered as he strode off back to his house.

Catherine watched as he stood next to his wife, who appeared to be locking their door. The distance between them wasn't vast but Catherine did not make it her business to eavesdrop into their conversation. However, she could just about make out him explaining in exasperated tones, 'she won't come ...'

Instead, Catherine exhaled deeply and looked down the length of their street. She spotted another of their neighbours walking briskly on the main road. Normally, it was his manner to tip his cap when they had passed in the street. She now noticed him pull up his coat collar, as though the weather was bothersome. However, this morning was fair. She did close her door and her hand hovered over the chain to lock it. Catherine paused, tutted to herself and busied herself with her daily chores.

* * *

The afternoon was drawing to a close when Reg came home. A broad smile adorned his face as he proudly held up a large fish.

'Superb!' Catherine exclaimed as she set about washing it. 'Any bother out?'

'Bother? What kind of bother?'

'Oh, it's just …' she was startled as his face appeared around the kitchen door. 'Mr Sealey from over the road. You were right, they were packing up. They left this morning, a right state he was in, I tell you.' She was aware that he had not interrupted her once throughout this explanation. She paused from scrubbing the fish, waiting for his response.

'Nothing that I could see,' he replied, 'but then again there weren't many people down the river. Must have more pressing matters I suppose.'

He was back in their front room in no time, sat in his favourite armchair, slowly turning the pages of the thin newspaper. His lips moved slightly as he read the articles. In fact, he had been so engrossed in the paper that he barely noticed his wife enter with their dinner.

'Anything exciting in the paper?' she nodded to where he had left it open on the chair. She craned her neck to see the headline. 'Whitehall Warmongers demand more blood …'

He nodded and opened this mouth to reply. However, a noise coming from their back garden drowned out their conversation. The loud voices, banging and clattering sounded like someone was outside their back door.

'Goodness me!' Catherine exclaimed. She was able to move quicker than her husband and stood looking out of the window, her hand raised to her mouth in shock.

'Reg, do something!'

He moved to the back door and stood blocking the doorway to face the gang of masked youngsters who now stood bold as brass amongst their flowerbeds. The flowers that they had spent so long tending were now carelessly being squashed by large, leather boots. The boys appeared to be laughing.

'Now then, lads,' Reg raised his voice to get their attention, his figure blocking the open doorway. 'Whatever you lot are doing in other houses … not here. There are people still living here, do you understand?' He paused and watched them look him up and down. If their faces hadn't been covered by hessian sacks, Reg assumed they would have looks of disgust on their faces, *who is this old man and what right does he have, telling us what to do?*

'On your way, boys. Do you understand?' They stood in a standoff, no one breaking the silence. Reg wondered for a moment if he was speaking the right language. However, after a short while, the gang fled out of their open gate, just as noisily as they had arrived.

'They're gone now,' he addressed his wife, her eyes wide but he saw her shoulders drop as the relief washed over her. Reg locked their back door the best he could before ushering Catherine back to their dinner table. They continued to eat the rest of their meal in relative silence, just small talk littered here and there. He tried not to let onto his wife at his growing concern that they had not seen the last of that gang.

* * *

'Reg, did you put your muddy boots out the back?'

He grimaced slightly as out of the corner of his eye, he spied his boots near the front door, where he had discarded them after yesterday's fishing. Catherine's voice was muffled from upstairs.

'I'll just put them out, dear,' he called out.

He paused at the back door before unlocking it ready to open. With a deep breath, he swung the door wide. Why should they be so fearful? This was their house and he'd be damned if any feral hoodlums tried to force them away... He looked at the gate, which gently brushed against the catch in the breeze. Reg tried to think if he had gone out last night to make sure it was closed properly. As he was unable to remember, he stepped out into their garden and pushed it closed. There. It was now secure. Sometimes the noise of it banging against the lock was irritating.

The wind stirred up a few loose leaves which had blown against the house. Dead, brown leaves with their sharp edges scraping on the paving stones. The gate lock squeaked slightly as the gate rattled in its closed position.

The silence around the neighbourhood, now devoid of any of the usual sounds of people going about their business. And then the scream, high pitched and urgent. A desperate call that sounded like a woman's voice …

Reg felt his knees buckle from beneath him from the blow to the head that he hadn't seen coming. The world was now a swirl of colours and sounds, his face felt wet from the light drizzle that had started that afternoon. He felt as though he was falling down a deep hole, as the light from the sky seemed to be just a pinprick now, a small white hole surrounded by black.

Catherine made it out of the door moments after. Cradling her husband's head, she saw in her eyeline pairs of rough, leather boots. She let out an almost animalistic howl as she looked down at Reg's eyes, glassy and now staring vacantly at the sky above. Unable to move, her legs cramped as she held him in her lap, rocking back at forth gently, her hand a poor attempt to stem the flow of blood pooling around them. She could hear the distant sounds of the gang as they moved further away from her.

She had no idea of what time it was. The only measure of time passing was the movement of the sun, the garden falling into shade. Reg's blood on her hands, warm and sticky at first, was now clotting and drying in flakes under her fingernails. All that ran through her mind was her past with Reg. She tried to recall when they had first met, her a shy teenager, him a handsome young man, asking her father's permission to court her. They had spent a lifetime together, Just a few years apart when he had been called up for the Great War. She had spent those years apart worrying endlessly, awaiting the telegram that every wife had feared in those days. But Reg had been discharged early due to a leg injury. He would never be called up again. They had spent their time together raising a family before eventually waving their children off too. Reg – a solid, dependable man, a pillar of the community. And now she was alone in every sense of the word. The residents around her had gone and it was down to her to survive. There was no one to help and it seemed as though the police weren't even interested in what was happening in the street.

Her legs felt stiff as she unfolded them from underneath her. At first, she feared she would not be able to get up at all, her knees weren't the best at times and sitting in the cold, damp air was not helping. Eventually, she managed to shuffle to the kitchen where she washed her hands in the sink, watching the water pool and swirl down the plughole. The water from her hands was a deep red colour at first, dirt and blood, before eventually running clear. Her mind felt foggy as though the last few hours had passed with her in a trance.

She moved towards the telephone with the intention of calling someone to help with Reg. However, her hand paused mid-dial. With all the vandalism which had happened in the last few days, why, she had not seen a single bobby on the beat for a while. Catherine thought of ringing one of her friends nearby. However, the memory of curtains being drawn, the world being shut out was still etched in her mind. *No one cares anymore and besides, the phone hadn't worked for months …*

Instead, she changed out of her house clothes and opted for something warmer. She pulled her overcoat around her and headed out into the dusky night. Unsure of her destination, she just knew that she had to keep moving. Staying sat in one position wasn't helping and she needed to take her mind off what had happened that day. All she concentrated on was putting one foot in front of the other. The streets were chillingly quiet, the only sounds interrupting her thoughts sounded like foxes crying out. It didn't take her too long to work out they were coming from people, not distressed animals.

The houses on these streets had not fared as well as those on Trafford Grove, that was for sure. Some looked as though they were burnt out, blackened shells of what once had been family homes. Catherine jumped in surprise as a gang of masked feral children raced out of one of the houses, narrowly avoiding a man charging at them with a stick.

'And don't come back!' he wielded the stick high in the air, the members of the gang dispersing as some were able to run faster than others.

'Picked the wrong house this time, didn't you?' the man called after them. In his anger, he seized an empty milk bottle laying in the gutter and threw this into their direction. Catherine could hear a dull thump as it made contact with something. The man gave Catherine a long, hard stare before retreating back into the house, bolting the door behind him.

She remained in the same position for a while, not daring to move. Catherine regarded the crumpled figure lying in the middle of the road. It did not move, just lay spread-eagled, face up where the bottle had hit him and knocked him out cold. Could this be one of the ferals that had killed her poor Reg?

A rolled-up and shredded yellow-stained copy of *The Beano* bulged out of the boy's back pocket. Catherine walked slowly to the figure and bent down on the cobbles beside him as the dawn was starting to break through the cloudy skies. She slowly lifted the grotesque mask from his head. She pulled her glove off and placed a hand on his shoulder. His body felt warm and Catherine could see his chest rise and fall with each breath. Looking around his head, she could not see any blood so assumed he'd just suffered bruising to the head, that was all. He gasped and opened his eyes slowly. The boy winced as he tried to move.

'Can you get up? I can't carry you dear. And I think if you stay here any longer ...' she looked up and down the street.

'I ...' he tried to sit up, his face grimaced as he did so. Catherine took one of his arms and helped guide him into a seated position.

'I think your friends have left you.'

The boy stared at her. 'They're no friends of mine.' His voice was quiet and his accent told Catherine that he was local. After he had sat for a few minutes, he attempted to stand and dusted off his trousers in the process.

'Where will you go now?' Catherine asked him. 'Won't your parents be worried about you?'

He frowned at her and cast his eyes downward. 'Don't know where they are. They went one day, don't know where …'

'What's your name?' she asked softly. By the looks of him, he couldn't have been any older than twelve.

He shook his head stiffly and put his hand to the source of pain in his head. The boy began to sniff and wiped his eyes with his sleeve.

'So you're alone then?' She continued to press him. He nodded, still avoiding her gaze. Catherine breathed deeply and thought of yesterday's events. She replaced her glove on her hand and stood up straight. *Reg – what would he have done?*

'Right,' she declared. 'Best foot forward, then.'

'What?' the boy stuttered at her.

'I can take you back to my house. I'll be able to fix your head up,' she announced before adding quickly, 'then send you on your way.'

She proceeded to walk back in the direction she had come from and made a few strides before looking back. The boy remained stood at the same spot.

'Come on, lad. I wish you no harm,' she held out her hand to him. Slowly, he walked to her but rather than take it, he walked alongside her.

They walked side by side for a while in silence. His feet scuffed against the cobbles in the road. Due to his injury, his pace matched hers. If she were being honest, the constant walking was starting to take its toll on her. Her joints felt stiff and she ached with every step. She noticed that every few minutes, the boy would anxiously look over his shoulder before facing the direction they were walking in again. She chose not to comment on it.

He spoke instead. 'My mum told me, before she left that is, not to trust anyone. To keep off the streets in the day, if I can.'

'Why?' She was just about to ask him why he had been left then but changed her mind.

He took her question as a prompt to explain. 'Mum and Dad said that there are people now who will take you as soon as they look at you!'

'What kind of people?' Catherine asked bemused.

'Bad 'uns, that's for sure.'

She frowned and nodded. 'You'll be safe with me for a while, until we find your parents that is.'

It didn't seem that long before they had reached Trafford Grove again. Catherine found the front door key and let them in, she took off her overcoat as the boy stood nervously with his back pressed to the front door. He looked around the room, an old stuffed armchair sat next to the dresser, within easy reach of the wireless. The fire had long died out in the hearth.

'I'll get that going again,' she motioned to him. 'You're quite safe here.' She felt as though she needed to reassure him again. 'We've an Anderson out back and can put the blackout blinds up later if you like.'

'We?' He looked around, his eyes wide. 'You said "we".' It was as if he expected a burly man to pop out at any moment, ready to finish him off.

'Oh, I meant me. It's just me here. Ever since ...' She looked in the direction of the garden and remembered Reg's body which still lay there.

'There are some logs out back, I'll get the fire going again and fix us something to eat.' She moved slowly before pausing, her hand resting on the back doorknob.

'I can help you, missus. I always helped my mum ...' He moved closer to her, forcing her to stop her train of thoughts and open the door. She remained stood on the doorstep, her eyes fixed on the paving slabs below. The boy breezed past her and walked over to the shed where the spare logs were housed. He balanced a few in his arms.

'You okay, missus?'

Catherine shook her head and broke her gaze from the spot where Reg had fallen. All she could see was a fading stain on one of the tiles. She put her hand to her head, puzzled and looked around their immediate area. She had not had any sleep for a while, and this added to her confusion. *Where was he?*

'I'm fine,' she answered eventually. 'I'm just a bit tired, is all.' She shuffled back inside and sat heavily on their sofa under the window. The events of the last day were starting to catch up on Catherine as her eyes began to suddenly feel very heavy.

'Don't worry, missus, I can fix us something to eat, make you a cup of tea …'

'Look in the pantry,' she waved her hand dismissively. 'Remember there's a war on though …' With that, she fell into a heavy sleep.

* * *

The warmth of the room roused her from her sleep. Catherine slowly opened her eyes in the direction of the fire in the hearth. It looked as though it had been burning for a while and was well tended. She lay in the same spot she had fell asleep in and breathed deeply, stretching herself.

She looked across the room, at Reg's chair, where he sat smiling at her. Her husband nodded approvingly at her. 'Good for you, girl,' he smiled in the direction of the kitchen. 'Just like you to take in any waifs and strays …'

Catherine gasped as she remembered this boy. She could hear clattering, coming from her kitchen. She turned to look back at Reg, but found his chair empty. Just the imprint of where he used to sit.

The pot bubbled on the stove in the kitchen. He stood with his back to her at the sink. Catherine decided to cough a few times as not to startle him.

'You feeling better, missus?' he asked.

'It's Catherine. But you can call me Cath.'

He nodded. She fully expected him to announce his name, but he did not. 'I'm making us potatoes. Bit of cheese on top, we used to have that a lot, when we got enough cheese, that is.'

She decided not to ask his name again. 'I'll set the table,' she replied. 'I've a few other bits in the pantry. I make my own bread, what with it being hard to get and all.'

'You grow your own greens out back?' he asked after they were settled down at the table.

'Yes. And if I need anything, I see what's in the houses in the street. I always leave a note behind, mind, with what I've taken. That's the right thing to do. I'm not stealing, it'll be paid back.' She paused. 'There's not much in the shops nowadays.' She looked at him and frowned. 'You seem to know a lot about my garden. Like where we keep the logs for the fire and all?'

'Oh …' the boy's cheeks seemed to turn a light pink in response. 'We spent a lot of time round here, that's all …'

'We?'

He placed his fork on the edge of his plate and swallowed hard. 'The gang I was with …' his voice was practically a whisper.

Catherine opened her mouth to speak. However, a noise from outside disrupted their conversation. She half-expected to see the boy's gang running wild again. However, this time, it was different. Frowning, she saw what looked to be officials patrolling the area. The boy joined her at the window.

'It's them!' he gasped and moved to cower under the windowsill. His eyes were round saucers, and he began to shake as he clutched his knees against his chest. The boy bowed his head as if to protect himself.

'Who?' she crouched to perch next to him, moving slower than he had. She squinted out of the window from behind the curtain. In the distance, she could see uniformed men, official looking hats but more worryingly, they were armed. She watched as they moved out of her sight. The knot that had formed in the stomach told her that they were not patrolling to investigate the graffiti which had sprung up in the area, or the broken potted plants on the pavement.

'It's okay now, they're gone. Here, give me a hand with the blinds …'

He moved quickly to help her, seemingly more reassured that no one from outside would be able to see in.

'They're the bad people,' he announced.

'And what are they looking for?'

He shook his head. 'I think they are taking people away. My uncle went with them and my mum and dad went looking for him. We heard on the news that people went to work in camps ... they were taken, I heard them crying and calling out ...' his voice trailed off.

Catherine cut in. 'Let's get back to our dinner.' She didn't want to hear any more from him, fully aware what he was referring to as she had remembered Reg telling her about it; the thought of being taken away from your family was enough.

He seemed to visibly relax once the room was blocked from the outside world. Catherine washed their pots from dinner and smiled as he joined her to help. The night began to draw in. This stranger in her house, whoever he was, would prove some comfort in what would be her first night without Reg.

'We used to listen to the wireless after dinner,' she announced. 'None of that nonsense on the news station though. No point in listening to things you can't do anything about.' Her fingers poised over the knobs on the radio set. She watched as the boy proceeded to sit in what had been Reg's favourite chair. Catherine was aware she was holding her breath.

'That was my husband's chair,' she remarked.

'Oh, sorry miss ... I mean Cath,' he jumped to his feet immediately.

'No, it's all right. You can sit there if you like.' However, he still chose to sit on the sofa instead. Catherine sat next to him as the music played quietly in the background. She watched as he stifled a few yawns and rubbed his eyes. It had been a long day for both of them. Wordlessly, she fetched an old blanket and draped it over him. Within no time at all, his eyelids grew heavier and eventually closed.

Catherine must have dozed herself too as she woke with a start. The light in the room had dulled due to the fire dying out. She blinked a few times at the shadows forming.

He sat, legs crossed like always. Pipe in hand, reclined in his favourite old chair. He tapped the ash gently in the ashtray beside him.

'You're letting him stay, then?'

'Just for the time being,' Catherine replied to her husband. 'Poor mite has no one. I don't think he'll survive on the streets by himself … I heard his story. He's lost his parents …'

'They're not coming back for him,' Reg stated. 'But I think he'll be wanted, out there …' he nodded in the direction of the door. '… for work and sorts.'

'Then I'll do what I can do keep him safe. He's not a bad 'un. Maybe just got mixed up with the wrong people. You know, got involved in things without thinking about them.' She looked over at the boy, his eyes flickering as he slept. Suddenly, he coughed a few times, waking himself up. His eyes darted anxiously around the room before settling on Catherine.

'I think I know why my house is familiar to you.' She studied him carefully. He looked very small under the blanket. 'Do you know what happened to my Reg?' She looked across to the now empty chair.

He cast his eyes down and fiddled with the blanket hem. 'I'm sorry,' he whispered. 'It wasn't me, I swear. But I know the boy who did it …'

Catherine studied him carefully, and swallowed the lump growing in her throat. Could this young boy really be responsible for killing her beloved husband? It didn't seem possible, he seemed so fragile.

He sniffed and continued. 'When you'd gone, left him outside, me and another boy came back. I felt so bad at what had happened …'

She paused and composed herself. 'What did you do with him? He was outside when I left, out back by the door …'

'Your shed,' he replied. 'We didn't want to leave him, you know, in case of any dogs or anything. Covered him with a sheet we found.'

Catherine's hands trembled and she put them in her

lap to calm herself. 'In the morning you will help me bury him, then? Reg will always be with me then.'

'Do you hate me? Do I have to go?' his eyes filled with tears.

'I don't hate you, no.' She replied to him finally. She wasn't sure of the conviction of the words that she spoke, but she could hardly tell a child of her resentment towards him. He had inadvertently left her all alone. But surely it was part of her civic duty to report a murderer?

'Go back to sleep,' she announced after a while. Catherine broke her gaze with him, blinking away the tears. Just as she did so, a shadow of a smile crossed his face. He seemed to be more at ease with her since they had first met. The boy turned his head away from her and in no time at all, she could hear his breathing change signalling he had fallen asleep again.

'Oh, Reg,' she sobbed to herself. 'What am I going to do?' Her head was in her hands as she wrestled with her emotions.

'He's alone and vulnerable …' Reg replied.

'But he's part of the gang that killed you!' Her voice was raised, and she looked across to her sleeping companion but he did not stir. 'He's showing remorse though and I believe him to be genuine.'

'There's your answer then, my dear,' he whispered back to her. 'Don't hold a grudge against this child, he just got mixed up with the wrong people, that's all.'

Catherine leant back on the settee. She felt her eyes grow heavy but didn't want to close them, she didn't want to let go of Reg's memory. A horrible feeling crossed her mind that if they did indeed bury his body tomorrow, she would no longer see him and be able to talk with him. It would be a final goodbye.

* * *

Catherine rubbed her eyes a few times as she adjusted to the light within the room. She felt stiff as she realised she was in the same position as she had fallen asleep in. It had been a long time since she had slept out of her bed. The boy stirred shortly afterwards as they went through the motions of eating breakfast together. Catherine had too much on her mind that morning, still wrestling with her emotions about the boy and what was the right thing to do. She found some old clothes for him as they prepared to go out into the back garden.

She looked around at the small allotment she and Reg had built together and tried to pick a suitable place to house a grave.

'What about there?' he seemed to read her mind as he pointed to the back of the garden. 'We could move the fence out of the way at the bottom ...'

She saw that he was referring to the garden that backed onto hers. The grass was overgrown and the weeds towered unruly amongst it. They had obviously not spent as much time tending to it as they had the rest. If they used that bit of land, then Reg would be close enough to the house to comfort Catherine yet far enough away not to disturb their allotment. She moved over to the back of the garden. The boy put down the shovels and helped her move the fence. Catherine took one final look around the houses. This one indeed looked abandoned as they all did now. She dug the shovel into the ground.

They worked together for what seemed like hours. The ground was fairly soft but the task in hand took much longer due to her advancing years and with him being a young boy. However, eventually they had dug a hole together big enough for their needs. Catherine trudged in the direction of their shed where the boy had said he'd put Reg's body. She breathed deeply and let the door hang open. Sure enough, a stained sheet lay concealing him. She wasn't ready to look at him yet and positioned the sheet so it would not slip off and signalled for the boy to grab his feet.

At their makeshift grave, she gingerly climbed in as they eased his body in. Catherine wiped her hands against her coat as they stood side by side in silence.

'He was my everything,' Catherine heard herself sob.

She bent to remove the sheet from his face. Reg's features looked grey as he lay, eyes closed. She studied his face, usually so full of life, she just wasn't used to seeing this expression – calm and peaceful. Catherine allowed herself to cry silently. As she raised one hand to wipe her eyes, she felt a small hand take the other.

Looking down beside her, the boy stared up at her, his large eyes glassy too. He said nothing but slowly used his other arm to wrap around her. He gave her a weak smile and squeezed tighter.

'I'm sorry Cath, this is my fault …'

She shook her head. 'No, no, it wasn't. Don't blame yourself. What's done is done.' She patted him on the back to reassure him. 'I'd like you to join me in a prayer.'

'Okay …' he shuffled his feet as they stood apart now, looking at the grave.

'Do you go to church?' she asked.

The boy shook his head. 'No, I've never been … we go to a …'

They looked up together as a distant noise interrupted them. Raised voices, breaking glass, heavy scraping sounds sounded far away but at the same time, close enough to pose a threat. She looked at him and saw the fear start to set in his eyes.

'Let's go inside,' she ushered him in, quicker than intended. Once they were back in the kitchen, she locked the door behind them.

'Have you got blackouts for this window too?'

'Yes, you'll help me.'

'Maybe we should do all the windows and keep all the blinds down now, you know, to keep us safe,' he panted at her, as the exertion of holding them proved to be an effort for him. 'Do you think they are looking for more workers, for the camps?'

'Maybe, I don't know,' she replied. 'However, they'll find nothing here …'

He smiled back at her, more genuine this time and full of hope. 'Does that mean I can stay with you then?' he asked tentatively.

'Yes, it does. You'll be perfectly safe with me, no one will hurt you, I'll see to that.'

'Thank you, Cath,' he beamed at her. 'I'll help start the fire again, it can be one of the jobs I do here,' he moved again to the back door. 'I'll just go out and get some more logs …'

'Wait …' she stopped him in his tracks. 'If you're to stay with me, I need to know your name …'

The boy looked at her and smiled. He was becoming more relaxed in her company. His smile showed they had developed an understanding between them and he had begun to trust her. He imagined now that the worst was behind him.

Finally, he replied to her, 'My name is Abraham.'

THE BUSKER

BY TALIESIN TROW

THE BUSKER

He woke up as he always did. What would happen if he didn't? Who'd know? Not even him.

He started the day again.

He woke up as he always did, looked around until he could focus on something. It happened to be a cigarette. A cigarette! A serious rarity. The majority of tobacco had been long since smoked, replaced with the remnants of factory floors, but this time, his tips had been good, his reviews favourable.

He leant over and took the yellowed fag from its resting place in the ashtray, he un-crumpled the butt and put it to his lips. He felt around in his pockets … searched in his bag … no lighter … a box of matches … all spent.

'Bollocks!'

'What is it?'

'Oh, hello, it was where's my lighter, but now it's, who are you?'

The doe eyed girl turned away with a blush.

'I thought I was your muse; at least that's what you told me.'

He looked at the girl blankly. She seemed nice; she was certainly pretty. He thought quickly, well, quicker than normal. 'Of course … got a light?'

The girl reached into her handbag and brought out

a hurricane lighter that her father had given her before he had gone. She handed it to him. He took it and lay back on the pillow reflecting on the burning embers.

'Ahhh, that's better.'

'Thanks'

'Oh, no. I mean, that's nice!'

The girl turned and rose from the bed, her slender form framed by the window.

'Good show last night' she said.

'Thanks.'

'It's nice to hear the oldies.'

'What do you mean?' he said guardedly.

'Well, I haven't heard Wagner for ages.'

'Oh yeah, I've always been praised for my Nibelung.'

'You certainly put a lot of life into it.'

'Thanks'

'I'm Sarah by the way.'

'Thanks'

He stood up and stretched his arms out. The sound of cracking joints from a life-time hunched over instruments was familiar to him but made his young companion wince.

'Breakfast?' she said.

'Is there any?' he said hurriedly; every meal was the last for a musician these days.

'Of course. We have eggs, bacon, even butter.'

'Butter!'

'Sheep's.'

'Ah, yes, sounds good.'

He stepped out of the room and began to piece his day together. He'd been working hard over the last few weeks, taking work here and there, labouring, driving, plucking chickens; the hooks on their feathers had ripped his hands to shreds. He'd nearly sold his guitar, but then, when he was playing on his usual corner, a woman had come up and put bottle of milk and fresh loaf in his case. It took a lot to make him stop midstream, but this was a week's work for him. He looked up and met the gaze of an auburn haired woman who looked to be in her fifties, but her manner belied her age.

'Many thanks; is there something you'd like to hear?'

'Play me one of the classics.'

He put down his guitar, and took his violin out of the case, began to rosin up his bow and played his finest 9th. He found this got the best response. He was halfway through the first movement when he opened his eyes, and saw his benefactor looking at him with a look of indifference. He lowered his bow. 'Something else?'

'Yes, one of the classics'

'Well, I know some other tunes, but I also value my freedom.'

'How about a private party?'

'Are you with *the* party?'

The lady laughed out loud. 'What does that even mean any more?'

It had been years since all unsanctioned music had been banned and in certain cases was punishable by death, but since the wave had passed over, there were pockets of people who turned a blind eye, even revelled in the old music. But there were also those who sought to trap people.

Music was dangerous, it meant freedom of thought, freedom of expression, and, crucially, freedom of movement.

'May I?' the auburn haired lady said, gesturing to his guitar.

'Of course.'

The woman gently picked up the instrument, as if it were her child, and began to pick out a melody.

He was impressed, what lovely tone, and even playing, and … what … no … no!!!

'You can't play that! You'll get us arrested!!'

'Private party?'

'Ok'

* * *

Angel Station led onto Upper Street. To the left was Pentonville's finest concentration camp, where many of his friends had lived and died; the Victorians had a strange ability to predict the future. To the right, restaurants, night clubs playing unimportant and inoffensive tunes, the drinks were good, but came at a price. Loose lips sank everything around here. The 200 yards between the two was a Nomansland inhabited by the deprived, depraved, and musicians.

He followed her past the Assembly Hall, The Union Chapel, what was left of Highbury and Islington, and into the park behind. The houses had been established as being on 'the safe list' during the troubles, and had remained pretty unsullied in the fallout after the violence had moved through; unlike Belgravia, once home to the elite, had now been left to the crows.

The house they moved towards was decked with the usual regalia of the past. Ionic columns showing the symbology of a new beginning which never came. The gateway was imposing, reminiscent of the Georgian houses that London was synonymous with, but were only home to the rich and famous.

'Here we are.'

'Great'

They turned before the gate to enter the local tunnel. When the troubles had reached their apex, and the underground could no longer hold everyone, any underground space had been utilised. The old postal tunnels in Holborn, the Victorian toilets in Shepherd's Bush, it was not unusual to use less than salubrious places for home.

But he was relieved. The idea of entering the home of one of 'them' was unsettling, at least his patron was a genuine fan of the classics.

Descending the stairs, they were met by a solid metal door; it would have withstood any type of blast the invasion could have thrown, but bizarrely had a 'Welcome' mat at its entrance. Once through the inches-thick door, he was bewitched by the sites, sounds, and most noticeably, the smells.

Marijuana mixed with candy floss, all wrapped in a

roast meat blanket. All either illegal or unobtainable, all unmistakeable, all probably courtesy of the John Bull Co-operative Society. The walls were festooned with posters of famous artists, Lautrec, Picasso, Beardsley all tattered and singed, clearly saved from the embers of burning homes before it was too late. The scratchy tone of an HMV gramophone blasted out fiddle and banjo, the likes of which he had never heard.

'Who's this?'

'Young family called the Seegers from America, they sing about freedom, three chords and the truth, you know.'

He didn't, but he loved the idea. This music was powerful, evocative, and very familiar. He turned a corner into the room from where the music was emanating, and stopped dead. He was met with a sight he had not seen for nearly ten years. A group of people sat casually in armchairs, drinking, smoking, talking in un-hushed tones, and, singing. Singing at the top of their voices, as if none would hear, none could hear in through the foot of steel and feet of earth that enclosed them.

The party turned to him, and all charged their glasses.

'The entertainment!'

'I'll try my best.'

'I'm sure you'll do just fine, is that your guitar?' a willowy woman with a stack of straw coloured hair asked.

'Play a tune or three,' joined a dashing man who looked like Noel Coward would be on his Christmas card list.

He opened up his case and pulled out his guitar. The A string was always his go to, always stayed true to his ear, tuning forks cost too much. He reckoned he knew his audience from his benefactor's demeanour, but he was still cautious, he'd spent too many nights in the cells for playing 'the wrong music' to risk in even these relaxed surroundings. He began to play preludes, slowly, softly, he saw that his audience were enwrapped. Eyes closed, heads on one side. He had never had such response.

Taking out his capo, he prepared to play a Guiliani

piece 'The Harmonious Blacksmith.' This piece had always been well received as it was based on Handel, and was in the key of E, which was one of the more popular keys after the troubles.

'No, no, no, you don't need to use that thing here.'

'I'm sorry?'

'Keys are immaterial, if the note rings true, that is enough for us. You were right Ems.' An older gentleman turned to the hostess, who smiled knowingly. He was confused; should he play something else?

'Try playing what you were going to play without the bar.'

He thought for a moment and spread his dexterous fingers across the fretboard. Normally, this would have worried him, last minute key changes, particularly of such classic tunes, were risky for so many reasons. But he felt a flow under his hands he rarely felt when playing the SC, Sanctioned Canon.

'Better, yes?' said the older gentleman, who had a viola at his feet.

'Yes?!?'

'May I join you?'

'Please!'

The older gentleman lifted his viola to his chin and awaited the nod to begin to play. The sound filled the room; fluid, warm, sensual, emotive. To his amazement, the rest of the guests all reached for various instruments, flute, oboe, cello, the willowy woman moved behind a curtain and appeared with a full-size harp. The hostess, stationed behind a fully stocked bar expertly poured Martinis with a violin resting in the crook of her arm.

The sound was exquisite, vital and like nothing he had ever heard. The notes mixed with the spiralling smoke and scent and filled him with the sense of power and love that had led him to become a musician in the first place.

Suddenly, the lights flickered, and all the electricity of the room seemed to go out. As soon as it had begun, the music was gone, as if it had never existed. Silence, it seemed endless, but must have only lasted for a moment. Then, pitch black.

'Give me your guitar,' a voice rasped in the darkness.

'Over my dead…'

'That is the only option if you don't give it to me.'

He handed his guitar over to the faceless whisperer. Shortly after, the lights came on, and the music resumed, but it was different. Familiar in a way he was only too aware of, his usual oeuvre, the oeuvre of fear. Nationalistic, stale, propagandist and SC. The postered walls were now plain, timber framed, with the occasional woodland scene straight out of the Black Forest.

'Schnapps all round!!'

The land of beer had quickly adapted to the far more alcoholic prospect of using apples and pears to make more knock-out libations. So it was for the army of civil servants who suddenly filled the room.

'Play us a tune!'

A sudden return to reality. He began the open strains of his Schlager medley. Mind numb, fingers on auto-pilot.

'You're a bit flat, aren't you?'

'Got a tuning fork?'

'I do, as it happens; the Islington Assembly Hall would be lost without it.'

Shit! A State Musician. That was a lucky escape! He took the tuning fork as if it were made of glass, and struck it against a…glass. Duly tuned up, he struck up with his best fake gusto, audience participation, arms linked and swaying.

After several hours and several encores, he put his guitar down, and went to the bar. The auburn haired woman had been replaced by a younger version, same twinkling eyes, same fiery locks.

'What can I get you?'

'Water, please.'

'I think we can do better than that!'

The young barmaid stretched up to the top shelf, reaching behind the bottles of schnapps and Trappist beers, puling out a small bottle with a wax top.

'Try this.'

'Bourbon!'

'Shhhh,' she winked as if to allay his fear he had aroused suspicion.

He looked around the bar, everyone was who was still there was pretty far gone by this point.

There was one pair of eyes which were not dulled by alcohol. It was the State musician, and he was staring with his piercingly sober eyes.

One of his drinking companions, who was definitely under the influence lurched towards the record player. He started rifling through the records in the boxes around it. He pulled one out and slowly started to focus on the label. His inebriated mist quickly lifted and he fumbled for his revolver. Quick as a flash, one of the 'locals' stood up and stabbed him in the neck. The place erupted into frantic violence, the steel door slammed shut, the lights went out, there was shouting and gunfire, smashing glass and cries of pain and death.

The busker was still frozen to his spot at the bar, and amidst the chaos, he felt a hand on his shoulder, and a whisper in his ear.

'Follow me.'

He did, and quickly.

He found himself in a small room, filled with manuscript and instruments. In the centre of the room, sat his hostess, in front of a strange machine, pushing faders and turning dials, green lights flickered to red, cables ran out of the machine into the walls. He had seen something similar at party rallies, it was a way of controlling the volume of the microphones which spread the word of propaganda and fear across the country. He also realised, that the sound of gunfire and shouting had all but gone.

She rose from her seat and spoke into a microphone suspended from the ceiling. 'All clear'

The busker was shaken and bewildered, and she knew it. She offered out a hand and gently led him back into the bar area. The floor was covered with the dead bodies of the government revellers, some with gunshot wounds, stab marks, bodies twisted, but all with blood issuing from their ears.

'We're going to have to move again, Ems,' said the old viola player.

'No, no more running. It's time to make a move, and I think we have the one to carry the sound for us.'

'What the bloody hell is going on?'

The young man was more than a little perplexed.

'One of the reasons I invited you here, was because of the way you played, but also, what you played. How many times have you been arrested?'

'A few.'

'So, you've been to Pentonville before?'

'The outer cells, yes.'

'Tomorrow night, I am hosting a gala event at the Assembly Hall for all of the camp's top brass, I want you to perform a classical set, on this.'

She reached under the bar, and pulled out a violin, but it was made entirely out of metal, pearlescent metal, and it had five strings.

'I've never played one of these before, I don't know if I can.'

'It's just like a normal violin, except this extra string; do not play this until the end.'

'What is this?'

'It's just music – and ... put these in your ears.' She handed him two metal earplugs.

'There is a story that a chap on the other side wanted everyone to play at 440hz tuning. This is not wholly true, plenty of orchestras tune like this, he is in fact searching for "the sound". A fabled tuning that can affect the body in many ways, taking it from ecstasy to agony. But it isn't just a frequency, it is a sequence, each melody produces a different response. Bach came close, Mozart, even Gilbert and Sullivan.'

'And you discovered it?'

'Me, no, my mother taught it to me, and her mother to her, and so on for generations, and now I am going to teach it to you. You have the gift, I know you are meant to play this music, will you?'

'Do I have a choice?'

* * *

Even though the enemy seemed to have no desire to run the country, the powers that had taken over in the aftermath, the **XXII** Committee, were happy to adopt the trappings of their old foe, fear and propaganda were more profitable than democracy, and it was cheaper to keep the camps open, cheaper labour, cheaper lives.

One of their haunts had been set up around the Islington area, and the Assembly Hall was where they met to discuss policy, such as it was, but mostly to party. The Busker arrived early, he was unusually nervous, he'd heard the phrase 'knock 'em dead', but this was ridiculous. He entered the huge hall and saw the speakers being erected at the front of the stage, and the machine he had seen for the first time only the night before being wheeled in to the centre of the room.

'So, you are the soloist?'

He spun around to see a smartly dressed man.

'Yes, that's right.'

'Emmeline speaks very highly of you.'

'Emmeline?'

'Yes, the Minister's wife, it's her event! All of the city's most important people will be here.'

'Oh yes, Ems.'

'Wow, you are on good terms.'

The hall was absolutely packed, with people dressed in the regalia of office, glasses clinking, tongues wagging. The throng was deafening. He stepped on to the stage as if a ghost, not even a head turned. He picked up his new instrument, a long cable linked it to the machine in the centre of the room. He played the opening strains of Stravinsky, the huge sound filled the hall, bursting from the speakers with a staggering sweetness and beauty. Everyone turned and took their seats. This was the largest audience he had every played to, and they were all his. This amplification thing was amazing! Even if he hadn't been a great player, the sheer volume could render an audience dumb.

He *was* a great player however, and the audience were in thrall to his every note. Polite applause turned to raucous shouts and cheers, as he took his artistic licence, and new sonic powers to the heights of his ability, a truly virtuosic performance. Then came the time.

'The 5th.'

He reached into his pocket and took out his ear plugs. He looked around the room, he caught the eye of Emmeline, almost unrecognisable with a tightly woven hairpiece and black dress, she flashed him a knowing look. He cast his eyes about and noticed something else. There were many here who were not members, there were servants, young and old, and looking to the balcony, there were children; were they protected? Collateral damage was not something he had considered, and not something he would entertain.

'For my final piece, I would like to play *The Ride of The Valkyries*.'

He saw Emmeline's eyes harden as he played at his most virtuosic. The audience erupted into applause and the obligatory encore was never more deserved. He turned to leave the stage.

'Wait!' came a voice from the audience.

He froze. Was this it, was he going back to the camp, had someone recognised him? Had Emmeline decided that his betrayal should be punished? He heard footsteps behind him walking up the steps to the stage.

He turned and saw the Minister of Pentonville approach him. He stretched out his arms.

'Fantastic!!! I think everyone would agree, come drink with us!'

* * *

He attacked his bacon and eggs as if he had never eaten before in his life.

'Coffee?' the young girl asked. He had already forgotten her name, his head woozy from the night before.

'Please. Do you live alone here?'

'I have this place to myself, yes, but I have to stay within the grounds, except for events like last night.'

'The grounds?'

'Yes, of the camp.'

He swallowed hard, spilling his coffee all over the table.

'Oh god, I'm so sorry.'

'That's ok, accidents happen, I'll just clean this up, then my father would like to see you.'

'Your father?'

'Yes, he loved your performance last night, he'd like to thank you in person.'

His heart started beating fit to burst. Should he try and make his excuses, had he let slip anything during the night before? He resigned himself to just going along with his new companion, who seemed strangely familiar, though he couldn't place her.

There was a knock at the door. He nearly spilled the rest of his coffee.

'The Minister will see you now!'

The busker was led from the girl's apartment through the grounds of the camp, to the Minister's quarters. These were as opulent as the Assembly Hall, but on a much smaller scale. He was led through a number of doors, all heavily guarded into an ante room.

'Wait here.'

He started to fidget, fingertips drumming nervous patterns on his knees. He looked up to see the auburn haired Sarah looking down at him.

'My mother said, you forgot this.'

She handed him a case, smiled sweetly and walked away, back to her apartment. The door to the Commandant's offices opened and the busker was ushered in. The Commandant was standing by a huge sash window. The room was filled with officious looking staffers, the sycophant brigade.

'Well, then, my young friend, quite the performance last night, most commendable. I trust your quarters were comfortable?'

Did he know where he'd stayed? He couldn't imagine that he would condone his staying with his daughter!

'Yes, thank you.'

'Ah good, Emmeline said that she had found you a nice spot, come, let me show you something.'

The busker came to the window and looked out on the scene below.

'The future my boy; industry, production, progress. Soon we will have enough raw energy to put Britain back on top.'

What he saw, he recognised only too well. He had never been on the inside of the camp, but you could smell it, and he knew people who had gone there, never to be seen again. The smoke stacks and man powered production lines would have filled a hundred factory sites, but this was all squeezed into a place the size of a couple of football fields. Guards with cudgels and whips kept every chain gang moving, boys as young as eight tethered to men old enough to be their great grandfathers. Women with tattered clothes, barely able to cover their dignity slaving away over vast cauldrons.

'Impressive.' he managed to force.

'Ah yes, let's make Britain great again! I see you have your instrument, let's have a tune!'

'Very well, I call this one … the 5th.'

THE ARBITRATOR

BY FAYE IRWIN

THE ARBITRATOR

D aniel threw the ball up in the air, his eyes followed the arc beneath his long dark lashes. In a clumsy motion, his arms rose up swinging the bat.

Thwack!

Thomas felt time return to a normal pace as he watched the ball fly out of the garden. It was so quick compared to the instant before. The ball zipped over the top of the bushes and disappeared into the street. Before Thomas could react, Daniel had dropped his bat. His dark curls bounced in step as he ran after it. The thumps of his footsteps were desperate. Thomas gasped, readying a cry.

'Stop, wait!'

But Daniel had the gate open and was out into the street.

Thomas couldn't see his face, couldn't see the blood. All he could see was his small body, limp on the street.

* * *

Thomas sighed heavily, forcing himself to concentrate. His ceramic opera mask pushed his breath back, drowning him in the smell of cognac. His black robes disguised him as a shapeless form of justice. All those attending were in their matching black robes and ornate masks. Above the din of ordinary conversation, there were exclamations in Latin.

Cryptic and overused phrases belied the shotty background some members had in Latin.

Shopkeeper ripping off the public?

'Qui vitulum tollit, taurum subduxerit idem.' *He that steals an egg will steal an ox.*

Boundary dispute between neighbours?

'Testis unus, testis nullus!' *One witness is no witness.*

Sisters arguing over an eligible bachelor?

'Veritas et aequitas.' *Truth and justice.*

The words were utterly interchangeable and had long since lost any meaning to him. He suppressed the urge to rub the bridge of his brow. There was no nuance nor suggestion of grey. He watched helplessly as guilt prevailed time and time again. The masks were a necessary evil, violent and bitter maniacs like the Blue Lampers, filled with impotent rage, would take out their anger on any magistrate, politician or policeman they could get their hands on. The masks protected the wearer, but they also, somehow, disconnected them from their own actions. They were just following orders, it was for the greater good, they'd tell themselves, and perhaps they were right, but the masks were here to stay. Thomas could never understand for the life of him why they had to be so theatrical though.

He shrugged off his wandering mind and came back to reality. He stood before a table at the head of the large Gregorian hall. On the table was a set of brass scales. Non-industrial scales had long since gone out of fashion in London, but this Portuguese set was ornate and too ceremonial. Two weighing pans hung from the bar suspended by chains as delicate as a jeweller would make a locket's chain. Bursting from the rod were engravings of sea and land creatures, topped by a sun emblem. Engraved at the bottom were the words, 'Julgue cada andar da vida como Deus nos julga.' *Judge every walk of life as God judges us.*

Each man, declaring his own Latin phrase and disguised, placed his judgement upon the scale. Left or right, guilt or innocence. It was all determined by the secret society in private.

Mr. Petska watched the proceedings. He swallowed.

And then swallowed again, watching anxiously.

'Excusatio non petita, accusatio manifesta,' said John. Thomas knew it was John due to his peculiar gait. He laid a few marks on the left pan. *A guilty conscience needs no accuser.*

From the back, another man came forward. His words were as clipped and crisp as his robes. 'Velle est posse.' Thomas couldn't place the speaker. He was as fooled as the rest of the crowd. Marks were placed on the right pan. *To be willing is to be able.* Or more commonly, where there is a will, there is a way.

One after another, they each came forward, having a say in the fate of Mr. Petska. Thomas's gaze slid across their faces. Each member returned his stare, unafraid. Their eyes were beady, glittery details beneath their decorated masks. For another week in a row, Thomas condemned a man. Mr. Petska and his family would be asked to leave by the end of the week.

Thomas took a shaking breath, unsure how to proceed. 'Vos amotum,' he boomed, declaring Mr. Petska an outsider.

The society boomed back a cheering chorus of approval.

An ache sat within his chest.

* * *

The scent of wet road and trees hit him as he stepped outside. It was laced with the cool flavour of night. Thomas tucked his head into his hat, hiding the grey-blue outline of buildings from his view. The scrape of his sole against stone punctuated his thoughts as he walked.

Mr. Petska had been the grocer on his street since before the war. Everyone felt that men like this were the cause of the taint. Thomas huffed, stepping harder, as he tried to outrun the oppressive shadow looming over London.

On the front step of his house, Thomas stopped to scrape his shoes on the U shaped brush. In two quick motions, he removed the filth of the street. He stepped inside to a dark house. On the side table sat a single oil lamp his wife left on, burning low. He hung his hat and outer coat on the mirrored coat rack, then turned the lamp down extinguishing the flame. He walked carefully down the hall trying not to wake his family. From the hallway he could hear the rhythmic breathing of his daughters, gently pulling the door closed as he passed.

Reaching his room, he noticed the darkness became a sea of ink. The curtains blocked the streetlamps from coming in. He stood at the window a moment, holding the heavy curtain open to look out at the street. No one was out. No sounds of footsteps. In so short a time, life had changed drastically.

'This time four years ago, I could buy sugar for your cakes and no one would think twice about staying out after dark.'

'Shut that curtain and come to bed,' June mumbled into the pillowcase. He pulled his hand back, letting the curtain fall. Little beams of light played across the floorboards from its sway.

* * *

Thomas stared at the bottom of his coffee cup. He was tired from his late night and tired of the grit at the bottom of his cup. He tried to tell himself it was thick like Turkish coffee, but he knew that it was just the quality ever decreasing.

Samantha and Helen bounced down the hallway and into the kitchen. 'Bacon!' Helen shouted. 'Oh, we haven't had bacon in ages.' She thumped into a seat and held her fork up like a weapon.

Thomas smiled into his cup, grateful for at least the small things. 'Where is your brother?'

Samantha shrugged. Helen, his wild four year old, slammed her cutlery harder on the table. A sharp look from him stopped her.

'Upstairs,' Helen replied, beaming.

Thomas dutifully headed upstairs to find his son was

a few lumps outlined by the drape of the quilt. 'Charlie. It's time to get up. I don't think the girls are going to save you any bacon.'

The lump shifted but did not comply. Closing the gap from the door to the bed in only a few strides, Thomas ripped the quilt off Charlie. His eyes were red rimmed and his cheeks were flushed. Thomas winced at the sight of him and then carefully sat at the edge of the bed.

'Helen doesn't cry like this about him,' his son said.

'Helen doesn't remember him, Charlie. She was only just talking when he died. She knows him as a name that has been repeated as many times as the alphabet. He is as real to her as a dream.' Thomas tucked Charlie's head under his chin and squeezed him. He breathed in the smoky scent of bacon and the faint scent of soap from Charlie's hair.

'You've got school. Chop chop.'

* * *

Thomas walked down the cobbled street, stones sliding under his shoes. The air was still damp and it curled around him. His satchel hung at his side and bounced rhythmically. The sounds were the percussive back beat to the spring birds' melodies. Others that passed him by in their morning shuffle, most surprisingly, were women. Their hair neatly waved and navy skirts stiff from starch. As he rounded a bend and entered the glass front door of his office building, he heard the bells of a school tolling. Children's laughter and pounding feet crescendoed and disappeared into the distance.

'Good morning, Alice,' he said to the building secretary as he entered. She dipped her head at him as he passed. Her sandy blonde hair caught the morning sun and looked like a halo. Alice never once stopped typing.

Thomas sighed and moved along as fast as he could. The lobby was a wave of bodies threatening to sweep him away.

Once he reached his office, he relieved himself of his

coat, hat, and satchel. Pulling a leather binder from his bag, he laid it across his desk and then smoothed the pages. After refilling his coffee, this cup worse than the last, he settled into the chart. This was a long table of numbers and figures of the Dalson's Steel Factory. He tallied up his last few figures before wrapping it up and scuttling down the hall.

Some men sat at a large oak table and a few stood in pairs around it. Their grey and navy uniforms blended into the haze of the room. Thomas choked on the cigar smoke and took a seat at the rapidly filling table.

When Steinbrinck entered, everyone stood or turned to face him.

Steinbrinck looked the room over and sat at the end of the large oak table.

'Whitten, you start,' Steinbrinck demanded. Thomas's grey business suit stood out like a blank canvas in the room of uniforms. He noticed for the first time that his hair was the darkest in the room. His palms sweated and heartbeat picked up a notch as he began the intonation of the month's figures. Alice appeared, handing out a simple table with Thomas's expenditure numbers and Bert's completed sales.

Paper rustled, creating the only airflow in the room. Steinbrinck nodded his head approvingly.

'See,' Steinbrinck said to the man on his right with a satisfied grin. 'It was worth taking the steel mill, listen to the prosperity we've brought to the region.' He tossed his hand out in a mix of contempt and pride.

The man on his right nodded in approval. 'A strategic move, sir. You will be Great Britain's richest man.'

'What do you say, Whitten?' Steinbrinck pinned Thomas with a stare. Another man, down further down the table, ashed his cigar.

Thomas looked up from his sheet, taking in the full room of navy, grey, and blond. He couldn't think of a word to say, so he pressed his eyebrows together willing something intelligible to come out. 'If Bert keeps selling like this,' he said at last. 'Then the King himself will be calling soon to borrow money.'

The men stared at him emotionless. Thomas let out a nervous laugh and the rest of them joined in. It was hollow – all of it – the laugh, the joke, the minor social graces.

Another man, at the end of the table, muttered something under his breath. His voice was venomous.

Steinbrinck nodded, then volleyed back a response. Thomas looked down at his papers, then sipped his water, trying not to give away how little he understood. Always though, his ears strained to decipher their words. It was like listening to a scrambled radio where sometimes the frequency would clear and the understanding would shine through.

Something about this weekend. About a woman. He couldn't tell as the words began to blend together. One man said something which rankled with Steinbrinck and within moments the meeting was dismissed. Thomas tried not to let it faze him.

* * *

'Mr. Whitten, I have your mail.'

Sitting at his desk, Thomas looked up from his coffee to see Alice standing at the door of his office.

'Thank you, Alice. You can leave it there.' He inclined his head slightly to indicate the left side of his desk. She walked in and placed a neat stack of envelopes there.

Alice turned to leave, the soft soles of her shoes whispered on the floor. 'Mr. Whitten?' she asked.

'Yes, Alice?'

'Are you any good at Latin?' She had his full attention now. Fear zinged through his gut.

'I used to know a great deal when I went to Cambridge, but I've lost quite a bit of it now. Why do you ask such a strange question, my dear?'

'Oh. Well, I received this letter and I'm not sure who it's addressed to. Can you make it out?'

Thomas took the letter. She clasped her hands

loosely in front of her, expectant. He felt it was too prim and formal a gesture. His eye raked over the ornate script, *for justice* sprang out at him and he knew just who this was addressed to. 'My, who writes like this anymore? I can barely make out the words. Why don't you leave it here and I'll see if I can puzzle it out later?' He tossed the letter into the stack, lifted his coffee cup, and met her gaze.

She looked down at the floorboards as though waiting.

He blew gently on the coffee before sipping. 'I'm sorry, but this will take a bit of time. I'll let you know when I have something useful.'

'Yes, sir.' She nodded her head in acknowledgement and left.

* * *

'Where are you going?' June demand. Her curly brown hair was escaping its pin.

Thomas didn't answer and instead continued to exchange the items in his satchel. Out came his leather binder and in went his black robes and mask.

'Are you going to do this every night? It's been twice this week and it's only Wednesday.'

'It's an emergency, June.' His voice was terse and he felt strung up like a bow.

'An emergency! And what about tomorrow and Friday? What will those be? Ah! I know, tomorrow you will be in jail and by Friday they will shoot you. Saturday I will be kissing your corpse goodbye and praying with lips shut because God only knows they won't let me pray any more - -'

Thomas cut the distance between them and grabbed her by the elbows. 'Stop. Do not ever say those words again and don't ever scream them. You have no idea whose ears are listening.'

She took a ragged breath and began to cry. 'Why do you keep doing this?'

He stared into her brown eyes. 'Shh,' he said,

brushing loose hair behind her ear. 'Shh.' He pulled her into his chest and tucked her head beneath his chin. June began to sob.

'Thomas. You could die for this.'

He nodded his head, unintentionally jabbing his chin into her head. He took a deep breath and let it out. 'I received a letter.'

'What did it say?'

He stepped back, his eyes searching. 'I have to go.'

'God damn you, Thomas, tell me right here and now. Before God and everyone why it is that you're risking your life – the livelihood of your family for this – this – cult!'. She stabbed one finger at the ground while her other hand rested on her hip.

'You wouldn't understand.'

With every ounce of his self control, he closed the door without a bang.

* * *

Robed and masked, Thomas stood at the dais, the brass scales behind him. He watched through the mask's eyelets as the crowd filtered in. Each wearing their own robes and masks. Each a participant in this intricate dance. Internally, Thomas marvelled at the silent orchestration of this event. Always at short notice, always when the need arose, and never spoken of thereafter.

As the temperature of the room was beginning to rise from the smash of bodies and drinks flowed liberally, Thomas saw the defendants enter. A young woman, a girl really, was thrust out into the widening circle of robed and masked figures. She wore a floral patterned dress with buttons down the front. The top half of her auburn hair was pinned up to the side and the rest fell in loose ringlets around her shoulders. Her chest rose and fell in gulps as she tried to escape the circle. Gentle but firm hands pushed her back. Thomas watched as she took him in, an imposing figure at the helm of the ship by the scales. Tears streamed down her face.

'Who are —?'

'Wait, sir! Another.'

From the crowd came another body, this one was much taller. A lean man with broad shoulders wearing a cotton workman's shirt coloured cream from dirt and sweat. His black hair stuck out in every direction from beneath a working man's cap. His face was deeply tanned, but clean and shaved. He was handsome with features too fine for the calluses on his hands.

'Is that all? Or do you have a third one coming as well?' Thomas asked. The crowd laughed, but no one else came forth.

'Who are you?' the woman asked.

Thomas laughed, unused to her boldness. 'Usually I'm the one asking questions, my dear.' A subdued chuckle rippled back at him from the crowd.

She squared her jaw and levelled her eyes at him. He admired her tenacity.

'What are your names?' Thomas asked.

'Beth.'

There was a pause. Ice swirled in glass tumblers. Everyone stared at the man.

'Greg.' The man nearly spat.

'Gregorio!' Someone shouted from the back. 'From Potenza.'

Oh, yes. I see the problem now, Thomas thought. *Star-crossed lovers indeed.* 'How long have you been seeing each other?'

'You've got the wrong idea!' Beth howled. The room exploded into angry shouts of eyewitness accounts and Beth's shrill denials. Thomas leaned back against the table, arms crossed, listening to the commotion.

'Every time she passes the docks, they stop and speak. There isn't a time I haven't seen it.'

'He touched her cheek.'

'He and his kind are mongrels, not worth —'

'You don't know anything! Those are all lies.'

'I saw them kissing at the park!'

'He flirts with her —'

The accusations came crashing in at him. An ocean of anger and bitterness, resentment and truth. It was Gregorio who betrayed them. Though he never said a word to defend himself, it was his eyes, framed by thick lashes, that told the story. They were the painful wounded eyes of an animal with his paw caught in a trap. Beneath that was something else, something more than the fear of being discovered. There was also the pain of losing her. Gregorio could see that inevitability now.

Thomas unhooked his arms, reached for his gavel, and smashed it, unrelentingly. Each hit was a sharp crack that assaulted the gathered members until order was restored.

'Beth or Gregorio. Tell me, how long?'

Gregorio eyed him seriously. 'A year.'

'Veritas et aequitas,' someone shouted. Their mask was green stained glass. Already this person was headed to the dais, to place marks on the scale.

Thomas panicked. He was losing control of the situation.

Another shouted, 'Excusatio non petita, accusatio manifesta.'

'Wait,' his voice filled the room. There was a quiet murmur, but he could feel the undercurrent of agitation. 'And you knew about his heritage? Who he was? Was he forthright with you?'

Her cheeks were flushed pink from defending herself. 'Yes.'

'He touched you without permission?'

'Never.'

Gravity weighed him down, pressing him into the table. Its ledge bit the tops of his thighs and the palms of his hand. *There is no crime. He has only the misfortune of birth and circumstance.*

Blood pooled by Daniel's head. Though he couldn't see the red in his dark hair, Thomas knew the wet clumps were from blood. His little boy cheeks ruddy from playing. Those thick angelic lashes. He rushed to him, his body numb. 'Daniel!'

The man got out of his car. He wore a white dress shirt tucked into slacks. He looked down at Daniel in disdain. This man ripped through Thomas with that one look. How quickly it hadn't mattered that he was born here, that he was well educated, or that he had fought in the Great War.

They were foreign somehow. They were less.

Even in that soul searing moment, they were less.

'Vade retro, Satana!' Jolted Thomas back. *Go back, Satan.*

No, they had taken his silence for permission.

'Enough.' Thomas smashed the gavel down again and again. 'This situation is delicate and cannot be decided tonight. I need more information.' *And more time.*

'You there and there,' he said, pointing to two masked figures.

They stepped forward encircling him.

'I need each of you to follow one of them and tell me more about what is happening. Is it as she says it is? Or is there more to this swarthy Italian then we are led to believe?

'I can follow Beth, sir.' The voice sounded forced down below its normal range. A woman? He was surprised.

He turned to the other and said, 'You will follow him then?'

'I cannot. Not without raising suspicion, but I can get more information.'

Thomas nodded satisfied with this answer.

'We will reconvene in three days.' He smacked the gavel a final time to adjourn. His wife's words rang in his ears. A little break would be good for them and would buy him time. Because he needed to save the reflection of a little boy who died four years ago.

* * *

The walk home felt darker than before. The weight of reality clung to him. Thomas knew that this was more than a simple matter of who would sell bread on Leman Street and who would set up a bakery on East Smithfield Road.

This was the fate of lives hanging in the balance.

Thomas looked up at the building, down at the street, and then examined his hands in his pockets.

A pool of crimson.

Dark hair plastered to his boy's forehead.

He blinked hard to suppress the tears. He could bless their union and hide them. He snorted at the preposterousness of that thought. And what? Force the council, the very members who brought the forbidden relationship to his attention in the first place, to condone, hide, and risk their very lives for? Of course not. The level of support needed within the community wasn't there. Whether he approved of their relationship or not, hiding them was out of the question. No one would take them in. No one would risk their lives for an atrocity.

Conversely, he weighed, he could condemn them. Turn them both in and see what happened. It seemed a shame to do this considering the lengths someone else went to bring the matter to a discrete kind of justice.

He turned a hard corner, picking up speed. At this pace, Thomas would be home in mere minutes, but his mind raged. He couldn't settle. Already his heart pounded and the back of his throat tightened. He knew that he couldn't walk up his stairs and simply fall asleep. Not now. Not with their lives undecided.

Light reflected off the wet stones of the street.

He kept walking past his home. Felt it recede into the night while the air lapped against his damp skin, cooling him. How could he keep this boy alive?

The broken bombed buildings.

The ghostly faces of children who should still have been alive had the bomb not hit.

Now here was Thomas. He could be mistaken for an 'other'. Each month more 'others' disappeared quietly. Thomas felt the pressure mounting on as he and his family became sore thumbs in a sea of blond. This boy was smart enough, durable enough, and held his tongue. He was trying to survive. It didn't matter where he came from, Thomas knew that to allow Gregorio to die, to turn him in was as good as killing himself. Murdering his entire family because they too were complicit.

Thomas walked faster, his shoes clipping on the cobbles and echoing back at him on the empty street. No official curfew had ever been announced but his late night walk was notable.

He could break them up but that wouldn't matter. Gregorio had a stain on him now. He had been 'other'. His life was already in danger from the rising voices of hate. A bead of sweat dripped down Thomas's back. 'Can't hide them, can't ignore it. Can't help them. Well, we all know that it must end.'

He pinched the bridge of his nose and then he looked up at the Thames. He saw the moon over it and a single cloud slightly darker than the night sky. He leaned heavily on a rail while he looked out at the ships. Light twinkled on dark masses as they glided across the water.

'He works for the docks. He knows ships.'

He couldn't get them both out, but he might be able to save Greg.

* * *

A beam of light cast across the room, hitting Thomas in the eyes. It was sharp compared to the dimness of the room. Thomas gathered up the stack which rustled too loudly. The well worn paper crackled in his hands. He had spent the night creating documents being careful to match his own. He packed up with fear and anticipation, tucking the papers in his satchel, snatching his hat and coat, and then he left. On his desk lay the newspaper folded open to an article, 'Cowardly Britons flee to Canada in their droves!'.

* * *

Thomas sipped an ale while he waited for Gregorio to appear, his eyes red rimmed from the lack of sleep. He took a deep breath, then drank again. It had all been a risk. Arranging for the passage, the passport, which was the most complex, was secured within a book. All of it would cost Thomas. He saw Gregorio enter and glance around confused. Tables were partially filled and people scattered across the room. The gold of the carpet blazed against the maroon. Thomas swallowed back acid creeping up his throat. They made eye contact and he glanced to the open chair at the two seater.

'You're the man, then?' Gregorio asked. Thomas noticed the smell of salt and fish as he took a seat.

'I am. An ale?' Thomas gestured to the bartender. The man quickly busied himself. The two men looked at each other, unsure of what to say next. The bartender sat the pint down and then swiped Thomas's marks off the table.

'You have family in Canada. Tomorrow, you will board the *Belinda* as Richard Foster. Do you like working on the docks?' Thomas asked.

Gregorio nodded. 'I do. It's an honest living.'

'When you are on the *Belinda*, it may be better that you conceal your knowledge.'

Gregorio cocked his head and squinted. This seemed counterintuitive. Certainly a captain would be grateful for extra hands.

'It wouldn't be within your skillset, Richard.' Thomas slid the book across the table to him. 'After you arrive and have settled in with your family, it may not be a safe occupation for you to take up again. I would advise against it. It's better to never look back.'

Without looking down at it, Gregorio took the book and tucked it into his pocket. It was a smooth motion.

'I understand,' he replied. He slugged down the ale and left.

* * *

It wasn't until he was home with the door firmly locked, that Gregorio dared to open the book and find what it concealed. There was a blue passport with gold lettering, a slip of paper, and a ticket. He opened the passport to look at the face of a man who resembled him. His skin was lighter in the photo, allowing him the opportunity to say how tanned he was. According to the slip of paper, he was originally from Canada and returning home from school. He sighed with relief. Nothing the past few days had made any sense. Why this man would try to protect him when Wednesday night he was certain he was going to be hung by a mob. Now he had the whole world ahead of him.

His finger traced the ridges of the embossed stamp. *A new life.*

* * *

Thomas crawled into bed next to June. She was asleep. He brushed her hair back and kissed her cheek. He felt elated. This was the right thing to do. He felt, in a way, that he had saved Daniel. That his son would live on in Gregorio.

* * *

Gregorio had to meet her one last time. Beth agreed to a discreet meeting near the shipyard. She stood in a shadow of an alley, waiting. Her dress peeked out from beneath the unbuttoned black coat. Gregorio leaned in, drawing her close. She tilted her head up meeting his embrace with her lips. Everything he felt for her welled up in him catching in his heart. From her pocket she withdrew a braid of hair. She pressed them into his hands, then pulled a package wrapped in brown paper out. 'I want you to have this. I'm sure you'll be robbed of everything at least once, so I sewed my necklace into this shirt. When you arrive, split the seam and you can pull it out.'

He tucked the brown package into his coat and held the braid of hair, rubbing his thumb across it. He knew it would smell like her perfume. 'I'm sorry,' he said, pulling her into an embrace. 'This isn't how …' he trailed off, unsure of what to say. The idea that there had ever been another way seemed ironic to him. What? That they would ride off into the sunset together?

'I'll write to you.' She sounded hopeful. It was almost a question.

'You can't.' He raked a hand through his hair. The dark locks fell immediately back to his forehead. For a moment, he allowed himself to think about what it would have been like to marry her. How she would have looked with her sandy brown hair pulled up with a ribbon and clutching a wildflower bouquet. 'I'll think about you everyday.'

He would think about who was lucky enough to have her, without guilt or fear, while he was forced to slink off into hiding.

He felt her smile as she nuzzled into his chest.

The murmur of the morning crowd began to grow. More people came to the docks going about their business. What little safety they felt was dissipating. He pulled her away gently. 'I love you.' He kissed her.

He saw the black line of tears down her face. Her makeup smudged.

'Goodbye,' Beth whispered.

He suppressed a grimace and walked away.

* * *

The morning salty tang of the sea and rush of waves at the docks felt different to Gregorio. He gripped the shoulder of his pack tighter, bringing it closer to his body. His breath felt ragged in his throat. 'Thanks, I'm going to see my mother again. Very excited to see their faces when I show up.' He practiced the words. He tried to make them sound natural and less rushed.

The *Belinda* was an ocean liner, grand with large stacks, a black bottom, and a white deck. She was small for her class compared to some of the other ocean liners Gregorio had seen. His boots clunked against the dock's boards as he approached. His heart hammered in his chest and his breath picked up. Though it was early, a line had already formed as passengers queued up to board. Two men stood at the deck looking at passports. Gregorio swallowed down his fear. He imagined one of the men looking from him to his passport, his face becoming angry, then betraying him there. He saw himself being dragged away by whoever was in charge now. He dreaded awaiting the awful fate of work camps. No one ever returned. There were only stories.

The line moved along. Time bent feeling both slow and rapid. Before he knew it, he found himself handing over his passport. The official looked at the photo, to Gregorio, and then ran a light finger over the embossed stamp. He nodded and stamped it, allowing him to board. There was no small talk nor exchange.

He tucked his new identity into his breast pocket, then boarded the *Belinda*. He did not look back.

Gregorio found his bunk as specified on his ticket. He slapped the bed, its crisp white sheet ruffling beneath his hand. A moment of claustrophobia crept in when he realized how close it was to the ceiling. *A week*, he reassured himself. *I only have to last a week.* Then he would be making a life for himself in green and glorious Canada. He had been given a small key to his locker in his bunk when he got his passage. This allowed him to store his things securely. He admired the rivets on the steel walls. It would take some getting used to, all the ducking, but he was getting a feel for this new life. He wandered around the ship taking in the sights.

The deck was grand, much larger than he thought it would be. He could see wood planking over the top of the metal where the passengers or crew could entertain themselves. He quickly found the canteen. There were a series of tables riveted to the floor with heavy chairs that didn't slide easily. Their tops were laminate and a garish yellow even in the darkness of the hold. Gregorio eyed the empty buffet, thinking what it would be like to take a seat amongst all the other passengers to eat his meals. He feared being the target of cold, staring eyes.

He continued on. The hallways were snug oval shaped doors with thresholds he would need to get used to stepping over. The ship was still boarding, and he was already at a loss for what to do. He went back onto the deck to watch the stream of passengers. The deck was becoming crowded, but he took hope in the fact that most of those getting on shared his complexion. They were families, chattering in all kinds of languages. Most dressed in the middle class way; homemade trousers and sweat stained hats.

His anxieties eased. This would be alright. They would all make it make it to this new home, this new life, for which they were venturing into the great unknown. Gregorio took a deep breath letting the tang of iron and salt fill his lungs. As the last of the passengers boarded, the sun began its crest toward noon. The freshness of the morning dissipated into a muggy heat. Still the hope and excitement of a new beginning buoyed him.

It bothered Gregorio that Beth had said 'Goodbye' instead of 'I love you' or 'I want to go with you'. A tinge of regret filled him. He looked down at his hands, rubbing the knuckles of his thumbs together. The clatter of the plank pulling up and the deep rumble of engines kicking on invaded his thoughts. He watched the empty docks fall away. Not a single person was there to wave goodbye as family and friends left for a new life. They vanished, slowly at first until the distance stretched and yawned.

* * *

Pearls clacked against the wood slatted floor. Thomas glanced up from the paper anxious. His children were arguing amongst themselves but were otherwise oblivious. There was something foreboding about that sound. He could hear June upstairs rustling around. Laying his paper down, he stood to investigate, but the headline caught his attention.

'Rents Down as Vermin Move Out' it read. Beneath was a photo of a building he recognized as housing a number of illegal families. 'An entire building has been renovated and cleaned for good families to move in. The filthy and diseased have been removed from London.'

A cold heaviness crept from his belly and into his hands, leaving them to ring with fear. Indirectly, the article said everything there was to say. Like a cypher the two short columns sandwiched between lies and news proclaimed in a loud voice the fate of those sad families.

Thomas went up the stairs, his feet catching on the treads. He saw June mumbling to herself, her head shoved firmly under the bed, and her butt in the air. Thomas stared at her, numb. The beads clicked as she gathered them into her hand. She looked up at him, surprised by his presence.

'Thomas, what's wrong?'

June placed the small pile of pearls on the bed, nestling her fist into the bed so that the fabric would cup them while she went to comfort her husband. She touched his wrist like a whisper hoping not to startle him.

Thomas grabbed her. She flinched at the suddenness and then relaxed into his embrace. 'Will you tell me?' She asked.

He ran his hand into her hair taking a shaky breath in. 'No.'

June reached for his face and felt wetness. Her heart sank and she hugged him tighter, returning the fierceness of his embrace.

* * *

Gregorio assumed they would be sailing for longer before a stop. It confused him that they were pulling into a port. Compared to London this was such a small port with empty docks and no activity. In fact, it felt secluded. A dense mist clung to those who were brave enough to stand on deck. It assaulted them, flicking sharp sprays of water into their eyes. He licked his lips savouring the freshness of it.

He hunched over the side of the rail, watching intently as the coast neared. Soon others crowded the deck, causing Gregorio's stomach to roll. They too felt engines slow and the wrongness of the moment.

A voice rang out in a foreign tongue, a language Gregorio could not quite identify, but he got the sense of it quickly enough from the others. They were being gathered. He itched to have a weapon, some way to fight. He looked around at the faces. Their eyes were tired, mouths set in a firm line, and fear etched in. Kerchiefs held down hair that would have otherwise been whipped by the wind.

The engines cut. 'Get your things' rang out to the crowd. *Get your things.*

'Is this Canada?' A boy asked his mother. Droplets of mist pooled and ran down his face like sweat.

'Enough,' she hissed. 'Hold my hand and be quiet.'

Gregorio couldn't quite catch his breath.

The crowd began to move, pushing him forward like the tide. He refused to move. This wasn't where they were supposed to go. *No one's resisting*, he realized. They simply followed, too worn to fight back. Many had spent all they had on their passage and brought only what they could carry. They had thought they were escaping, but oppression rose its hand and smacked them down again.

Anger, searing as acid, rose up in him. *The man with dark hair sliding the book across the table to him, his face hopeful.* Whatever his motives had been, it wasn't this fate. No one had known.

'Where are you taking us?' Gregorio screamed out. Finally brave enough as rage coursed through him. A few murmurs of dissent joined him; curiosity, anger, betrayal. They all felt it in their blood.

The smacks of rifle butts hitting flesh were the only response.

Screams and the push of human bodies lifted Gregorio from the deck. Each moment he felt himself being funnelled off the ship.

A thought of the shirt in his locker caught him unawares. They would soon be going through everything he had left to him in this world. The necklace, Beth's braid of hair, even his only photo of his family.

The violation filled him with more rage. *Fight*, his

body screamed.

The muzzle of a rifle stared him down. Would it sting when his blood bloomed on the deck? Or would it feel like floating away? Gregorio could grab the gun, turn it on the soldier. He could push him into the bay. He could create a diversion for families to escape. It was then that he looked out at the wharf. A line of men waited to herd them into large open bed trucks.

The urge to fight left as suddenly as having the wind knocked out of him. When he was a boy he had fallen from a tree. The unforgiving group left nothing in his lungs, only the sharp pain of no air.

There was no escape. Fear burned within him, leaving his chest heaving and his throat tight.

* * *

June read her book with the maroon hardcover and gold embossing. Thomas was sure it was a romance. It was something light and airy for her to forget the life they were living.

'If you could move anywhere in the world, where would you go?'

'Aren't you just something, Thomas? What is this all about now?'

'Just tell me. Where have you always wanted to live?'

June set her book down on her lap, a finger tucked between the pages, and gave him her full attention. 'Why, I thought I'd always live here.'

Thomas paused, considering her words. Then he said, 'I was thinking about the Caribbean a lot lately. Charlie and I have been reading *Treasure Island*. The way he describes the water, I bet it's quite wonderful.'

June stared, quizzical. 'What's brought this on? Aren't you happy?'

'It's not that I'm not happy. I just don't feel safe. Can't you see what's happening?'

'Thomas. Say what it is that's on your mind. I can't stand this.'

'When Daniel died, I thought that there was nothing so dark that could touch me again. But something woke me up. I realised that as terrible as it was to lose Daniel, that I could never forgive myself as a father, as your husband, as a man, if I didn't do everything within my power to protect our family.'

A quietness fell between them. June waited.

'Each year the face of London changes more and more. Don't you see it? When you go out how the faces have grown paler?'

June shook her head. 'No, I haven't.'

'I notice. I feel their eyes on me when I'm the only one who looks different in a room. There's a taintedness now in the way that people speak to us. As though we might steal their child or their livelihood ... we have to leave. We have to sell the house and get away.'

A knock at the door startled June. Thomas felt his whole body go white with terror. He scrambled out of bed to put on his robe.

His legs felt like water as he took each step. His hands as he reached for the knob shook.

There stood Gregorio. His hair was windswept by a wind that wasn't present in the stillness of the night. It was the small boy next to him that caused Thomas's breath to hitch.

Thomas sank to his knees, letting the door swing open to hit the hallway wall. He reached his hands out but couldn't bring himself to touch him.

'I love you, Daddy,' Daniel said. 'I'm safe now.'

'Thank you. Goodbye,' Gregorio said. His words were soft wisps, barely reaching his ears.

On his knees, looking out into the empty night, Thomas sobbed.

THE SOLDIER

BY RICHARD DENHAM

THE SOLDIER

'Here's a health unto His Majesty!' Enid raised her glass.

The others looked at her.

'It's an old toast,' she explained. She was feeling a little testy. This was her youngest son's send off party before he joined up, her two neighbours could at least show a bit of enthusiasm. 'Eighteenth century, Jack used to say. All old soldiers used to raise a glass to the king.

George instinctively looked at the photograph. From what had become a shrine on the mantelpiece, a smart soldier smiled at him. He was technically Corporal John Williams, Royal Welch Fusiliers and he was wearing his bandsman's uniform, complete with bugle and lanyard. Jack had joined up on the first day that he could, not merely slapping on Lord Derby's armband as a promise. He'd passed the physical, 'taken the king's shilling' as he used to say, and the rest was history.

Tom had served with the Royal Welch too, but he wasn't a bandsman and he hadn't gone in until 1916 when the brown envelope had hit the doormat and he'd had no choice. Tom always admitted to everybody that he wasn't very brave; certainly not brave enough to be a conchie, so he had taken the shilling, just so that he wouldn't stand out in the crowd.

'A health unto His Majesty!' George took up his mother's challenge, momentarily wiping the years that had passed since 1914. And Enid smiled at him and Margo looked optimistic.

'Sorry it's not champagne,' Enid said. There'd never been much of that particular commodity in Neath and George had never sampled the stuff. It was what other people had – and then only occasionally – the black marketeers and Those In The Know; TITS as Tom called them, ignoring the 'K' that spoiled the acronym.

'His Majesty,' Tom echoed, although no one had heard anything about the royal family for years. In 1940, when the balloon had gone up, it was widely believed the Windsors, along with their government and the exiled governments of at least eight other countries hiding in London, had gone. Some said this was hogwash, Edward VIII had been, and still was, in London the whole time. Others said his stuttering brother was the head of 'Free Britain' in Canada, widely dismissed as a fantasist and warmonger, ruling over an imaginary kingdom over a thousand miles away and certainly not recognised by the United States of America. All of this was rumour of course, but it was hard not to believe them when rumour was all there was.

Since Fleet Street had taken that direct hit on the night of 17 November, news as the older generation knew it had gone. The BBC was still going, but its broadcasts kept breaking down and there were rumours that its once-bustling corridors were deserted and the whole mish-mash run by infiltrators from the Church of the Remnant.

'Any news from the boys?' Margo asked.

Enid's face said it all. Jack had gone forever. And her boys? Who knew? But Enid Williams was a stoical woman. Her own parents had lived through the trouble before the Great War. She had lived through that and the General Strike and the Depression. Disasters, she knew, came in battalions. Yet, no news was good news. What passed for the government these days still sent out death notices when they could. And Enid had not received anything.

'Nothing,' she smiled. 'But that's the Merchant Navy for you.'

She remembered the day perfectly. A review of the Fleet at Spithead. Jack was in hospital at the time, but Enid had taken the train and little George and they'd had a couple of minutes for a mother to hug her boys – little Jack and Alan. They'd both towered over her and kissed the top of her head. They'd told George to behave himself and to look after her, especially now Dad wasn't well. They'd be back, they said, when the whole thing was over, laden with souvenirs.

Yes, that was the Merchant Navy, all right.

'Well, look at you.' Margo beamed at Enid's remaining boy. 'Your Dad'd be so proud, George.'

George beamed. He'd known Margo all his life. She'd been his babysitter, his confidante, his Mam's best friend. Tom and Margo didn't have kids; George was their surrogate son. He hadn't got his uniform yet. In fact, the papers that had come through had been rather vague on all that. There was no mention of a unit, still less a regiment. Only a date and a venue – the old dance hall behind the bus station. No doubt, all would be revealed.

'This going to the wars stuff is exciting, isn't it?' Margo was a simple soul, a throwback, Tom sometimes thought, to those silly girls of 1914, with their white feathers and it'll all be over by Christmas mentality. 'It's like the crusades!' Tom almost groaned; it was worse than he thought. 'Richard the Lionheart riding out to take Jerusalem.'

'Except, he didn't,' Tom muttered. He half expected his wife to unfurl a poster of 'Women of Wales Say Go!' 'Have you got a minute, boy?' he turned to George. 'Pop outside. I've got something for you.'

The men left the table, with the dubious soup and apple juice and walked out of the dark little kitchen into the garden.

'Smell that?' Tom asked.

George breathed in. 'What?' he said.

'Exactly,' Tom nodded. He perched on the low stone wall and folded is arms. 'Nothing. When I was a boy … Hell, when *you* were a boy, the air over Neath was acrid with coal and steel. Where's it all gone?'

'Well, I …'

'Where've the Welch Fusiliers gone, boy? Your father's regiment and mine? Where …' and he hated himself for making the boy think of it, 'is the Merchant Navy?'

George blinked.

Tom put a hand on the lad's shoulder. 'Where are you going? Later today, I mean?'

'The old dance hall,' George said, 'behind the bus station.'

'Yes,' Tom nodded. 'I know where it is. Then what?'

'I don't know,' George told him. 'It's hush-hush. That's over for you.'

'This isn't war, boy,' Tom said. 'It's a bloody way of life. The new normal.'

'You and Dad …'

'Me and your Dad were boys,' Tom said gently, 'just like you are now. Tell me, when you're over there … wherever there is … what will the enemy look like?'

George frowned. He hadn't really thought about that, except that he'd just walk over the lot of them. 'Beast men,' he said, not that he'd thought about it.

'Go on,' Tom looked at the boy from under his eyebrows, his chin on his chest. 'They always said to your Dad and me in training, "There's the enemy. There are his eyes. Look into his eyes. When you kill him, look into his eyes." So, go on, Georgie. Look into the eyes of your enemy. What do you see?'

'Um … he's ugly,' George said, frowning with the concentration. 'Hideous, in fact. He's taller than me. Broader. He's got huge fists and feet, giant boots. And he's snarling. I can't understand what he's saying, of course, but it's a guttural sound, deep in his throat. His teeth …'

'Yes?' Tom raised his head. 'What about his teeth?'

'They're sharp,' he said. 'Pointed.'

'And what kind of man is this beast you're going to kill?' Tom asked quietly.

'He's mean.' George was warming to it now. 'Vicious. He's a killer and a liar. He feeds like a ghoul on the flesh of others. And he's coming this way, Uncle Tom. He and all the other jack-booted bastards are coming across the Channel. We've got to turn them back.'

'Of course you have, lad,' the older man said. 'Now, let me tell you what's actually going to happen.'

George sat back on the low wall on his side of the path. The men could hear the women laughing from the kitchen, still doing, after all this time, what Winston Churchill's government had once told them to do. They were keeping calm and carrying on; carrying on because there was nothing else to do. It was said that the short-lived Prime Minister shocked the old leadership by refusing to flee, probably to Canada, with the rest of them. His pride and stubbornness would have been a boon to the British if they were still in the fight, but a man like Churchill was useless to a lost cause. Some said, or liked to believe, he went down in a hail of bullets, clutching his tommy gun and with a cigar between his teeth at the windows of Downing Street. Others said at least he gave a final defiant two-finger flick, a 'V for Victory', to his executors, most dismissed all of this as wishful thinking. Either way, the official line was that he was a thug and a warmonger and his disastrous short-term had been nothing but failure after failure and his was a name best to forget and let die with the way things were.

'I had that picture in my head too,' Tom said. 'So did your Dad. It came from the recruiting posters you used to see on walls all over the place. On the way into the pits, the factories. It was outside the picture palace, even on the chapel door. I can see it now. There was a beast man, a gorilla-like monster wearing a pickelhaube, those stupid pointy helmets the enemy used to wear. He wore a field-grey uniform and his mouth was open in a roar, blood dripping from his fangs. He had a girl in his arms. She was beautiful, blonde of course, and she'd fainted. Oh, the posters didn't spell it out in so many words, but they didn't need to. We all know – either the beast man had raped the girl, or he was about to. And next, it would be *our* girls, our wives and sweethearts, our sisters and mothers. That's why your Dad joined up when he did ...' There was a pause. 'That's why you can't wait to go now.'

George smiled. He'd heard nothing wrong so far.

'I never really bought into all that stuff,' Tom said, 'for King and Country.' He jerked his head towards the kitchen. 'Your Mam still believes it; so does Margo. Then, in 1916 when I got my call-up papers, I saw for myself. Your Dad did, too. It was probably a pretty little place once, like Glamorgan used to be once upon a time. Fields, a valley, quiet woods. Except that all that had gone by 1916. The trees were twisted, shattered stumps, the fields were a sea of endless mud. The quiet had been replaced by noise, the howl of the shells and the thunder of the guns. Day after day after day. I remember the first time I crossed No Man's Land – men beside me falling on the barbed wire, chests riddled with bullets, heads blown to buggery – but not me. Whoever looks out for soldiers was smiling on me that day. I got through. I jumped down into the enemy trench. I saw the beast men. And you know what?'

George shook his head, open-mouthed.

'It wasn't a beast at all. It was a kid, just like me. He'd lost his helmet and he was staring at me, gaping. There were no blood-encrusted fangs, there was no raped girl lying on the ground, just a photograph, flapping slightly in the wind. There was a girl there, pretty, smiling. Girlfriend? Maybe. Sister? Perhaps. He seemed too young for it to be his wife. He'd pinned the photo to one of the posts that held the trench up.'

Tom half-turned from the scene he was reliving.

'The kid pointed his rifle at me and squeezed the trigger. There was a click. The thing had jammed. I'd witnessed a miracle and I hadn't even noticed.'

'What happened?' George asked, ashen-faced.

Tom breathed in. 'I killed him,' he said. 'Shot him through the head with my .303. mine didn't jam. I saw his blood spatter crimson all over the girl's photograph.'

There was silence now. Then Tom's hand was on George's shoulder and his face was close to the boy's. 'Don't go, Georgie,' he whispered, 'because it's all a lie. It was a lie in 1914-18 and it's all a lie today. Except now, there are no trenches and there are no regiments. We've all lost our way. The war has torn up all the maps of our lives. We've got nothing left. No Royal Welch Fusiliers. No steel mills. No coal mines. No Winston Bloody Churchill to tell us to fight them on the beaches. *Nobody* wins a war, boy. *Nobody*. Remember your Dad, how he looked when you saw him last?'

George did and a lump rose in his throat.

'He was a shadow, wasn't he? In bed all the time, sick and raving. The gas. The guns. It'll be different for you, but the result's the same. Find people. Make them your people. Find a way out of this; God knows how, but somewhere … there has to be a better place.'

'Georgie!' The boy heard his mother's voice from the kitchen, saw her smiling face, beaming with pride, she who had lost three men already. 'They're here, lovie. You haven't finished your dinner and they're here.'

George looked into Tom's face. Then back to his mother's. He could hear the thud of boots on the road outside and the bellow of the NCOs. He broke away from Tom, from the nonsense he was talking and dashed through the passage to the front door.

A column of soldiers had stopped just outside and a huge man momentarily blocked out the light. He had stripes on his sleeve and a swagger stick under his arm. He saluted smartly. 'Mrs Williams,' he said. 'I'd like to make a soldier out of young George here.'

She squeezed to the boy's side; Margo was already manhandling his coat.

'Oh, he won't need that,' the recruiting sergeant said. 'It's not far to the old dance hall and he'll be given his uniform there.'

Tears of pride welled in Enid's eyes, her George was now a man, and was off to do his bit. The soldier's wage that George would send back would mean she could survive and the house would stay, as it had for generations, as a Williams house. Now if they could just finish off, well, whoever the enemy was nowadays, and get her boys back. Yes, that was enough to hold onto; one day Little Jack, Alan and George would all be reunited and leave all this bloody business behind them.

'My Dad was a soldier,' George told him cheerily.

'Really?' The recruiting sergeant feigned interest.

'He was a bandsman in the Royal Welch Fusiliers.'

The recruiting sergeant chuckled. 'Well, lad,' he said, 'that was then. Come on. You're in the Free Corps now.'

THE ENTREPRENEUR

BY JUSTIN ALCALA

THE ENTREPRENEUR

Sir Montgomery hated the sun. He assumed the feeling was mutual. There was never an official declaration of war, but the star the Earth revolved around was one of the few things daft enough to defy him. So, when a beam of dawn pierced through Sir Montgomery's curtain and spit on his face, he wasn't surprised. Another shot fired in their great war.

Sir Montgomery peeled open an eye. He massaged his temples. The blonde woman next to him snored.

'Piss off,' Sir Montgomery grumbled at the light seeping through his large framed window.

Sir Montgomery sat up. He belched before swallowing whatever erupted from his stomach. He thought back to last night's Great Smith Street soiree. He'd lost count of how many drinks he'd had, but it was enough to make all of parliament merry. He inspected the room. It stunk of sex and cigarettes. His lipstick-marked tuxedo shirt hung from the lamp. He gave the blonde woman next to him a once over. *She looks like a baby* he thought. .

Sir Montgomery recalled the chance encounter. A hundred chaps with parsnips in hand wanted a go at her, but she had other plans, and Sir Montgomery knew it. He watched her from a cluster of conversing penguins eying him— her eyes transfixed on his knight's sash. She'd later feign a serendipitous bump of the elbow at the bar. After a few drinks, she sprung her pitch. Daddy was in hot water with the powers that be and needed a man of Sir Montgomery's influence to help. He assumed she knew the price.

Sir Montgomery removed a cigarette from his case, lit it and shambled out of bed. He withdrew the curtains to face his ancient enemy. The birds gave morning praise from the begonias. *Today was a big day*, Sir Montgomery reminded himself. The XXII Committee, twenty-two men whose authority was second only to the gods, was sending a delegation and stopping by – all the way, wherever they were from — for tea. Everything needed to be spot on.

When last they met, the Committee had taken his oldest son for cultural indoctrination. Sir Montgomery saw it for what it really was, ransom. Today, they'd return Montgomery III along with a new business strategy for England's future. Sir Montgomery expected a request for another donation. He'd secured payment. He felt it a price well worth his great legacy for England.

'Tickety-boo,' Sir Montgomery whispered as he daydreamed about the future.

He puffed the coffin nail down to his fingers before retrieving the servant bell and giving it a jingle. The blonde in his bed stirred. She stretched before opening her eyes. It was likely the chandeliers and gilt ceiling that told her she wasn't home. The blonde woman sat up fast as if buried alive.

'Morning.' Sir Montgomery leaned on the window glass. The blonde woman wiped at her runny eyeliner.

'Monty,' her voice shook.

'Tit-tit. Sir Montgomery my dear. Today, it's *Sir Montgomery*. Now, why don't you gather your things and return to your little mouse hole.' The blonde woman cocked her head.

'And my father?'

'Yes, yes. Leave his name with my steward. I'll handle everything Monday.'

'How can I be sure?'

'Because I'm an important figure, and a family man, and I don't want to dance around blackmail plots.'

Just then the bedroom door opened and the staff drew in. The footmen, George and Noah, kept their heads down as they hurried to lay out Sir Montgomery's wardrobe. Meanwhile, Megan and the new girl, Barbara, pulled away the blankets, seemingly blind to the naked woman beneath them. The blonde gasped and shielded her breasts. Her lips pressed hard as she glared at Sir Montgomery. *She doesn't trust me*, Sir Montgomery considered.

'Think of it this way,' Sir Montgomery tucked into his monogrammed satin robe, 'I am a businessman, and you are a service. You named a price and I paid it. The transaction is complete.'

The blonde woman stood up, exposing herself. She gathered her sparkled dress and slipped into it. She shoved past George to collect her shoes from under the velvet ottoman at the foot of the bed.

'Is that all people are to you? Resources?' She sneered and walked out the door.

Sir Montgomery smirked at George and Noah. They nodded straight-faced while handing the knight his toothbrush and towel.

After a long shower, Sir Montgomery dressed in one of his best suits, a double-breasted wool tweed, then left to meet with his Steward downstairs. Nicholas stood at attention next to the breakfast table in the dining hall. Sir Montgomery ignored Nicholas and melted into a chair. He rubbed his forehead. When his head felt a little less like a dry raisin, he took a sip from his steaming cup and unfolded the herald. The headlines read *XXII Committee Strategies for Economy Prove Useful.*

Sir Montgomery recognized it was controlled propaganda. If one could read between the lines, they'd see that the Committee was trying to earn England's trust. He knew the daily news put their own spin on what the global chessboard looked like. All the reader had to do was sharpen their knack for underlying meanings. What really caught Sir Montgomery's eye today though was the side column. *Earl Wathmere Embarrasses Himself on Radio … again.*

Sir Montgomery mulled it over. This was the fate worse than death. Wathmere was a defector of the incumbent government, and a party leader with great promise. Had the politician played ball a little more eloquently, he could have been where Sir Montgomery was now, an essential piece in the game. Wathmere went rogue, though. For it, the powers in charge exiled him. He stayed in government reserved housing, making a fool of himself on a stray radio broadcast. Sir Montgomery wondered if his bravery had cursed him to forever be one of history's punchlines.

'Well, then,' Sir Montgomery looked up to Nicholas, who was hovering over his shoulder, 'out with it.' Nicholas cleared his throat.

'Sir.' Nicholas kept his nose up, 'we expect the delegation from the Committee with your son Montgomery III near noon. We have met all the preparations, including the change of flags.'

'Any opposition?'

'Of course not, Sir. Your staff understands they are in a most desirable position of employment.'

'Oh Nicholas, I appreciate your candour. No dillydallying about loyalty or honour. Just the hard facts.'

'Thank you, Sir.'

'What about the girl last night?'

'She gave me the name of her father. Apparently, he's in Shepton.'

'Cornhill?'

'Yes Sir.'

'Right. Find out who the warden is and write to him. Stuff the envelope with confetti.'

'Yes, Sir. How much confetti?'

'Enough to put an end to it.'

'Yes, Sir.'

'These requests grow bolder. It started as free drinks. Now it's husbands and fathers. Anyhow, see that it's handled.'

'Yes, Sir.'

'And the tarts?'

'Apologies, Sir?'

'Monty's tarts? Have they been prepared?'

'Ah, of course, Sir. It will be a fine homecoming.'

'Yes,' Sir Montgomery flipped the paper to the business section, 'yes it will. So then, what is it you need from me?'

'Well Sir, I don't know how else to put it, but your lawyer has become rather pushy about you signing the updated inheritance. He came by again this morning to check on it.'

'Yes, visits from the Committee gives people the jitters. I'm sure our pushy friend wants his fee before the world changes again. Money is tight amongst the commonwealth. Do you have the papers?'

'Yes Sir,' Nicholas beckoned George, who stood to attention near the silverware cart. George hurried to Sir Montgomery's side and handed over a stack of rolled documents. He straightened them on the table, then clicked a ballpoint pen before handing it to Sir Montgomery. 'He highlighted the newly added arrangements for your son.'

'Yes,' Sir Montgomery checked the old clock in the corner. There was little time left before his guests. He flipped to the last page and signed. 'The kingdom is his when I'm gone. Now, get this back to our pushy legal team.'

'Immediately Sir.'

* * *

Sir Montgomery spent the rest of his free time in his private office adjoining his bed chambers. He reviewed his proposal. The Committee expected affairs to run cleanly in England, but Sir Montgomery knew people can't be managed upright. There were syndicates to pay off, officials to bribe and a mistrust to seed in every village's insurgency. *White gloves hide dirty hands,* he thought to himself. Luckily,

Sir Montgomery felt he'd done it discreetly enough. The Committee never need know.

All of it cost money, however, extensive amounts of it. Whispers from insiders and old banking friends helped with that, but it took daily effort on Sir Montgomery's part. So, as he sat in his office waiting for guests, Sir Montgomery purchased several bullish stocks by phone. When he'd completed the trades, he signed off on the last bribes of the day before putting the pen to rest. The marker rolled next to the only framed photo on his desk. It was his favourite.

Sir Montgomery sipped his finger of early scotch before picking up the frame, falling backwards in time. In it he was on holiday with his family. Montgomery III and Thaddeus huddled under Sir Montgomery and their mother on a beach in Greece. Thaddeus smiled wide with his thick chalk teeth at the camera, but Montgomery III didn't stare into the camera at all. He stared up at his father with pride. Sir Montgomery had taught his son how to sail that morning. *The boy showed a real knac*k, Sir Montgomery remembered. *He showed a knack for everything I showed him.*

The front bell rang. The Committee was a tad early. Sir Montgomery thought it a forgivable breach of etiquette. He waited for Nicholas to handle introductions. Sir Montgomery gave himself a look in the mirror along the wall. His hair had been combed neatly but greyed along the edges. He was clean shaven, but wrinkles cut beneath his nose. Hi suit was crisp, but it couldn't hide the swell of his belly. *I'm an old alleycat* he brooded to himself.

Time had aged him, though Sir Montgomery blamed the sun for the wrinkles. At one point, he believed he could have had last night's blonde without paying for it in favours. Now, he supposed he was just another old man with money. His shoulders felt heavy. Then, from the distance, another voice rang in his conscience. *The oldest alleycats have the longest claws.* Sir Montgomery nodded and picked up his chin.

Nicholas's trademark knock wrapped at the office door.

'Come in,' Sir Montgomery called as he straightened in his chair. Nicholas squeezed his pink face in the door.

'Sir,' Nicholas announced with teeth clenched, 'an unexpected guest has arrived. I warned him of teatime, but he insists.' There was shuffling outside the hall. Sir Montgomery knew whoever it was heard the exchange. Sir Montgomery took a deep breath and exhaled. He waved a hand and played pretend.

'That's Nicholas. Whoever it is can have a moment.'

A short, brawny man shoved through the door. He was near Sir Montgomery in age, bald on top with greased white along the sides. His ears and pockmarked cheeks looked like dogs had chewed them. Sir Montgomery watched as the man straightened out his wrinkled suit coat before picking his incisors with a toothpick. Ivan Piłsudski, local street boss, entrepreneur and Spiv King, was one of Sir Montgomery's least favourite people to do business with. It wasn't because Ivan held a lot of cards, *which he did*. No, Sir Montgomery hated fraternizing with him because the odious man had as much refinement as a wild boar.

'Ah,' Sir Montgomery smiled as Ivan helped himself to a seat across the table, 'Mr. Piłsudski. What a pleasant surprise.'

'Zamknąć się,' Ivan grunted. 'Your charms can't skin this snake. I wish to talk alone.' Nicholas stood behind Ivan, arms folded. Sir Montgomery nodded for Nicholas to leave them. The steward obliged.

'Well then, this must be dire.' Sir Montgomery removed a cigarette from his gold case and offered one up. Ivan shook his head. Sir Montgomery lit the tip and breathed in the soothing tobacco. 'Alright, on with it.'

'Pinfield is out.'

'About being a mandrake?'

'No. Out of cooperating with the Committee.'

'Has he gone mad?'

'Perhaps, but maybe I'm feeling mad too.'

'Good God, man, stop speaking in tongues. This is serious.'

'In English?' Ivan hoicked up snot before going back

to picking his teeth. 'The Roundheads are looking more profitable by the hour. They need weapons. They need information. And now, they have people like Pinfield.'

'The bloody Roundheads? They're not a resistance movement, they're a gang of murderers on their last legs. Are you saying Pinfield is a turncoat?'

Ivan ignored him. Sir Montgomery watched as Ivan reached for the scotch and sniffed it before sipping. Ivan's mouth turned crooked. He leaned back in his chair before spitting it back into the glass. 'Horse piss.'

'Ivan. I am busy. Now, did you come here for riddles, because I'm sure I can find you a crossword puzzle in the library.'

'Pinfield is simply out. Well, for now. We'll follow his money. Perhaps he'll join the Roundheads, perhaps not.'

'Ivan, let me spell it out. We are the government now. We have the money. We say what goes.'

'We? Don't you mean the Committee?'

'They've allowed us to run ourselves.'

'Us?'

'Yes. England.'

'As long as you follow their guidelines?'

'We can do this all day, Mr. Piłsudski.'

'Do you like history Montgomery?'

'What?'

'Do,' Ivan leaned in, 'you like history?'

'When I'm on the winning side, yes.'

'I like history. The past always shows the future. And if it's taught me anything, it's that the rich and powerful will maintain the idea that they're better than everyone else until their neck is on the block.'

'Is that a threat, Ivan? I don't deal well with those.'

'You'd know if it was. I'm giving advice, one businessman to another.' Sir Montgomery resisted a cringe as Ivan tried to put himself the same league. 'No one ever settles when you take away freedoms. You're fighting a losing effort. The resistances may seem small now, but they won't go away. And for men like me, there's profit.'

'So what is it then? You want more money?' Sir

Montgomery asked. Ivan shrugged. 'Fine, double it.'

'That only covers Pinfield's losses.' The doorbell rang. Either today was a game of *Surprise Monty* or the Committee was here.

'Triple it.'

Ivan smiled, showing his gold tooth. 'That works today, my friend. I'll update you on my efforts.'

'Please don't.' Sir Montgomery stood and buttoned his coat, eager to get away. 'It's why I pay you. I don't want the bloody details. Now, that's a delegation from the Committee at my front door. I don't know how you square with them, but the back door is yours if you wish to take it.' Sir Montgomery rang the handbell.

'They butchered my family. They put me in a cell twice. Now, they've chased me to London,' Ivan's knees popped as he took to his feet. He stretched calmly as George entered the office. 'Yes, we play bridge together on the weekends.'

'Well then, back door it is.' Sir Montgomery turned to his footman. 'George, see that Mr. Piłsudski makes it to his car through the gardens.'

George nodded. Ivan followed, but paused briefly in the doorway. He gave a hyena smile.

'Remember, the past always shows the future Montgomery.'

'Yes, I'll consider it,' Sir Montgomery showed Ivan away with the flick of his hand. Ivan shook his head before following George. Sir Montgomery gave it a moment to put some space between him and his visitor, then left his office to meet the Committee in the parlour. He had suffered being cornered enough for one day.

Sir Montgomery hurried to the foyer, looking down from the white marble mezzanine as Nicholas directed staff to take coats. A dozen stiff men standing in some ridiculous pecking order studied art and furniture. They wore top hats and long coats, even though it was late Spring, black shoes shined to mirrors and matching gloves. A handful of suits and pen pushers accompanied them. George and Noah scurried to collect coats for the cloakroom.

Sir Montgomery cleared his throat, ready to make an entrance. But before he could say a word, something took his breath away. Standing at attention was Montgomery III in his khaki service dress. His face was stern and his beautiful auburn hair cropped short. *What the deuce did they do to him?* Sir Montgomery's inner voice fumed. While he teemed with disgust, the old alleycat voice reminded him that this was the biggest meeting of the year. He needed to stay focused. Sir Montgomery could learn about Montgomery III's holiday when it was all over. He swallowed the spur in his throat, cleared his mind and readied to play ball.

'Good morning, sirs,' Sir Montgomery called out while descending the staircase. The Committee stared with steely expressions. All except for one, the one who Sir Montgomery recognized – Sir Francis Teck. The clean-cut scoundrel smiled as Sir Montgomery made it to the bottom of the staircase.

Sir Francis was Sir Montgomery's contact during the British Union of Survivors debacle. He was hardly a player in that era. Sir Montgomery partnered up with Francis to iron out several early wrinkles in England's caste. It's where Sir Montgomery learned Francis's true colours. Unlike most of the Committee, who pretended to be part of some noble line, Francis was like Sir Montgomery, if not scarier. He'd used treacheries of many forms to move up the ranks. Sir Montgomery half respected him, and half feared him. Francis was brilliant at the game, and willing to sacrifice anyone at the altar to climb further up. Now, here Francis was dangling Sir Montgomery's poster-boy looking son in front of him.

It dawned on Montgomery, what a queer fate the British Union of Survivors had received. It seemed the smartly dressed thugs were once on the cusp of glory. 'Join the B.U.S', the old half-torn posters said, 'Get on board the B.U.S!' said another, smiling maniacs waving the viewer onto their red double decker. Pencil-moustached lunatics dressed up in their beach attire promoting their Margate rally, the rally that was going to change the world. One would have guessed they were the closest things to allies the Committee had, but the unspeakable purges, men dragged from their beds at the dead of night never to be seen again said otherwise. The B.U.S and the Committee really *did* seem like two sides of the same coin, so why the antagonism. What was left of the B.U.S, the lunatic fringe who dared not gather openly still considered themselves equals. Yes, yes, that was it. The B.U.S were so dangerous to the Committee because they considered themselves equals. Some said the same thing happened in other countries, the brown-shirted ones being obliterated for whatever reason by the black-shirted ones. A friend of the cause would naturally see himself as a comrade and an equal, not a submissive coward, and, in the eyes of the Committee, that naturally would never do. A man who thinks himself a friend is the most dangerous foe of all. What was good for the goose was good for the gander; no, that wasn't right, that was a saying about women wasn't it? The man's tangent was reaching record levels, this bizarre distraction inside his own mind, just a few more seconds reprieve from reality, just a second more.

'Good morning, sir.' Francis stepped forward and offered his gloved hand to Montgomery, startling the reluctant host back to the present. 'Such a warm welcome.' Sir Montgomery shook Francis's hand and smiled. He considered the man pressing his hand like a vice. Francis looked like an average black haired man, but he was strong. In the morning, when Sir Montgomery snored off his latest hangover, he thought Francis likely sweated to whatever fitness routine the Committee indoctrinated. *It likely had to do with drinking milk while marching ridiculously in your undergarments to Wagner* Sir Montgomery deliberated.

'Well,' Sir Montgomery smiled back, 'Tell me, how were your travels?' The group remained quiet. Francis nodded.

'Very good. Very good indeed. The countryside has a certain charm to it.'

'Yes, well, it's no Swiss Alps, but it'll do.'

Francis's grin stretched to a full smile. 'And how is

everything in London treating you? Fair?'

'Of course. Everything is in order.'

'Oh good,' Francis turned to his group of blonde-haired, blue-eyed clones. 'The British Empire has been conquering people for so long, we feared it had forgotten how to bend the knee.' The clones laughed.

'Ah, ah,' Sir Montgomery wagged a finger playfully, 'Parliament is cooperating fully with the Committee's guidelines, remember?'

Francis patted Sir Montgomery on the back. He fought off a shiver. 'Yes. What was I thinking?'

'So,' Sir Montgomery straightened his suit coat, 'Who's ready for some tea?'

Francis frowned. 'Mr. Brown,' Sir Montgomery's ears almost twitched. He could tell Francis stripped Sir Montgomery of his title intentionally. 'Don't you wish to say hello to your son first?' The top hats parted so that Sir Montgomery and his son shared a path.

'Of course,' Sir Montgomery smiled, walking over to Montgomery III. The young man stared at his father, expressionless. *What had they done to him?* Sir Montgomery fretted. He took a deep breath and stretched out his arms. Montgomery III stood still. Sir Montgomery forced his son into an embrace, slapping his back hard before pulling away. Montgomery III's face ran flush. 'Son, welcome home.'

'Hello, father,' he said lifelessly. *At least he hadn't caught one of those ridiculous lisps*, Sir Montgomery joked with himself.

'So much catching up to do my boy, I look forward to hearing of your adventures,' Sir Montgomery squeezed at his bicep before turning to Nicholas. 'But first, let's get down to the matters at hand.'

'So much to catch up on, indeed,' Francis spoke up as he gathered his men with a snap of his fingers. 'Come, let's get ourselves some of this famous tea everyone keeps talking about.' Francis turned to Sir Montgomery. 'We *fancy a cuppa*, Mr. Brown. Is that how they say it?'

'Looks like I'm not the only one polishing up on my

accent.'

Nicholas led Sir Montgomery and the delegation into the parlour for noon tea. Sir Montgomery took his prearranged seat near the fireplace as staff helped the Committee into recliners and sofas. It took longer than expected. Sir Montgomery half assumed it was because the Committee had forgotten how to bend their knees. Francis took Nicholas's direction and sat in one of the pair of antique chairs across from Sir Montgomery. A turret top table adorned with a silver tray of condiments, tarts and a miniature globe sat between them.

'Monty,' Sir Montgomery called out. Montgomery III's eyes widened as he sat in a lone chair near the garden window. 'Come, son, see how it's done.' Montgomery III turned to Francis.

'Yes, Montgomery,' Francis patted the empty seat between him and Sir Montgomery. 'Come sit next to your father. See how it's done.'

Montgomery's eyes danced between Francis and his father. He stood up, swallowed hard, then walked to the table. Sir Montgomery watched as his son rubbed his fingers together. He was nervous. Montgomery sat, hands blanketed over his lap.

'I had Nicholas prepare tarts for you,' Sir Montgomery offered Montgomery III a plate. 'They're your favourite, brown butter apple.'

Montgomery nodded. 'Apologies, father. I had a big breakfast.'

'No need to apologise, boy,' Sir Montgomery did his best to fake a smile. The sun slipped through a drawn drape into his eyes. Sir Montgomery waved at Megan, directing her to secure the drapes. 'Glad they're feeding you well.'

'He's eating very well,' Francis took a tart and bit into it hard from the sides of his teeth. Sir Montgomery imagined it was how he bit the pin off of a grenade. 'So, Mr. Brown, why don't you tell us the progress of Parliament. When last we left, there was much turmoil.'

'Handled,' Sir Montgomery directed the new girl, Barbara, to the table as she balanced a teapot on a tray.

She bowed her head and poured steaming water in each of our cups. 'People are tired of war, we bled every warmonger out from our legislature and replaced them with proper representatives, men of peace. I've also followed a few leads and peacefully suffocated the small bands of lingering resistances in the villages.'

'Suffocation is not peaceful, Mr. Brown,' Francis said as he selected black tea from the refreshment box.

'Yes, I'm sure you're right.' Sir Montgomery picked a cigarette out from his case before offering it up to Francis. He shook his head. Sir Montgomery lit the tip and took a puff. 'Regardless, I've used some of my connections to reach out to the radio services and daily papers. I have notified them that any misinformation around the governance of this nation will be met with swift justice. I've kept a close eye on them since the initiative, and I'm glad to say they're behaving well. Well, everyone except for crazy Wathmere.' Sir Montgomery snickered. 'So, Parliament, the people and the media are all on board.'

'Very impressive Mr. Brown,' Francis lifted his saucer of watery tea. *A man could go to the gallows for not letting tea steep properly* Sir Montgomery thought to himself. The visitor took a large sip, unflinching. 'Your son has much to learn about the art of negotiation.'

'He'll get there,' Sir Montgomery said with a cigarette dangling from my lips. He slapped Montgomery III on the back again, trying to get a reaction. Montgomery III said nothing.

'It is as if this great nation is waking up,' Francis put his cup down on his saucer. He spun the globe around, pressing hard on England. 'We must purify ourselves of the old shadow that once loomed over us, decadence, perversion … corruption. A new dawn is amongst us.'

'Well then,' Sir Montgomery breathed in hot tobacco smoke, letting it snap off the rubber bands tightening around his spine, 'Just call me Apollo.' *I hate the sun,* Sir Montgomery sneered inwardly.

'Yes,' Francis spun the globe. 'Each of us must do our part to purify the masses. It takes resolve and dedication to scrub the system honestly – clean it of its corruption, and corrupt it has been for far too long. We must be willing to sacrifice ourselves for the good of the whole.'

'I hear that, old boy,' Sir Montgomery exhaled like a locomotive. *Teck was crafty* Sir Montgomery cautioned himself. He couldn't get a read on the man. Sir Montgomery didn't know if he were laying the groundwork to ask for money or something entirely different. Sir Montgomery focused on the cigarette to keep calm.

'We are having trouble elsewhere,' Francis rotated the globe and then carelessly spun it round. 'People are being fed for free in order to keep this hard-won peace. Can you imagine that?'

'Let them eat cake,' Sir Montgomery crossed his legs and laughed. He was uncomfortable and didn't want to show it. Exhibiting fear sabotages negotiations. Pretend to hold all the cards. Let the other side think you have more that they want.

'Cake indeed,' Francis looked to Montgomery, who quickly stared at his tea as it settled. 'What a funny thought. Only,' Francis paused, thinning his lips. He leaned in towards Sir Montgomery. The two men traded stares like predators crossing paths in the wild. Sir Montgomery assumed Francis was trying to learn something about him. Sir Montgomery kept the smirk but didn't break from the exchange. 'It's not funny at all Mr. Brown.'

'No?' Sir Montgomery crushed his cigarette in the ashtray and crossed his legs again.

'No,' Francis shook his head. 'You cannot bribe people to comply with the future. It gives the notion they are in charge or the future is somehow negotiable. People in charge can never truly be assimilated. If one truly wishes to expel the corruption, to cleanse the land of dishonesty, you must demand change. It is not enough to go along with it, we must, all of us, believe it with all our hearts. Each citizen must believe it, or they will go astray.'

'I hear you Sir Francis,' Sir Montgomery crossed his legs once more to the other side, 'and sometimes it can be like teaching a fish to fly. It takes an inordinate amount of coaxing.'

'Indeed,' Francis's eyes grew wide as he leaned in over the tea table. The blacks in his eyes dilated. Sir Montgomery felt like he was being hypnotized. 'And many will fall to their deaths trying to grow wings. Still, we must demand this evolution.'

'Well then,' Sir Montgomery shrugged, forcing a smile to spread across his face. It was harder for him than lifting a car. 'I'm your wing maker.'

Francis's face went blank. He stared at Sir Montgomery with intense pupils for an uncomfortable amount of time. Sir Montgomery licked tobacco from his lips, peering back. Montgomery scratched at his temple. Finally, after a long game of *Flinch*, the visitor's face cracked into a smile. He belted out a loud laugh like some deranged Father Christmas.

'Fish and birds and wings,' Francis slapped the table. 'Hilarity!' Francis looked all around him. The top hats reacted quickly, stirring up fake laughter. Sir Montgomery joined in, pressing out the helium from his belly with each chuckle. Before long, everyone in the room was in on the guffaw. Everyone except Montgomery III. His stare locked on the uneaten tarts.

It took several minutes for the room to cool off. When the last of the tittering died down, Francis straightened his jacket and finished the cup of black tea.

'Well,' Francis took another tart and bit into it, 'where were we?'

Sir Montgomery noticed that Francis's remarks didn't show any signs of want or need. The man either liked to play with his food or he'd lost track of his goal. The Committee needed money. Sir Montgomery knew that. It was time for Francis to make his proposal. *A good salesman always pushes to close the deal* Sir Montgomery deliberated. *Perhaps I should help him out.*

'I believe that you were going to test my loyalty, Sir Francis,' Sir Montgomery's brain begged for another cigarette. His hand tried to oblige. He pressed it hard on his lap.

'What ever do you mean?' Francis tilted his head. 'Should I need to test it?'

'Come now,' Sir Montgomery pressed his chin into his thumb and index finger, framing his cheek. 'We're both smart men. We've worked together in the past. I know the efforts can't move forward without funding. So why don't you just ask me?'

'You think I want money?' Francis's head cocked back.

'I do,' Sir Montgomery raised his lips to reveal a toothy grin. 'No need to dodge the issue. I understand how it all works. I've planned. Nicholas has a case with routing numbers and signed documents. It's all there.'

'Impressive, Mr. Brown,' Francis sifted through the serving tray and removed a lump of sugar. He placed it in his mouth and sucked on it. 'Only, I don't need your money.'

'You don't?' Sir Montgomery cleared the glue in his throat.

'Your money had been important to get us on our feet, and for that the Committee is grateful. Tell me Mr. Brown,' Francis paused for a moment, weighing up the words in his mouth, eventually he pinched his chin with his leather covered hand, 'who is Ivan Piłsudski?'

'Who?' Sir Montgomery sunk in his seat. His stomach twisted.

'Ivan,' the visitor enunciated slowly, 'Piłsudski. Who is he?'

'Oh yes,' Sir Montgomery waved his hand. 'A local street thug, I believe.'

'You believe?' the brows on Francis's brow raised to their peak. 'I was told you two work together.' Heat surrounded Sir Montgomery's collar. He recalled how resourceful this damned man was.

'I deal with a lot of rabble,' Sir Montgomery shrugged. 'It's difficult to remember them all.'

'But this Ivan,' Francis tapped his chin, 'he just left your home, yes?'

'He did?' Sir Montgomery slapped his forehead. Montgomery III shuffled in his seat. 'Oh, yes, you mean Ivy. I haven't heard him called by his proper name in ages. Yes, we work together. He feeds me information on the locals – ensures that the rabble are behaving.'

'I thought,' there was a pause while Francis tapped the table, 'it was all taken care of?'

'It is,' Sir Montgomery blurted while tugging his collar. 'But I always like insurance. Ears to the ground and all that. One must be pragmatic when dealing with, situations.'

'And is that why you pay him?' Francis tilted his head. *He knew* Sir Montgomery fretted. *I have to recover quickly.*

'That money is a donation,' the sun bled back out from the drapes onto Sir Montgomery's forehead. He adjusted in his chair to try to escape it. 'I ask him to spread it to the masses. Damn my gold heart.'

'Yes,' Francis slithered his tongue out and licked his front teeth. 'Mr. Brown, working with that sort, can start nasty rumours. The kind no one of an honourable position should want. The days of whispers and back-alley dealings must end. Speaking of rumours, I also hear that you may be taking advantage of your position with the markets, and the daughters of London? You wouldn't be abusing the privileges awarded your position, would you Mr. Brown?'

'No,' Sir Montgomery shook his head hard. 'Jealousy, I tell you, I must have upset a lot of people on my rise, supporting the Committee. Bitter people are always trying to twist an earnest man's profit. It's hearsay.'

'Oh,' Francis bobbed his head, 'very good. And you're right. Your lawyer's office seemed rather desolate. Tough times for all.'

Sir Montgomery knew he was being outwitted. Francis knew about Ivan. He'd checked in with the legal team. Sir Montgomery assumed Francis was aware of everything. Sir Montgomery's conscience told him to confess, to throw himself at Francis's mercy. *Means to an end. I did it for Englan*d he almost blurted. *I did it for peace, I did it* *all for the Committee*. The old alleycat in him roared though and told him to calm down. *You could turn this around.*

'Oh Francis,' Sir Montgomery put his hand to his heart, 'you wouldn't happen to be spying on me would you? I thought we did things upright nowadays?' Francis's men froze, fingers pinching saucers with teacups. Francis's face froze. Sir Montgomery didn't think he liked being on the wrong side of accusations but hoped the contradiction would warn Francis to back off.

'Yes,' Francis wagged his finger, 'well, a parent must keep an eye on their children to ensure they're raised accordingly.' There was a pause. 'Also, I wanted to ensure that this country's future leadership was all in order. The Brown lineage must be ready for whatever the future holds.'

'Sir,' Sir Montgomery lifted his tea and tested a sip. It was still too early. 'I've made the proper arrangements to ensure my legacy is in line with the Committee's needs. It's been a testing few years. I'm ready to play ball, be it money, connections. Whatever it takes.'

Francis licked his lips. He adjusted his body, so it was parallel to Sir Montgomery. Francis's hand raked through slicked hair before reaching out and landing on Monty's shoulder.

'No, no, Mr. Brown,' Francis shook his head, 'not your legacy. Your *son's* legacy.'

Now Sir Montgomery understood.

The sun cut through the razor thin slit in the curtain and onto Sir Montgomery's forehead and neck. Sir Montgomery looked to Montgomery III, who winced as if his father were about to strike him.

'You devil,' Sir Montgomery muttered, paused in time. 'But I've done so much for the cause. Every move, every measure I took, I made it for us, for England!'

'Was it though?' Francis nodded to the men sitting at a nearby sofa. Hard soles hit the ground from Sir Montgomery's backside. A pair of young soldiers stood attention at each of Sir Montgomery's shoulders. 'Your efforts were for yourself, Mr. Brown. The Committee agrees that intent such as this does not run parallel with our objectives. Luckily, your legal team was eager to arrange for Monty's immediate inheritance.'

The papers Sir Montgomery screamed inside. He didn't read the fine print. Sweat ran from Sir Montgomery's collar. He massaged his forehead. The two men by his chair inched so close to Sir Montgomery that he could smell the starch in their clothes.

'Wait just a minute,' Sir Montgomery leapt up as if he'd been buried alive. The men shoved him back down, and hard. Francis smiled at his men. Sir Montgomery took a deep breath. 'On what grounds? You can't steal my money and give it to Monty. It's mine.'

'We're not stealing it, Father,' Montgomery III spoke up. His voice was firm. Sir Montgomery gave his son a once over. He saw the same icy glare that rested in the other soldier's eyes. 'Bribery, adultery, illegal trade, shadowy meetings with criminals and warmongers. You've committed crimes against England. You're being stripped of any authority. Father, we are grateful for the good you have done previously, but you are a man of a different time, a different era. You're a man of the past and only men of the future can hold the reigns now. There can be no blemishes in the new Sun. Do you see their benevolence? Their mercy? Our House will endure, your legacy has been permitted to continue through me, your memory will remain.'

His words shot a bullet through Sir Montgomery's heart. His mind flashed back to little Monty staring up at him in the photograph. Sir Montgomery's mind raced. This was perhaps the only betrayal he could have ever faced. He took a deep breath then exhaled. The tension in his body released.

'Then I am broken,' Sir Montgomery fixed on his son. There was a moment of silence. The soldiers garbled something to the house staff. Nicholas, George, Noah, Megan and Barbara shuffled out of the room. None of them so much as glanced at Sir Montgomery. Montgomery III didn't cower any longer. Sir Montgomery watched, stunned, as his son continued to shoot daggers at him. Sir Montgomery was in such a stupor that he hardly noticed Francis point at him and then the men behind him.

The soldiers lifted Sir Montgomery by his arms. He felt how strong they were. They balanced him up onto his soles. Sir Montgomery felt lightheaded. Francis stood up and came uncomfortably close. Sir Montgomery could smell the black tea on his breath.

'Mr. Brown,' Francis put his hands behind his back,

'By the orders of the XXII Committee, you are being placed under arrest. You will face expedited justice for your crimes of bribery, illegal trade, moral decency and espionage.'

Sir Montgomery let the words bounce off him. He felt nothing.

'So, what'll it be, Francis,' Sir Montgomery seethed through his teeth, 'firing squad? Gas? Or is it burning me like a witch? I know how much your lot enjoys torture.'

'Mr. Brown,' Francis puffed out his chest, 'who said anything about execution? We will process you like anyone accused of a crime.' He stepped to the side so that Montgomery III could see. 'We believe in justice, due process and structure. Without institution, foundation is easily corrupted.'

Montgomery III nodded.

'Well then Francis,' Sir Montgomery tugged at his arms feebly, 'are we off to the Isle of Wight for my free haircut?'

'How I enjoy British humour,' Francis shook his head slowly. 'No, Mr. Brown. Should you be found guilty, we will show clemency. With unquestionable authority we have that luxury now. No bars. No haircuts. You will continue to serve the Committee, in a sense. We have someplace far more merciful than that wretched island. Now, shall we get our coats?'

* * *

The sun baked through Sir Montgomery's face. There were

no drapes in the cottage. He stared at the beams that made up the ceiling. A web stretched from the rotted wood. The spider was busy eating one of its catches. Sir Montgomery read that they eat their prey from the inside-out. He sat up alone in his twin bed. His window faced east, allowing Apollo to fill the room.

'Piss off,' he swore at the window. He reached for a pack of cigarettes. There was only one left. *Resupply wasn't until Sunday* Sir Montgomery thought. *This would be a long week.* He lit the cigarette, slid on his moccasins and shuffled out of the back door. The frigid air bit his cheeks. The fields were barren. The only trees in sight were dead. The ugly broadcasting tower, complete with its ceaseless red blinking light, was Sir Montgomery's lone scenery.

He tugged at the outhouse door. The cesspool hadn't been emptied in weeks. Sir Montgomery searched for rats before grabbing last week's herald. He'd read it several times, but it had a way of battling the isolation. He could stay connected with the world, even in exile. He sat down and flipped to the business section again. *I must be a masochistic* Sir Montgomery ruminated. His eyes hurried to the small article at the bottom. He'd read it at least fifty times.

Montgomery Brown III to be Knighted for Contributions to England.

He was my son Sir Montgomery accepted. *That was undeniable.* Yet, Sir Montgomery knew he shared him with another father. Francis saw to Sir Montgomery's legacy now. The damned man used what Sir Montgomery built and fuelled it for The Committee's desires.

Sir Montgomery finished the article, smoked the last of his cigarette and did his business, then returned to the cold yard. Plumes of soot spewed from the crooked chimney. He hurried inside. Smoke from wet logs were stinking up the cottage. *He was trying to build a fire again,* Sir Montgomery swore to himself.

He hurried to the main chamber where Wathmere was stabbing flames in the fireplace. A microphone chord dangled from his neck like a noose. Montgomery paused to study the pathetic man in front of him. A once noble and celebrated politician, now a drunk laughing-stock, whose listeners did no more than laugh at his rambling calls to arms. The man who styled himself as the leader of the resistance was in fact the worst thing to happen to it. Now that Montgomery was here to share the broadcasts, things could finally be different. England would be keen to hear what *he* had to say.

The fumes were far too close to the radio transmitter for Sir Montgomery's liking. He hurried and disarmed Wathmere before opening the flue.

'Damn it, man,' Sir Montgomery pointed to the transmitter. 'I told you I'd make the fires from here on out. You will ruin the equipment.'

'Apologies,' Wathmere straightened the sides of his hair. 'But this damnable sun just isn't cutting it in this god forsaken place.'

'Don't get me started,' Sir Montgomery sat down at the lone chair sitting next to the radio desk. Wathmere handed him the headphones. The room was spartan, save for the equipment and Wathmere's leftover cans of dinner. Sir Montgomery tuned the dial until the transmission feed sounded clean. 'How'd the night go for you?'

'I believe I delivered my finest speech yet. I wouldn't be shocked if England's uprising took full flight by next week.'

'You said that last week.'

'Yes, well, these things take time. What great monologue will you be providing today, then?'

Sir Montgomery sat in the chair for a moment, his finger over the microphone's button. There was only one thing he ever wanted to talk about.

'England's future,' he said as he straightened the microphone.

'You're not going to rant about your legacy again, are you?'

'I might. There's a lot of airtime to fill.'

'Right then,' Wathmere rolled his eyes. 'Tickety-boo.'

THE HOUSEWIFE

BY SAMANTHA EVERGREEN

THE HOUSEWIFE

A nne Routy awoke to the sound of the warning sirens; the ones that made her heart stop every time. The ones that meant more bombs would be dropped and more of the life they knew would be lost once again. But her only thought as she sat up in bed was that she needed to get her boys to safety.

She jumped from her and her husband's warm bed, her bare feet landing hard on the cool, wooden floor. Anne didn't dare turn on a light as she ran across the room, even as she hit her toe on the dresser that sat next to the bedroom door, knowing that it would only mean death from above.

As she threw open the door, she could hear the humming of the planes that flew over her home and all of London. Hundreds of planes flew across the night sky high in the freezing air, hiding in the gloom of darkness to rain more chaos down on them.

Anne rushed down the hall and crashed into the room where her two boys slept peacefully.

'James, Tommy, wake up! We need to go to the basement,' Anne said breathlessly as she shook them awake.

'The sky is screaming again, mummy,' Tommy whispered as she reached down to pick him up from his bed. She took James' small seven-year-old hand and pulled him to his feet to stand by her side.

'I know, sweetie, but it's going to be okay. We're going to the basement, and we'll be safe there.'

Through the dark, Anne held onto her boys as they made their way down the hallway. As they passed the windows, Anne looked out and saw the flashes of light in the far distance, lights that looked a lot like fires. She turned away, terrified at this glimpse of what tomorrow might look like, and was thankful that her husband was out at the factory a long way off from the fires.

Finally, they reached the freezing cold basement, and Anne walked her boys over to the corner of the dark room to sit down with them.

Tommy cried silently in her arms as she hugged him to her chest, and James held onto her hand as he lay close to her side. Even though she knew that he didn't want her to know, Anne heard him softly crying too.

Anne closed her eyes as she rocked back and forth, in the hopes that doing so would calm her babies and herself. Warm tears started to fall from her eyes, dripping onto her lavender nightgown as the sound of bombs exploding got closer. Anne knew that the world they had once known was never going to be the same.

Anne sat up in her bed as the booming rang in her ears. Without thinking, she leaped out of bed and ran through the cottage to where her boys slept. She pushed open the door so hard that it slammed against the wall, but she only found them both sleeping soundly, without a care in the world.

Anne closed her eyes as she let herself lean back against the wall, at least until her heart slowed down to a normal beat once more. Even though it had been years since they had lived in London, the war now over and lost, the nightmares haunted her still, even in the picture-perfect port of Isaac.

After letting out a deep breath, she stepped away from the wall and took one last look at her boys, who shared a bed even though they had their own. Ever since the war, Tommy could only sleep if his older brother was by his side. The passing of the years had made no difference to that.

She felt a soft smile play at her lips before she turned away and started for her bedroom to get dressed. After all, a housewife's work is never done.

Anne pulled on a dress with a purple flower pattern and stepped into some old brown flats before making her way to the kitchen to start a simple breakfast of eggs and toast for the boys to have before school.

She cracked eggs into a red-hot frying pan, the sound of sizzling filling the room, but even the mindlessness of cooking didn't let her escape the images from her nightmare and the memory of her life she'd had before. Of course, maybe it had been that interview she did last week, with that kind journalist talking to her about her life before losing the war, that was the reason for her thinking of the past so much lately.

The life she had once had in London was so different from the one she had now. Going from a two-story house to a two-room cottage, from living a city life to a life by the sea, and, of course, having to leave her family behind in that gray, crumbling world once known as home. But the biggest heartbreak that seemed to be plaguing her lately was the loss of her husband, though that had been after the war and seemed a lifetime ago.

Anne knew just how lucky they had been in getting out when they did. It was only that her husband had family here, and that they could be given a place to live when so many had nowhere to go.

She knew that, even with the world so different from the one they knew, she still had her boys, and they could live somewhat well off.

Though money was no longer used here, she could buy food and goods with the baked sweets she made and, of course, by teaching the other housewives higher quality recipes from London, from corned beef fritters to cheese and potato dumplings.

But Anne had learned much from the people here

as well. She had learned how to debone every type of fish you could imagine and how to make the best use of her land. With the help of Mrs. Smith and Mrs. Green, Anne now had a blooming green garden, full of all kinds of fruits and vegetables. From arugula, which would do best in the spring and autumn, to Belgian endive in the autumn and winter. Broccoli, cabbage, mushrooms, and every type of herb you could name now grew tall and thick.

Still, even with all of the help from everyone, there was always something about the people here, a coldness. Of course, she could never quite put her finger on it, or on why she felt that way, but there was something ... off. They were kind but they never let you into their life.

'Mummy, is breakfast ready yet?'

Anne snapped out of her thoughts and looked over her shoulder to see James standing there, seemingly half asleep as he rubbed at his eyes, but at least he was dressed. She saw that Tommy looked much the same as he followed behind his brother.

'Yes,' Anne answered with a bright smile as she placed the eggs and toast on two plates. Her boys slid into their seats as she set the dishes in front of her children, and they started eating like there was no tomorrow.

For a moment, she watched her boys as they ate and admired them as the sun cast its beaming light over the table. James looked so much like her late husband, Robin, with his black hair and bright green eyes, even as a ten-year-old, he was tall for his age. Which was good, he would be able to work hard and stand tall even in this world they lived in now.

Tommy, on the other hand, looked much like Anne herself, with his brown hair and blue eyes. She knew that he was smart, smarter than any six-year-old should be, but the war had made him grow up too fast. Of course, it had forced everyone to age and grow up too fast.

'Are the two of you ready for school?' Anne asked them as she washed the pan that had been used to cook that morning's breakfast.

'Yes, mummy,' James answered with his mouth

full.

'Good, because I want you two to walk straight to school and right back home afterwards, got it?'

'I know, mummy,' James said, sounding a little annoyed that he had to promise her the same thing every day, but it made Anne feel better. Because, though she knew they were lucky, they had made it out of London and were able to live a somewhat normal life. The planes that flew overhead a hundred yards away on the other side of the port told another story.

They were a reminder that they had lost, and that, at any moment, everything they had come to know could be blown away once more. After all, that's what had happened to her husband and that man Jerry.

Her kids finished their breakfast then, and she came over to take their dishes as they got up to grab bags loaded with their books and homework before heading out of the door to school. Anne was always thankful for this time she had alone. After all, she never had much time for herself while taking care of the house duties, cleaning, cooking, maintaining the garden, and, of course, making sure that her boys had everything they needed.

After she finished washing the dishes and placing them out to dry, she went over to the hook on the wall to grab her bag of gardening tools before making her way outside.

She stepped out into the sunny, cloudless morning, the weather perfect as she made her way to her garden where she would be picking garlic, tomatoes, and red peppers for the spicy white fish stew they would be having for dinner tonight. And, maybe, she could even grab some rhubarb for a pie if they looked good.

As she walked, a light breeze carried the smell of the sea to her it was the same sea that made their little port run. It gave their men jobs, gave them their food, and something to trade for goods, and provided them all with something to do besides think about what lay on the other side of the port.

Out of nowhere, a strong breeze blew a piece of

her brown hair into her face as she walked onto the overgrown, grassy path to where her garden lay. It made up part of their land, the other dominated by their cottage and animals. A half dozen chickens gave them fresh eggs, and the few pigs they had were good for breeding and selling.

Anne kneeled down in the damp grass and started to pick the bright red tomatoes, the noise of the little children playing in the meadow and birds singing filling the warm summer air as she started to fill her basket with the ripe, red fruit.

Of course, another sound hung in the air in the far distance, the ever-present hum of planes that flew over the Navy ships that sat on the other side of the port. Anne had learned to block it out a long time ago but, still, it let them know that they were never truly safe.

Out of nowhere, every sound seemed to stop suddenly, and Anne felt the hairs on the back of her neck stand on end as an icy fear seeped into her veins.

She looked around herself slowly as she stood up, wondering why it seemed like the world had gone silent out of nowhere. The kids' laughter seemed to be muted, and the birds had stopped moving altogether. Even the breeze had seemed to stop as if everything was waiting for something to happen.

Then she heard it; the sound of footsteps coming from behind her. Anne turned and saw Mrs. Taylor and a few of the other women that she would make small talk with at the market walking through the large group of trees that sat a little way off from her land, their arms laden with baskets covered with fabric.

Anne watched them for a moment, not understanding what they were all doing here. The way they were headed would only lead to the burned out cabin on the other side of the port, a place they knew not to go. She frowned and stepped forward to get a better look only to stop herself. Instead, she hid behind one of the large trees and peeked around it, feeling as if this was something she shouldn't be seeing and that would get into trouble if she was caught.

As she watched, they kept walking through the trees heading further and further into the woods. All of them had baskets, pails, or buckets full of something, and she had a feeling it wasn't fish.

After what felt like hours but could have only been minutes, they had gone so far into the woods that Anne couldn't see them any more. They were now only moving shadows.

Anne stepped out from behind the tree after a moment and stood there, her mind racing as she tried to make sense of why just about all the women in the port were walking toward what they all knew could be their death if they were seen.

She was snapped out of her thoughts suddenly as a group of black birds took off from the trees startling her. For a moment, she watched as the blue summer sky was blacked out with crows, their frantic cawing matching the beat of her racing heart.

After a long second, Anne took one last look at where they'd been before she turned away and went to finish picking her vegetables, running back to the cottage in a hurried blur.

She tried not to think about what she had just seen as she started to heat some oil in a pot and cut the vegetables up. But as she dropped the diced tomatoes into the stock and lit the burner with a burning match, she couldn't help it; the mystery of why they would put themselves in danger was just too much for her to pretend that it didn't happen.

Anne watched as the match she had just used burned for a moment, the fire dancing down the piece of wood as her mind raced with what she was about to do. She closed her eyes for a second before she blew it out and threw it onto the counter without looking back.

She let out a breath as she made her way back outside and started walking through the trees once again. As she did, Anne saw that the once tall grass had been knocked down and yellowed, meaning that it had been walked over many, many times before. She wondered once again why anyone would go near the other side of the port.

Anne slowed her pace, then she realized just how quiet it was, and it was then that she felt her blood run cold, even in the summer heat. It was far too quiet for all of the women in the village to be walking here. She would have heard something by now, and the hum of planes seemed to have moved away, which was rare.

'What am I doing?' Anne asked under her breath to no one but herself; at least that's what she hoped. What was she doing here? She was a single mother had who lost her husband after something like this, something they should have never got into in the first place. They should never have saved that Jerry, because if they hadn't then her husband would probably still be alive today. After all, she didn't really know the people here. Behind their kind small talk they all could be someone else.

The only person that she really knew was Robin's cousin Mr. Shipham. The others were just people that she said hello to when she passed them in the market. If she got into something she shouldn't, it would be all too easy for them to throw Anne and her kids out and leave them with nothing or, worse, put them on a boat, and send them toward the Navy.

It was that thought, the thought of her boys, that made her turn back and make her way home once more. She would not be the reason for more death, especially not for the little family she had left.

Back at home, Anne made herself stop thinking about what she had seen as morning turned to a burning hot afternoon, and she finished deboning the white fish. She carelessly cut it into pieces and dropped it into the pot with the rest of the stock that had been left for far too long. The tomatoes were now nothing more than paste but at this point she didn't care much.

Mindlessly, Anne prepared and baked the rhubarb pie, doing it more from muscle memory than anything else as her thoughts still raced around her head, trying to make up a simple reason as to why they were in the woods that morning. Maybe they were going to pick the Queen Anne's lace flowers that grew in between the trees ... No ... She couldn't make herself believe that.

As the pie baked, Anne went and sat in Robin's old armchair and started working on her half-finished needlepoint. But, as she picked up the needle, she could only sit there looking down at the half-done quote. The words Keep Calm and Carry On. looked back at her, stitched into the fabric with a deep red thread.

Anne had seen it on a motivational poster produced by the British government before it fell as they were leaving the place they had once called home.

She heard that the poster was intended to raise the morale of the British public after the mass air attacks on the cities, in the hopes of invoking the old Victorian belief in a 'stiff upper lip'. The idea was to promote self-discipline and remaining calm in adversity.

In a way, the poster became recognized around the world, not on the surface, but in the dark corners; no one talked about it openly. It was shared where people still hid their tea boxes and pipes. Where people still hummed 'God Save the King' under their breath when they didn't think anyone could hear. Where people still believed that not all was lost.

But Anne wasn't sure why she had written it, not when she knew that there was no going back at this point. There was no hope left for the world, home, and family that she had once had.

'Mummy, is something burning?'

Anne snapped back to reality suddenly and saw that James and Tommy were back from school. They were standing in front of her. She hadn't even heard the door open, let alone noticed the time that had passed.

She looked out of the window in shock and saw that the afternoon had turned to evening, the sky now a deep red and orange and mixing with angry-looking clouds that she knew meant a storm was coming.

'Oh no,' Anne said and ran into the kitchen. Opening the oven, she found her once beautifully made pie was now an ugly, deep brown.

Taking it out, she placed it on the counter and prayed that it was still salvageable.

'Mummy, are you okay?' Tommy asked, tugging at her skirt. The worry clear in his little voice was something that a six-year-old shouldn't have, shouldn't know.

'Yes, honey, I'm fine. Are you ready for dinner?' Anne asked, looking down into his deep blue eyes.

'Yeah,' James answered from where he stood next to Tommy, watching her face as well. Anne put on a smile to set them at ease, and it seemed to work as the worry faded away. 'Great, go clean up and I'll get dinner served.'

They nodded and turned away, starting down the hall to get changed and wash up for dinner.

Anne swallowed and let out a breath. This day had been weird enough. The idea that she had sat in the living room and didn't even notice the time passing didn't help things.

But that's what she got for thinking about a time now gone forever. Shaking her head, she got to work grabbing bowls and ladled the stew, cutting thin pieces of bread to have on the side.

She set down the steaming dishes as her boys came running back to sit in their chairs, and she did the same.

Steam rose from their bowls as thunder shook the windows suddenly. Rain started to fall outside, the sprinkling sound of it filling the air as it hit the ground and windows.

At least it would cool the summer air down Anne thought as they all started eating.

Soon, the room was filled with the sounds of spoons hitting the edge of clay bowls. Anne once again made herself smile and look at her boys before she spoke. 'So, how was school today?'

'Fine as always,' James answered. 'We read for most of the day.'

'Really? What are they reading to you?' Anne asked, not really paying much attention until James answered.

'Nothing. We had to read on our own. Mrs. Kelly

wasn't there.'

'Is that rare for her not to be there?'

'Not Really. She normally has Wednesdays off.'

'Since when?' Anne asked, forgetting about her dinner now as lightning flashed across the sky, lighting the candle lit room for a split second.

James gave her a very confused look as Tommy went on eating, blissfully unaware.

'I don't know ... since we started going there ... why?'

Anne felt goosebumps run down her arms, but she still put on a small smile, as if she was just wanting to know about their day like every mother does.

'No reason, just wondering is all,' Anne answered, and James rolled his eyes.

As they finished their meal, Anne took Tommy's hand as she led her boys to bed, her head spinning. Whatever the women in this port were doing, it had been going on since Jerry had come into their lives so many years ago. She hadn't seen her, but could Mrs Kelly have been with them?

Anne made her way back into the kitchen and started to wash the dishes; after all, a housewife's work is never done, but it also gave her time to think. How long had this been going on? Since they moved here, or maybe even before that?

Did the women know about Jerry even before she and her husband had found him? Did they have something to do with it? All she had was questions, but what she needed was answers. And she knew there was only one way to get them.

Lightning flashed across the night sky then, making Anne realize just how late it was and that she needed to start making her way to bed, because she would be getting up early tomorrow morning.

Mindlessly, she undressed before slipping on her old, lavender nightgown. The silk was cool against her skin as she undid her bun and let her brown hair fall around her shoulders. For a moment, she stood in the middle of her bedroom, thinking.

Anne was happy with the life she had made here, even if her husband wasn't here with her. But that could all change tomorrow. She moved over to stand before the small, cracked glass window of her bedroom and looked out into the darkness.

Once again, lightning lit the world up for a moment, and she saw that the rain hit the ground so hard that it bounced upward in the grass. Her breath fogged the window pane in front of her.

How long had she waited for answers? Answers about why no one came to get Jerry when they had first found him. Answers to why her husband had been killed trying to take him back to where they believed that he belonged. Answers to why everyone in the port seemed to live in a bubble, away from the war that they had lost and the consequences of it. But she promised herself that, when daylight returned tomorrow, that would all change.

Anne turned away then and made her way over to her bed. She flipped the covers up and lay down, her eyes closed, and had the feeling that nothing would be the same again, though she couldn't have told you why at that time.

She awoke early the next morning, far before even the sun rose, and got dressed in the same outfit she had worn the day before, not even bothering to put up her hair as she hurried to get her chores done. She made a simple breakfast for her boys of cottage cheese with strawberries cut up and set on top, and washed the clothes, laying them out to dry by the fire she started.

With all of that done, she grabbed the large basket that she used for running errands and stepped outside only to be met with a world that seemed to reflect her own mood.

The sky was a deep, ashy gray as a misty rain fell, and as Anne walked, she knew that the yard would be full of puddles. Tommy would have to jump in them on his way to school, getting himself all wet and muddy. Of course,

James would try to stop him a few times before joining in himself, even if they both knew how mad it made her. But today she wouldn't say a word about it, so focused on what she was doing and the answers she needed.

The ten-minute walk seemed to go by in a blur, and before she knew it Anne was at the market. As she started up the path that led to the walkway, she was struck by the smell of freshly caught fish and salty seawater. The sea lay only feet away from the stalls that lined the road where people sold their goods.

But there was also the smell of baked bread and simple brown sugar cookies, not to mention the fresh fruits and vegetables of the season.

There was a clothes stall, too, one she hadn't seen before. A couple of jackets, trousers, a cap and three dresses. All a little shabby, all a little second hand.

One of the great things about getting up so early was that only a few people milled around besides the sellers and herself, and that made this the perfect time for spying.

Anne put on a bright smile as she walked over to where Mrs. Green was selling her jams and seasoned butters. 'Mrs. Green, how are you doing today?'

The older woman looked up at Anne, her gray hair stuck to her face a little from her walk here in the rain. 'I'm as well as I can be, dear. Are you looking for anything in particular?'

'I'm not sure yet. Which jam would you recommend for something a little sour?' Anne asked.

'Well, over here I have a blackcurrant jam that would probably work well.'

Anne nodded and picked up the jar, pretending to listen as Mrs. Green went on about the taste, but Anne took that moment to look around the small wooden stall. She was trying to find anything that didn't belong, but the problem was that she didn't know what would be out of place.

There were papers with the sales of the day, empty jars, lids, and a bag of bread, all getting wet from the weather, nothing that would stand out.

Anne kept her smile on as she bought the jam and moved on to Mrs. Smith, one of the best fishmongers in the port. Anne started making small talk about the catch of the day as she looked around and again there was nothing out of place. Bones and scales lay all-around, along with a brown bag of rye bread that Anne guessed that she sold to go with the fish.

'Is there something wrong?' Mrs. Smith asked, looking up at her with brown eyes. Her black hair fell around her shoulders.

Anne blinked at the woman and put her smile back on in a flash. 'No, just looking at the bread. Is that the recipe I showed you last week?

'Why, yes, it is,' Mrs. Smith said, looking back at it as if she was surprised Anne had noticed it in the first place.

'That's great. I'm so happy you tried it. Can I buy one from you?'

'Oh no, dear. I'm sorry, but this is for someone else.'

'Oh,' was all Anne said in reply, looking away from the bag and trying to find anything else. Her thoughts were drawn back by Mrs. Smith's next words.

'Have you seen Mr. Shipham lately? I know he talked about you the other day and wished that you would come to see him more.'

'Did he?' Anne asked, feeling guilt run through her. She hadn't seen Robin's cousin in a long time, and she knew that wasn't right, given that he had offered her husband his job and, her a deal on the cottage after his death ... He had been a comforting shoulder to cry on in that first year afterwards. It had been a few weeks since she had last seen him and that was too long. He had no family left beside her boys and herself, not since his wife died a few years back.

'He did. You should see him. I heard that he was down at the dock today,' Mrs. Smith said.

Anne nodded slowly and turned away, feeling as if she had just been dismissed by a teacher... As if she had been caught doing something that she shouldn't.

She walked down the path that led to the docks, the sound of seagulls and the normally-heavy, crashing waves of the sea deafening as she went, but everything seemed muted as her mind worked like the gears of an ever ticking clock.

It really did feel like Mrs. Smith had just wanted to get rid of her... but why? Were they going back into the woods, and they just didn't want her to see them? Suddenly, the idea that maybe she had been seen yesterday terrified her... What if they get to her boys?

'Oh, God,' Anne said out loud as she whipped around to run back up the path, but instead ran right into a hard body.

The impact knocked the wind from her lungs, and she was almost sent to the ground, but a strong hand wrapped around her wrist and pulled her back up just in time to save her.

'Why, Mrs. Routy, where were you going so fast?' Mr. Shipham said, letting go of her as she righted herself. Anne felt her cheeks pinken as she brushed away the sand that had got on her dress from his hands.

'Nowhere. I was actually coming to see how you were doing. I haven't been to see you in a little while, and I have to say that I felt bad about all of the time that has passed.'

He smiled down at her, his green eyes full of delight as she spoke. 'Well, I understand, Anne. You're a single mother, after all, and as my late wife used to say, a housewife's work is never done. And with two boys, I could only imagine the workload you have cut out for yourself.'

Anne smiled at his words because he was right; her days never seemed to end.

'Would you like to have a cup of tea with me, Anne? I just put a pot on after I finished checking my crab traps.'

Anne looked up at his kind face, lined from all the time he spent in the sun while on the sea.

'Of course, I would love a cup.'

Mr. Shipham beamed at her before he held out

an elbow for her to take.

She let a smile find its way to her lips as she wrapped her own arm around his before they started walking the rest of the way to his cottage that sat a little way off from the market.

Mr. Shipham slid away from Anne and held open the door for her as she stepped into his humble living room and was immediately hit with the smell of rose tea and freshly baked bread.

'Please, have a seat, Anne. I'll grab the tea,' Mr. Shipham, said and Anne happily did as she was told, sitting down in one of the faded green armchairs.

Anne watched as he pulled out a beautiful tea set one with, pink and red roses lining the thin glass cups. He poured the steaming liquid into them and placed them on a silver tray along with, to her surprise, a pat of butter and a few rolls before he came and sat down next to her. Set the tray on the table that sat in-between them.

Anne picked up her cup and took a long drink of the hot liquid, the incredibly-floral taste coating her tongue. It tasted almost exactly like how a rose smelled, fragrant and flowery, leaving a smooth, wonderful taste in her mouth.

'Like it?' Mr. Shipham asked, taking a drink from his own cup.

'Of course. You always knew how to make a good cup of tea,' Anne answered, looking at him before her eyes fell to the tray. For some reason, the rolls caught her attention.

Anne blinked a moment at them, not understanding why she was so keen on the bread; it wasn't like they were anything special. They just looked like the perfect treat to have on a rainy day.

'You know, I've always felt that rain is the white noise of nature. You can't even hear those damned planes today.' Anne looked up to find Mr. Shipham looking out the window at the rain that still fell as he went on. 'Of course, some people love white noise like me and others find it off-putting. You can't hear as well, the ground wet and muted ... One can be followed so very easily.'

Anne was only half-listening as she picked up one of the rolls and simply held it, turning it repeatedly in her hand.

Bread never rises well in this kind of weather; the flour absorbs more water from the air on rainy days, making it come out flatter than normal.

Anne felt her eyes widen then, realizing now what had been bugging her all day... A bag of bread sitting out in the rain was wrong. Not only would it be soggy and stale, but no one in these times would just leave food out to go bad.

That was, unless it wasn't supposed to be eaten.

Anne almost wanted to laugh at how simple it was. But she still needed answers to the questions she had.

'Have you figured it out?' Mr. Shipham asked.

She looked up at him, her heart pounding in her chest like it wanted to make a run for it ... or maybe that was just her.

'What have you done?' Anne asked, looking him right in his eyes.

'The right thing.'

'If it was the right thing then why did no one come for Jerry? Why did my husband have to die? What did he even die for? What is this?' Anne asked, trying hard to keep her voice steady.

'All good questions, my dear Anne,' Mr. Shipham said, looking down into his tea as if the answers lay in the steam that still rose from his cup.

'So, answer them!' Anne hissed, slamming her teacup down and, no longer caring about how she sounded.

'The answers are not as black and white as you may want them, Anne. But I can see that you're ready to know.'

'Know?' Anne asked angrily, 'Know what?'

'Have you ever wondered why we seemed so untouched?' he asked her looking her in the eyes as well.

'We're just a little fishing port. They probably don't care what you do as long as we keep quiet,' Anne answered him.

Mr. Shipham gave her the same smile that you would give a little kid that had just told you the sky was blue and the grass green. 'You're right, we are just a little fishing port. A port that is right next to the Navy and prisoner ships.'

Anne felt her eyes widen in surprise. She had seen the ships every day since she and the boys had arrived but she hadn't known they were floating prisons.

'What kind of prisoners?'

'British ones.'

'Our own men imprisoned next door...' Anne said in almost a whisper, her heartbreaking at the idea of what they must be going through, remembering the horrors that she had seen in the papers years ago.

'Yes, they're only a boat ride away from us. We're so close that they get much of their fish from here, it's why we're not as bad off as others. They count on us for many things, and they think that if they let us have more freedom, it would tranquilize us. That freedom would make us forget about our men, but they're wrong.'

'What do you mean? What are you talking about?' Anne asked.

'It's not as much as I would like to do, trust me. But we send messages to the prisoners back and forth, from family, from spies, and from people in much higher places than I have a right to know about.'

'And you have the women doing it?' Anne asked. 'Aren't you worried they could get caught?'

'I've taken care to make sure that, even if one was caught, no one would be able to jail them for anything besides being a little too close to the border. I've made sure that the women can talk their way out of it,' Mr. Shipham answered simply.

'How can you be so sure? They have children to take care of, Mr. Shipham. They have homes. The women make this port run.'

'I know that all too well, Anne. You housewives are far stronger than many men would like to believe, but I've hidden the messages well, and I think you've already got an idea of how it's done.'

Anne raised an eyebrow at him in reply, not understanding his meaning.

She watched as he grabbed the roll she was still holding and held it out for her, as if that was some kind of answer. A moment later, he broke the piece of bread in half and to Anne's surprise, there was something hard and short in the middle of the fluffy interior.

Anne felt her mouth open a little in surprise as he pulled out whatever it was and held it in his hand for her to see better.

'Did you know that wood can be hollowed out fairly easily, and can burn over a thousand degrees Celsius?' he asked her.

'You're hiding wood in the bread,' Anne said, taken aback. 'That doesn't seem very suspicious, now, does it? If it's found.'

Mr. Shipham let a little smile spread his lips at her words. 'You're not wrong, but we can't just throw sticks in the direction of the ship and hope that the wind is on our side. That wouldn't work, but there are people on the other side that hate what has happened to the world and want to help in any way they can.'

'Who would risk their lives?' Anne asked.

'We call them runners, men who have been wronged by their own country and want to get revenge. These runners buy the bread that the women make, and they pick it up on the other side of the port. Afterward they deliver it to the ship and, sadly, the guards happily give the moldy bread to the men that are imprisoned, thinking it's funny.'

'But what if one of the guards eats one?' Anne asked.

'It's well known that the guards like to put things in the food, from razor blades to nails. A piece of wood would be nothing to them.'

Anne felt her stomach turn at that idea and had to close her eyes a moment at the terrors that humans could do to one another, how one person could be so evil, let alone a whole country… No, she knew it wasn't the whole country, it was just the people in charge.

'Jerry was one of the runners, wasn't he?' Anne asked, meeting the other man's gaze and watching as they filled with guilt.

'Yes, he was a runner. I have to say that I didn't know him, just that something happened with his cover, and he was able to escape.'

'How did we end up finding him? Why didn't you tell me and my husband about what was happening?'

'Anne, I wanted to trust you both, but we didn't know how you would react if you found out about what we were doing. The other side can give you a lot of money for information.'

'But we never wanted money! We helped him! My husband died thinking that he was doing the right thing by taking him back to the Navy. You could have saved both of them! He was your own blood!' Anne shouted at him as she stood and, in a flash of anger, made her way toward the door. Her heart was pounding in her chest once more, but this time it was from anger, not fear.

She reached for the handle but was stopped by a hand on her shoulder.

'My dear Anne, Jerry was a dead man walking. Trust me, I wanted to save him. God, I wanted to tell you both, but by the time I got the go-ahead to tell you, Robin had already stepped onto that boat. And after everything that happened, I couldn't bring myself to tell you.'

'You couldn't bring yourself to tell me?' Anne hissed, turning back to face him.

'Of course, I knew that you couldn't stay oblivious for much longer and I would have to tell you about what we were doing after that plane shot them down, but I didn't want to hurt you any more than you already were. But, Anne, I want the world we once had back.'

'You will never get it back! The world we knew is gone, and it will never be the same. And you can't fix it with bread and the labour of housewives!' Anne shouted in his face, her anger boiling over.

She grabbed the stupid piece of bread from his hand and this time when she turned away from him she didn't look back as she walked out into the gray world.

Anne made her way back up to the market with the rain pouring down now, and in a blur she was back home to her to quiet cottage.

Even dripping wet, Anne felt only red-hot anger still boiling inside her, and it only seemed to keep rising. However, there didn't seem to be anywhere for it to go besides out.

Anne threw the soaking wet piece of bread she was still somehow holding against the wall and before she knew what was happening, she grabbed a clay vase that held long dead roses and threw that too. She watched as it smashed against the wall, pieces of it flying across the room.

She stood there for a moment, her breathing heavy as the anger faded, and Anne was left with a mess to clean up, this time one of her own making.

Letting out a long sigh she went over and started to pick up the broken pieces of vase and roses, feeling now like a little kid who had thrown a temper tantrum. As she lifted a large piece of the vase, she found the hollowed-out piece of wood under it.

Anne picked it up and looked at it for a moment before she broke it in half with a crack, wanting to see what the inside looked like. She found a folded letter inside.

She bit her lip as she pulled it out and held it, hesitating a moment as she wondered what could be written within. Could it be a love letter from a girl? A letter from a father to his son?

Anne unfolded it, knowing that it was immoral to look at someone's personal life and loved ones but, still, she read on.

Dear James,

I hope you're doing well. I know that things aren't looking very bright at the moment, but please, remember that we will be together again.

Oh, I could just picture us all sitting down together eating, talking, and enjoying ourselves as soon as this is all over. And that won't be long now, at least, that's what some are saying. Maybe next year you'll be here for Purim, and we'll all celebrate twice as much. Tonight, I am going to the secret service held in the baker basement with your father.

It's a very quiet room, we can't even make a sound after nine pm, but it's better than nothing. I even got to see Mrs. Merry, and we made small talk about how to get even more women in on this type of thing.

But again, please stop worrying about me so much. I'm in the best of health, and I hope to hear the same from you. You know I love doing this. Just the idea of the joy this brings you makes it all worth it.

Oh, and James send us some news about the other boys. We are all curious to know how they're making out.

I'll write again as soon as possible.

Love, Mother & Father

Anne felt her heart melt at the words, the letter written so beautifully on the ever yellowing paper. A mother only wanting to comfort her son ... a son with the same name as her own.

As much as Anne didn't want to admit it, she understood now. She understood what they were trying to do. No, it wouldn't change the world they now lived in, but it could save this one mean's hope of it changing.

Anne stood then as she heard the door open and folded the letter back up, believing it would be her boys coming back from school. Instead, she turned around and found Mr. Shipham standing in her doorway, dripping wet.

'So, you read it, then?' he asked her, looking down at the letter in her hand as he moved further into the room.

'You knew that I would read it, didn't you?' Anne asked him, even though she already knew his answer, and he knew that she did.

'I'm sorry, Anne, about Robin but if you join us, you will be helping men and women who need it. I can't promise that you'll be safe, and I can't promise that you won't be in danger at times. But I can promise that you will be helping to change this world, even if it's just a letter at a time. Will you join us?' he asked, looking down at her.

'You really think that I'm capable of this?' Anne asked, her heart pounding. This time, it was with excitement.

'I think that you're more than capable, my dear Anne,' he said looking at something that sat behind her.

Curiously, Anne followed his gaze and found that he was looking at her half-finished needlepoint. The words 'Keep Calm and Carry On' stood out to her like they were glowing.

Anne closed her eyes for a moment. She wouldn't lie it was scary. But then she thought of her boys on that ship, wanting a letter from home, their only solace being the world that they once knew and the promise of a better future. Anne wet her dry lips, opening her eyes before she spoke.

'But there's something else,' Mr Shipman took her hands in his, 'before you commit to joining us.'

'What's that?' There was something in the man's face that made Anne's blood freeze.

'Have you noticed that no one else has come here since you arrived? There are no passing strangers.'

'Well,' the thought hadn't fully occurred to Anne, but she tried to rationalize it now, 'we are a port,' she said. 'No one's allowed to leave it, so we're hardly likely to get passing trade, are we?'

'Oh, but we do, my dear. The flotsam from the cities, the dispossessed. Their numbers were greater once, but now, they've slowed to a trickle.'

'What about them?'

'We can't have them here, Anne,' he explained. 'Can't risk having our little operation's cover blown. Any hint of what we're doing with the bread and the ships and it would be over for all of us.'

'So …?' Anne was afraid to hear his answer.

'So they have to be silenced, Anne,' Mr Shipman said. 'Eliminated. The women do it – they're far more efficient than the men. They carry knives in their baskets – you've probably seen them on their way to the woods. The refugees are kept there, in the little abandoned cottage. Then, when the time is right, the women form a circle, putting them out of their misery. They're buried out there, in the woods. You may have seen their clothes in the market stall – it all adds to our little economy, doesn't it?'

Mr Shipman looked into Anne's horrified eyes. 'We do it,' he said, 'the women do it, to keep you and your boys safe. Is there anything wrong with that?

'Well,' she said, after a silence. 'I suppose not. I guess a housewife's work really is never done.'

THE PARTISAN

BY BETHAN WHITE

Various Authors

THE PARTISAN

'Mama?'

'What is it, darling?' The child's mother was busy, as she was always busy. She had enough food for her family, let no one say she didn't, but it wasn't always the food they liked. She reckoned on any average day, she spent as much time making food look and taste like something else as on any other three tasks together. Today, the challenge was making sprouts taste like chicken pie. It could be done, but it took time.

'You know that man?'

Her mother turned in exasperation. She shouldn't be surprised. This girl had been born with a question on her lips. Once, memorably, they had spent a whole day discussing the ins and outs of 'why is grass?'

'You'll have to give me a few more clues, Elena,' she said. 'I know lots of men.' She regretted saying that almost as the words left her mouth. Elena's father, no longer what could strictly be called resident, was nonetheless pathologically jealous and it wasn't unheard of for him to quiz his children on his visits.

'Lots of men, Mama?' Elena slid off the window seat and came round to where her mother was working at the kitchen table. 'Are those *sprouts*?'

'Yes, but they're not for us,' her mother told her

hurriedly. 'I'm making them for Mrs Jones next door. We're having chicken pie.'

Elena clapped her hands and said, 'My favourite. Lots of men, though? Daddy says ...' she wrinkled her forehead, 'that you are no better than you should be. What does that mean, Mama?'

Her mother smiled as best she could. 'It's just Daddy having a joke,' she said. 'Daddy and his jokes, eh?'

'Why doesn't Daddy live here any more, Mama?'

This question was a perennial. The answer was always the same. 'Daddy's busy, Elena. You know that. He has to patrol, to keep us all safe.'

'But he could still live here, though, couldn't he, Mama?'

'He stays here sometimes.' That was nothing but the truth.

'But he makes you cry when he stays here.' The child was relentless. 'Why does he make you cry?'

Her mother wished she could say, because he beats me. Because he rapes me. Because he can spend hours telling me how worthless I am, how ugly, how I smell before he takes me against my will, over and over again, with so much hatred. Instead, she said, 'I'm sad because I know he will have to go.'

Elena leaned her chin on her folded hands on the table top. 'Mama, can I tell you something?'

'Always.'

'Sometimes I'm not sad when Daddy goes. He isn't like my Daddy any more. He's rough and he isn't polite.'

Despite herself, the mother laughed. 'Not polite?'

'Please. Thank you. That kind of thing. And he asks us questions. All the time.'

Her mother's hackles rose. 'Questions?' she said. 'What about?'

'You. Who you talk to. The neighbours. Who they are and if anyone has moved. That kind of thing.'

Her mother nodded, but her lips were tight and her eyes hooded. 'Well, if you don't want to answer them, just tell him no.'

'That would be rude.'

'Not really,' her mother said. 'I've told you and your sisters about being nosy, haven't I?'

'Well … yes.'

'So. There you are. It applies to daddies as well.'

Elena unfolded her arms and reached out a tentative finger. 'Are you sure these sprouts aren't for us.'

'Of course I'm sure,' her mother said, glad to change the subject. 'I told you. Chicken pie for us tonight.'

'With veg?'

Her mother raised her eyebrows. 'Since when did pie not come with veg?'

Elena nodded. 'True. So, what about that man?'

Her mother sighed. How could the child hang on to a subject so relentlessly.

'What man?'

'You know. The man. The man up the hill.'

Her mother took off her apron and folded it neatly, covering the sprouts against the flies of the early spring afternoon. 'Let's go into the other room. Sit comfortably and you can tell me properly what you want to know.'

The child's father wasn't expected any time soon. His patrol had only left the day before and it would be a merciful while until they got back. Time for the bruises to heal. So with any luck, anything the child found out, she would have forgotten by then. Even this child.

The sitting room was comfortable, if a little shabby. A few ornaments were missing, broken in her husband's rages or swapped, when such swapping was possible, for food or clothes for the children. She considered herself lucky that they were all girls, so hand-me-downs weren't a problem. The biggest one was getting to the age when she could wear her mother's clothes but when they were worn out, who knew where that would leave them. They sat on the sagging sofa, curling into the corner as she always did, the little girl, her baby, squirrelling down into the space between her hip and the cushions of the back. One day, and it would be soon, she was going to have to tell her she wouldn't be the baby for much longer. On his visit before last, the child's father had left her with a present that would go on giving; another mouth to feed. Already, the neighbours were beginning to talk. Perhaps she needed to tell the child sooner rather than later. But not today.

'So. What man?'

Elena screwed her head round to look up into her mother's face.

'The *man*. The man up the *hill*.'

Not for the first time, the child's mother wondered where the girl got her brains and her tenacity from. She would be the first to admit that schooling had not been her favourite occupation and yes, when the soldiers had come she had picked Henry, the most handsome one, and had given him whatever he wanted in return. He had given her her eldest daughter and when he had disappeared, she had had to think quickly, which is why she ended up with the oaf she was still shackled to now. The baby had been small for term, so she had managed to get away with it, but she knew he looked sometimes at his dark-eyed daughter and wondered. Thank goodness that he was as stupid as they come; genetics was a mystery to him and long may that continue. But this child was definitely his – so how she was so bright was anybody's guess.

'It's no good, baby,' she said, dropping a kiss on her daughter's curly head. 'There are lots of men, even men up hills. Tell me more.'

'Well.' The girl squirmed down, getting cosy. 'He's a man, I don't know how old he is.' She knew that this would be the first question. 'He's older than Daddy, younger than Granny.'

That didn't narrow it down much. Allowing for her child-centric view, the man could be anything between thirty and a hundred.

'He's not handsome, but he isn't ugly.'

Again, almost anything.

'He's got dark hair, it's really long and kind of wild.' She sketched some mad hair with her hands. 'It's curly, like mine, but he doesn't have anyone to comb the tangles out, so it's a bit …' she wiggled her fingers together. 'Untidy.'

Her mother frowned. 'I don't think I know anyone like that.' That was true. Most people kept themselves tidy, even when they didn't own much. It was a way of controlling their lives, to have neat hair, clean clothes, even if they were patched and worn and ten years out of date. 'Are you sure you haven't imagined him?' She knew her daughter had a vivid imagination, the sort that kept her – and sometimes the entire family – up at nights. She had once refused to go into the garden for over a week because of the dragon under the gooseberry bush that had turned out to be a fallen branch. 'What colour is his hair?'

'Hmmm.' Her daughter thought deeply, dramatically drumming her fingers on her chin and screwing up her mouth. She kissed her head again. The child did nothing by halves. Finally, she said, 'Some of it is kind of pale, the bits at the ends. Then there is some darker, but there's some grey bits in that, like Granny sometimes when she doesn't have any of that stinky stuff in the bottle.'

Her mother laughed out loud, throwing her head back. Her erstwhile mother-in-law kept a weather eye out for misbehaviour in her son's possession and to hear her bottle blonde head described so very accurately was the best thing she had heard for weeks.

'What, Mama?' Elena looked up, anxiously. Her mother didn't laugh much, and she had come to learn that it often was the precursor to more tears.

Her mother wiped her eyes. 'Sorry, darling, it's nothing. Go on.' She was still chuckling as her daughter continued with her description of the man up the hill.

'He's really skinny.'

Her mother immediately had an image of a poor old man, not eating enough, not looking after himself properly and her maternal instinct rose up and tapped her on the shoulder. She was always like this when she was pregnant, taking on the troubles of the world as if she didn't have enough of her own. 'Does he have food in the house?' As she asked this, another thought struck her. Were her children going into some strange old man's house? What kind of mother was she to allow this to happen?

'I don't know. I never go in his house. I just like feeding the chickens.'

Well, that answered two questions at once. He had food and he wasn't inveigling her daughter into his house.

'He's skinny but strong. He had to move a hen house when they had pecked up all the worms and he did it by himself.'

So, probably not that old, then. But she immediately stopped herself – if her own father could hear her thoughts he would tut sadly and shake his head. Not all old geezers are weaklings, he would say, tousling her hair. God, she missed her dad sometimes. But he had gone about the same time as Henry had, there one day, gone the next. Her mother had cried for a while then dried her tears and gone off with a soldier somewhere up north and she had never heard from her again. She sighed.

'All right, Mama?'

She hugged the girl tight. They had been pretty much her first words, this golden child who took on the problems of the world. She had given her her own golden curls, her blue eyes and her disposition. If only we could choose what we gave to our children, she thought. She wouldn't have passed on that; she was on a hiding to nothing that way. 'All right, baby. Tell me more about your man up the hill.'

'He's very funny,' she said. 'He can cross his eyes and talk in a funny voice. He pretends to be one of the chickens and the chicken tells me a story. He makes me laugh. Sometimes, he has boiled some eggs and I have one.'

'You don't like boiled eggs!' Her mother was amazed. Ever since one of her sisters had told Elena that eggs came from chicken's bums, she had refused to touch one.

'I don't mind Clara's eggs,' the girl said, solemnly. 'I've seen Clara's bum while she waddles around and it looks pretty clean. So that's all right.'

There was nothing to say to that, so her mother just waited for the next nugget of information.

'The hens tell some funny stories. They tell me about

before the soldiers and it sounds like a lot of fun. Before, hens could go anywhere in the world, because they could fly then. They went on holidays in the sun and lay on the beach and got brown.' She furrowed her brow. 'But that's a bit funny, Mama, isn't it, because hens are already brown. Anyway, they did all sorts. Clara even climbed a mountain. It must have been difficult with her little legs.'

'It must,' her mother laughed. Even so, this sounded worrying. If her father were to ask … perhaps she would have to stop Elena seeing her friend up the hill for a while. Apart from anything else, it was making her unaccountably sad. She never thought of anything before. Her life had both begun and ended when she met Henry. Although everyone looked down on her as being loose and free with her favours, she knew that Henry wasn't just after one thing. She always thought of it in her mind as her mother said it – After One Thing. For someone who had run off with a soldier, her mother was full of wise sayings. Henry had lived. Henry had been places, like the hens. He had one picture in his wallet that she liked to look at, of Henry, with a rope around his waist, climbing a mountain, she didn't know where. Geography had never been her thing. Henry would wrap her in his arms and take her to wherever he wanted her to go. On holiday to somewhere he called the Big Apple. She hadn't been listening, as she had been tracing the muscles of his chest at the time, running her finger round the lines of the tattoo that he had over his heart. But it was somewhere far away, and it sounded wonderful. He had seen some famous people, too, film stars. She sighed again. She did miss the cinema, you could lose yourself there, that was a fact.

'I think the man up the hill is a bit lonely, sometimes,' Elena volunteered. 'He's always very pleased to see me, anyway.'

Her mother looked down into the innocent eyes. Her daughter was welcome wherever she went. Even her father wasn't as hard on her as he was on her sisters. Her smile could – in the over-worked phrase – light up a room. 'Of course he's pleased to see you, baby,' she said. 'Everyone's always pleased to see your pretty face.'

Her little girl rubbed her cheek against her tautening belly. She would have to tell her soon. She would have to tell her father soon as well, and that was going to be no fun. She flinched in anticipation.

'The man says he knows Daddy,' Elena said, suddenly. 'He knows he goes off doing important things.'

Her mother stiffened. She hated her husband, with every fibre of her being, but she knew that what he did, hunting out the partisans and people who would cause trouble, was important work. 'Does he ask where Daddy is?' she said, trying to keep her voice level.

'Oh, no,' Elena's voice was bright. 'He knows where Daddy is. His friends tell him, I think.'

'Friends?'

'Sometimes, when I go to feed the hens, I have to wait because there are men there. But that doesn't happen very much. Two times, I think.'

Elena was bright, but numbers weren't her thing.

'They are a bit smelly,' she volunteered. 'They come from further up the hill.'

'From the woods?' Her mother was trying not to let her alarm spread to her daughter, nor to the child within her. She had had a few tentative flutters from her child to be and she knew that alarm made him – surely, it was a boy this time – spin in her womb.

'I dunno.' Elena shrugged.

'Don't say dunno,' her mother said, automatically.

'I don't know. Sorry, Mama. They are just there, and then they aren't.'

How lovely, to be like a child. To just take things or leave them alone as the fit took you. 'How many are there?' She saw the confusion on her daughter's face. 'Umm ... a lot? Just a few?'

Logic, child-style took over. 'Well, the house isn't very big, so just a few, I suppose. Unless ...' she began to giggle.

'Unless what?'

'Unless they sat on each other's laps.' The giggles

became an all-encompassing gale of laughter. 'That would be so funny, Mama, wouldn't it? If those big smelly men sat on each other's laps?'

Her mother smiled in spite of herself, in spite of her heart being in her mouth. 'It would,' she agreed. 'Does ... does the man ever tell you things. Like ...' How to explain indoctrination to a child?

'He tells me lots,' Elena said. 'He tells me about the hens, which ones have had babies. He said, the next time one had babies, when they get bigger, we could have some. He said that we could have eggs then, from a nice clean hen's bottom.' She bounced with excitement. 'Could we, Mama? Could we have some hens?'

Her mother thought of the mud patch outside the back door that she had once hoped would be a garden, full of vegetables and laughing children. Instead, it looked like a battle ground, the children scattered through the village, playing with friends, anywhere but here, where the sadness and fear had soaked into everything and everyone except this golden child at her hip. Hens could certainly not make it any worse. And eggs would be nice.

'We could name the hens after people we know, Mama, couldn't we? We could call them Mama and Granny and Daddy ... but hens are girls, aren't they? So not Daddy, perhaps.'

'No. Perhaps not Daddy. And anyway, my name isn't Mama, you know. Granny's name is Margaret. Some people call her Molly. So we could call two hens after her, couldn't we? Margaret and Molly. So that's two.'

Elena looked confused. 'Do all grown ups have names, then?' This was a new idea.

'Of course.' Her mother smiled.

'What, even Daddy?'

'Yes. Daddy's name is George.'

Elena's eyes grew enormous. '*George*?' She giggled. 'That's a silly thing to be called.'

'Possibly. But it's his name, all the same.'

'So ...' Elena was thinking. 'You have a name? The man up the hill has a name?'

'Yes. Everyone has a name. As soon as you're born, or soon after, you have a name.' I will call this boy Henry, she thought to herself. So I can say it every day.

Elena was silent for so long that her mother thought she had gone to sleep and started to ease herself upright, to get on with her sprout transformation.

'Don't go, Mama. I wasn't asleep, just thinking.'

'Sorry, my little one. What were you thinking about?'

'I was wondering what your name was. Why does no one call you by your name?'

That was true and the thought caught at her throat. She had no friends to speak of, her husband called her things no husband should ever call a wife, her mother-in-law called her nothing – her look of contempt said it all. Her father had called her by any number of endearments. Her mother had, latterly, called her slut. But no one used her name. Henry had said it was the most beautiful name in the world and, on his tongue as he held her in the dark, it had seemed that it might be true.

'Oh, I'm too old for names,' she said, as if she meant it.

'No, Mama. No one is too old for a name. I think the man up the hill has a name. I heard one of the other smelly men call him it.'

'Don't tell me!' Her harsh tone made Elena jump. The less you know, the less you can tell.

'But Mama …'

'No. If you know it, forget it. It's best you don't go there again, at least for a while. Wait until Daddy has been and gone.'

Elena's eyes were on hers. The child could see into her soul, she was sure of it. 'But, Mama, if I don't tell you, the name will be on my tongue and I might just say it. So, can I tell you?'

'No.' But now she was less certain.

'Can I guess your name?'

Her mother laughed. 'All right. But this might take a while.' She thought of the millions of names out there and the chances of her daughter hitting on the right one.

'Does it begin with A?'

'Nope.'

'B?'

'Going through the alphabet it cheating!'

'All right then – umm – S.'

'My goodness, that was a lucky guess. Yes, it begins with S. What made you choose that?'

'It's … the man's favourite hen. Her name is Suzanne. Is that your name as well?'

The woman gathered up her child and held her close, so no one could hear what was being said. 'Yes,' she whispered. 'My name is Suzanne. Now, let's play another game, but quietly, quietly.'

'Okay.' Elena giggled. She loved whispering, though she didn't always remember to do it quietly and often did it up the other person's nose, or in their mouth. But right now, she had no choice, she was held so tightly. 'What game?'

'Let's play, guess the man's name.'

'I thought you said …'

'I made a mistake. Does it begin with an A?'

'No.'

Her mother was trembling. 'Does it begin with an H?'

'Yes! I mean,' the child dropped her voice to a whisper again, 'yes, it does.'

'Is it … and you must be quiet, Elena. Please, be quiet. Promise me.'

'I promise, Mama.'

Their hearts were beating together like drums. This was a moment they would never forget, whether they lived for years or moments. Elena knew her mother would guess right; it was the only thing that would make any sense.

'I must tell you first,' the woman said, 'that the man isn't bad, though some would say he is. Don't forget that.' Her heart was already flying up the hill, to where the man stood, among his hens. 'I think … I think that his name is Henry.'

And her tears flowed over the little girl's golden, nodding head.

Other titles by the authors for your consideration:

No Faff, No Fuss, Just Food
By Maryanne Coleman

No Fuss, No Faff, Just Food is a cookery book for people who have better things to do than slave over a hot stove. Filled with suggestions as well as recipes and thoughtfully peppered with pages for your own ideas, this book takes the lid off the simmering worries which many people have when cooking for themselves, family and friends – cooking should be fun, not scary, and reading this romp through possibly the most relaxed kitchen in the world will have you laughing as well as, very soon, cooking like you mean it!

Recipes in *No Fuss, No Faff, Just Food* include main meals, snacks, basic techniques and – of course – chocolate cake! There's no point in a recipe book with no chocolate cake in it and as a bonus, it is gluten and dairy free! Safety in the kitchen, from sharp knives to anaphylactic shock, avoidance of, is covered as well as some yummy recipes.

If you only ever have one cookery book, make it this one.

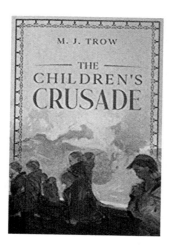

The Children's Crusade
By M. J. Trow

In the summer of 1212, 30,000 children from towns and villages all over France and Germany left their homes and families and began a crusade. Their aim; to retake Jerusalem, the holiest city in the world, for God and for Christ. They carried crosses and they believed, because the Bible told them so, that they could cross the sea like Moses. The walls of Jerusalem would fall, like Jericho's did for Joshua.

It was the age of miracles – anything was possible. Kings ignored the Children; so did popes and bishops. The handful of Church chroniclers who wrote about them were usually disparaging. They were delusional, they were inspired not by God, but the Devil. Their crusade was doomed from the start.

None of them reached Outremer, the Holy Land. They turned back, exhausted. Some fell ill on the way; others died. Others still were probably sold into slavery to the Saracens – the very Muslims who had taken Jerusalem in the first place.

We only know of three of them by name – Stephen, Nicholas and Otto. One of them was a shepherd, another a ploughboy, the third a scholar. The oldest was probably fourteen. Today, in a world where nobody believes in miracles, the Children of 1212 have almost been forgotten.

Almost... but not quite...

The poet Robert Browning caught the mood in his haunting poem, *The Pied Piper of Hamelin*, bringing to later readers the sad image of a lost generation, wandering a road to who knew where.

Love Bites
By Kyt Wright

Elisabeth Bathory wears a police uniform and patrols the streets of London at night.

Elisabeth Bathory is over four hundred and sixty years old.

Elisabeth Bathory is a vampire.

Elisabeth Bathory enforces the Edict ensuring humans are never killed by vampires.

Humans are starting to turn up dead and it's obvious her people are behind it!

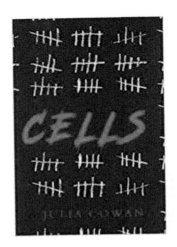

Cells
By Julia Cowan

CELLS tells the story of an unofficial, covert prison designed to remove repeat offenders who have upset the balance of society.

Jim, a troubled seventeen year old, finds that he is imprisoned with his absent father.

Jim is torn between his desire to expose his violent abductors and the desperate need for a new beginning.

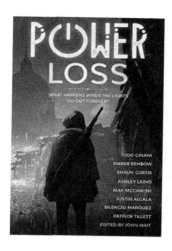

Power Loss
By various authors

What happens when the lights go out forever.

The day the lights went out is remembered as *Day Zero.*

It wasn't just the lights, it was the phones, the computers and just about everything else that made modern society what it was.

Power Loss tells the story of eight individuals, by eight different authors, each trying to come to terms with the blackout and survive in a world that has changed forever.

Consumed
By Justin Alcala

Sergeant Nathaniel Brannick is trapped in Victorian London during a period of disease, crime, and insatiable vices. One night, Brannick returns from work to find an eerie messenger in his flat who warns him of dark things to come.

When his next case involves a victim who suffered from consumption, he uncovers clues that lead him to believe the messenger's warning. Despite his incredulity, he can't help but wonder if the practical man he once was has been altered by an investigation encompassed in the paranormal. That is, until he meets the witch hunters, and everything takes a turn for the worse.

Prester John: Africa's Lost King
By Richard Denham

He sits on his jewelled throne on the Horn of Africa in the maps of the sixteenth century. He can see his whole empire reflected in a mirror outside his palace. He carries three crosses into battle and each cross is guarded by one hundred thousand men. He was with St Thomas in the third century when he set up a Christian church in India. He came like a thunderbolt out of the far East eight centuries later, to rescue the crusaders clinging on to Jerusalem. And he was still there when Portuguese explorers went looking for him in the fifteenth century.

He went by different names. The priest who was also a king was Ong Khan; he was Genghis Khan; he was Lebna Dengel. Above all, he was a Christian king who ruled a vast empire full of magical wonders: men with faces in their chests; men with huge, backward-facing feet; rivers and seas made of sand.

Was he real? Did he ever exist? This book will take you on a journey of a lifetime, to worlds that might have been, but never were. It will take you, if you are brave enough, into the world of Prester John.

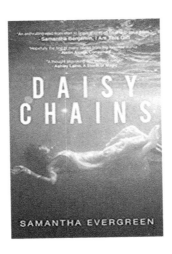

Daisy Chains
By Samantha Evergreen

After a wild night of partying on the last day of spring break, three seventeen-year-old friends Rose, Lily, and Violet wake up to find their best friend Daisy Young is missing and in the small town of Watkinsville, Georgia in 1975 that's not normal.

As the days go by, everyone starts to wonder how the girl who spent her days with her head in the clouds and had no enemies could go missing. Rumors start that she ran away; that's until Rose, Lily, and Violet find bones in a riverbank.

Watkinsville descends into madness as Chief Thompson and the newly instated 21-year-old Officer Mark Hollow look into what had happened that night. But only more questions arise as men from around town start to confess for no reason, all with the same story. So Rose, Lily, and Violet and Officer Hollow take it upon themselves to find the killer.

But little do they know they're running against the clock and things may not be quite what they seem.

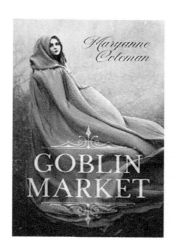

Goblin Market
By Maryanne Coleman

Have you ever wondered what happened to the faeries you used to believe in? They lived at the bottom of the garden and left rings in the grass and sparkling glamour in the air to remind you where they were. But that was then – now you might find them in places you might not think to look. They might be stacking shelves, delivering milk or weighing babies at the clinic. Open your eyes and keep your wits about you and you might see them.

But no one is looking any more and that is hard for a Faerie Queen to bear and Titania has had enough. When Titania stamps her foot, everyone in Faerieland jumps; publicity is what they need. Television, magazines. But that sort of thing is much more the remit of the bad boys of the Unseelie Court, the ones who weave a new kind of magic; the World Wide Web.

Here is Puck re-learning how to fly; Leanne the agent who really is a vampire; Oberon's Boys playing cards behind the wainscoting; Black Annis, the bag-lady from Hainault, all gathered in a Restoration comedy that is strictly twenty-first century.

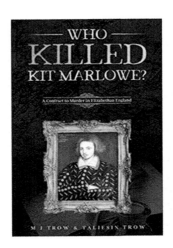

Who Killed Kit Marlowe?: A Contract to Murder in Elizabethan England
By M. J. Trow & Taliesin Trow

Kit Marlowe was the bad boy of Elizabethan drama. His 'mighty line' of iambic pentameter transformed the miracle plays of the Middle Ages into modern drama and he paved the way for Shakespeare and a dozen other greats who stole his metre and his ideas. When he died, stabbed through the eye in what appeared to be a tavern brawl in Deptford in May 1593, he was only 29 and many people believed that he had met his just deserts.

But Marlowe's death was not the result of a brawl. And it did not take place in a tavern. The facts tell a different story, one involving intrigue, espionage, alchemy and the highest in the land.

The brutal murder of a young playwright at the peak of his powers has intrigued and captivated for over 400 years. This compelling journey through the evidence allows us to know, for the first time, who killed him.

Fade
By Bethan White

Do you want to remember?

Do you want to forget?

There is nothing extraordinary about Chris Rowan. Each day he wakes to the same faces, has the same breakfast, the same commute, the same sort of homes he tries to rent out to unsuspecting tenants.

There is nothing extraordinary about Chris Rowan. That is apart from the black dog that haunts his nightmares and an unexpected encounter with a long forgotten demon from his past. A nudge that will send Chris on his own downward spiral, from which there may be no escape.

There is nothing extraordinary about Chris Rowan   ...

BLKDOG

www.blkdogpublishing.com

Printed in Great Britain
by Amazon